BY THE
Sword

Also by Greg Costikyan:
Another Day, Another Dungeon

MAGIC OF
THE PLAINS:

BY THE
Sword

GREG COSTIKYAN

A Tom Doherty Associates Book
New York

BY THE SWORD

Copyright © 1993 by Greg Costikyan

This book is printed on acid-free paper.

A Tor Book
Published by Tom Doherty Associates, Inc.
175 Fifth Avenue
New York, N.Y. 10010

Tor® is a registered trademark of Tom Doherty Associates, Inc.

Edited by Debbie Notkin

Library of Congress Cataloging-in-Publication Data

Costikyan, Greg.
    By the sword : magic of the plains / Greg Costikyan.
       p. cm.
    ISBN 0-312-85489-7
    I. Title.
    PS3553.O7633B9   1993
    813'.54—dc20   93-12759
                                        CIP

First edition: June 1993

Printed in the United States of America

0 9 8 7 6 5 4 3 2 1

For Victoria

CAST OF
CHARACTERS
▶▶▶

The Vai

Poai: A member of the Women's Council of the Va-Naleu tribe; wife of the shaman Tsawen; mother of Nijon.

Tsawen: Nijon's stepfather and shaman of the Va-Naleu.

Mo'ian: Great Chieftain of the Va-Naleu.

Nijon Oonitsaupivia: Nijon, son of Mongoose, the Trickster; our hero.

Vauren: Nijon's rival.

Dowdin: Vauren's close friend and Tsawen's apprentice.

Lai'iani: Nijon's sometime girlfriend.

Naenae: Nijon's horse.

Jutson: A warrior.

Dihaen: Another warrior.

The Caravaneers

Mika Nashram: Mountebank and palter.

Fela: Merchant and leader of the expedition.

"Chief Mo'aloo": Actor and sometime confidence trickster.

Dana, Mosha: Soldiers.

The Court

King Manoos: Ruler of Purasham.

Princess Nlavi: His daughter.

Prince Poran: His son.

The Satrap Mesech: Ruler of the Motraian satrapy of Noshen; Nlavi's betrothed.

Marshall Nyekhon: Commander of Purasham's army (such as it is).

Grand Vizier Vakhan: Chief minister of state.

Chancellor Zhemen: Head of Purasham's diplomatic corps.

Divers Others

Mongoose: The Trickster; Nijon's dad.

Brother: Nijon's half-brother, a mongoose.

Detros: A member of the Royal Guard.

The Dragon

Matli: Matriarch of the dragon's collection.

Shemli: A maiden.

Dekh: A pest.

Meshed: The keeper of Hekhat Castle.

Laelai: Daughter of the count of Ik.

BY THE
Sword

PRELUDE

▶▶▶

The world is wide and high and young: unbounded steppe. The early-morning sky is tinged with blue and rose; green vegetation ripples in the breeze. Out there are herds of antelope, mastodon, wild horses, aurochs. Of all its inhabitants, only the humans know this world is bounded, and they only because they raid and trade with the settled lands of the north, where the people are tiny and quick.

High soars the eagle; low creeps the snake; but the true master of these plains is not the lioness, nor yet the mastodon. The masters of the world are men and women, bowlegged with lives ahorse, herding cattle, hunting, warring. They are hardy, well nourished on cheese, animal flesh, and blood. For the nonce, their manner of life is secure, for no hoe nor ox-drawn plow will cut the sod of these great plains.

Atop their hardy, hairy mounts, they roam the wide world at will, and none may stay their path; for as they are bred to the horse, they are bred to war. The northlanders call them Vagon, barbarian; for they are the terror of the north, who sweep out each generation to plunder and burn. To themselves they are merely the Vai, the People. Among them did Nijon come to manhood. This is his tale.

* * *

The encampment was at peace, though the people were not.
About it were scattered the horses and cattle of the folk,
each marked with the symbol and color of its owner.
Young men and women tended the herds, lest animals stray
or a predator strike. Women worked at curing leather,
mending tools, smoking meat, but always with a sense of
anticipation that centered on the north. They awaited
word.

Led by Dikon Khan, the warriors of the tribe, all the men
save the youngest and oldest and those who voluntarily
surrendered the warrior role, had ridden north in search of
booty. The wind might bring back word of triumph or
tragedy. No metaphor, that: One of the Women's Council
sat always by an oddly shaped pot that hung by horsehair
from a post, listening to the whistle of the air as it passed
through the pot's mouth. This was the compact that
Tsawen, the tribal sorcerer, had made with the North
Wind: that it would bear tidings.

A gray-haired woman sat there now, head cocked to
listen to the whistle. Above, the sun crept toward the
meridian.

At precisely noon, the North Wind spake: "Victory,"
whistled the pot. "Triumph."

With a shriek, the woman sprang up. Glad cries rose
skyward.

They built a great bonfire at the camp center, and brought
forth three white calves to sacrifice in celebration. The liver
and lights they would offer to the North Wind in thanks for
its assistance, but—"Where is Poai?" the women asked
each other. For she, wife of the sorcerer Tsawen, must
preside over the rite.

It was nearly sunset now. Flagons of kumiss had been
brought forth and a great feast prepared. Women, children,

"Perhaps you should sleep now, dear," said Tsawen, pulling a skin over her torso. She murmured thanks.

Tsawen soon joined her in slumber; she might be tired by the labor of birthing, but he was no less exhausted by his magical exertions. He had spent hours and considerable power, breathing the sacred fumes, sending forth his spirit. The hawk had been no great feat: a simple compulsion laid on a bird. But the two-headed calf had been the very devil to arrange.

Ten-year-old Nijon peered from behind a boulder at two other boys, Vauren and Dowdin by name. They labored over a fire. Nijon did not envy them; they had been given a hard task, largely in punishment for tormenting Nijon himself.

Several large stones sat in the fire. Using sticks as levers, Vauren and Dowdin were rolling one now, out of the flames and toward a pit. The pit, lined with hides, was filled with water. In the water floated skeins of wool and several splits of wood from the tsaemol tree.

Laboriously, the boys rolled the hot stone into the water. It hissed as it met the liquid. They rolled another stone into the pit, and a third. As the water steamed, a green tint infused it, the hot water cooking dye out of the tsaemol wood. The wool would pick up the dye and turn green; then the women would spin it, and weave blankets and coats from the richly colored yarn.

At present, Vauren stood between Nijon and the pit, bending over to pry at a hot stone. "Hyaah!" Nijon yelled, springing up and bounding down the slope. He gave Vauren a strong shove—and the boy tumbled into the pit, green water splashing everywhere.

Nijon stood laughing as Vauren sputtered up. Vauren stood in the pit, examining his limbs; his tawny skin now had a definite viridian cast.

"Why, Vauren," Nijon taunted, "you look positively green. Nauseous perhaps?"

"You bastard," Vauren said between gritted teeth. There was murder in his eyes, but his parents had been quite clear that there were to be no more fights with Nijon. Nijon only laughed.

Dowdin, standing to one side, smiled faintly. "Yes, bastard," he mused. "Has Poai told who your true father is yet, Nijon?"

Nijon lost his grin.

"Rumor has it it's Doowaien," Vauren said nastily, naming the tribal idiot. He stepped out of the pit and shook his legs.

Dowdin cackled. "A likely candidate," he agreed.

"My mother does not lie," said Nijon, advancing on Dowdin with balled fists.

"True, true," said Dowdin hurriedly, backing away. "She's an honest woman—eh, Oonipivia?" He omitted the "-tsau-" in Nijon's patronymic, turning it into an expression of contempt: not "Son of the God Mongoose," but "son of *a* mongoose"—a deadly insult.

Nijon snarled and struck out at Dowdin, who dodged aside and circled behind Vauren.

"Yes," said Vauren, "who could doubt Poai's veracity? It must be true; Nijon's father is a mongoose. Have you been growing claws, Nijon? How about your teeth? Prominent incisors, perhaps?"

Nijon turned to face Vauren, hands clenching.

"That must have been quite a sight," said Vauren, "Poai and the mongoose."

"Yes, yes," said Dowdin, laughing, keeping the pit between himself and Nijon. "Can't you see it? 'Oh, darling,' " he said in a falsetto quite unlike Poai's deep voice. " 'A dead snake? For me? How precious, my pet. Let me smooth your pelt. Oh, yes! Yes, there! And now—' "

With an inarticulate roar of rage, Nijon charged Dowdin.

Vauren put out a leg. Nijon tripped over it—and fell, face-first, into the dye pit.

Vauren and Dowdin took off for the camp, giggling hysterically.

Nijon and Lai'iani lay in a hollow not far from the camp, skin wet with the dew that drenched the grasses all about. Lai'iani's tongue played with Nijon's; through the net of her hair he glimpsed purple sky, tinged now with rose as the sun's rays broke over the horizon. The only sounds were the song of insects, horses cropping grass, their own hearts and breathing.

"But Nijon," said Lai'iani, "what if you do not return?" She tucked her head under his chin; one hand stroked down his side, toward his hip.

"Can you doubt that I shall?" asked Nijon, a little insulted that she would even consider that he might fail. Against the bare skin of his chest pressed her doeskin tunic, and softness within; he felt his breath quicken.

"Then," she said, one hand moving inward from his hip, toward more intimate parts, "then I should never see you again." Gently the hand moved; Nijon felt himself harden.

"True," said Nijon, heart racing, divining where her thoughts were tending. His own hand moved up her smooth flank, beneath her short kirtle. . . .

Heavy footsteps crunched through grass. "There you are, lad," boomed a contralto voice. Two strong fingers belonging to Poai, Nijon's mother, took a grip on his right ear and heaved upward.

Guiltily, Lai'iani rolled away into the grass. Poai hauled Nijon upward by his ear, ignoring his clothing's disarray. "I've been looking all over for you, boy," Poai said, yanking him toward the tribal camp.

"Ma!" Nijon protested, trotting sideways along behind that viselike grip on his ear.

"Time to apply your ritual paint, my son," Poai bellowed.

Nijon was led in this undignified fashion, cursing under his breath, toward his family's tent. Lai'iani pouted behind.

Clad in nothing but bold stripes of ocher and patterns in red paint, Nijon faced his tribe, the sky achingly blue above him. They had all come to see him off, as tradition demanded. Closest stood Mo'ian, chieftain of the Va-Naleu, wearing the bonnet and holding the staff that together dignified his office. The staff was adorned with feathers and mummified snakes; the bonnet bore the horns of an aurochs, carvings in mammoth ivory, the tail feathers of eagles. The chief was older now, standing painfully, perhaps wishing that the ceremony were over and a nice lunch of raw antelope liver about to commence.

A little behind him was Tsawen, Nijon's foster father and the tribe's shaman. The sorcerer wore his spirit mask, an intricate carving of wood and bone; at his belt was his medicine bundle, the repository of the tribe's very soul. With him stood Dowdin, now Tsawen's apprentice. Dowdin wore no mask; he would not make one until his apprenticeship was over and he was ready to become a shaman in truth. His face bore as close to a grimace of contempt as was politically wise; there was still no love lost between Nijon and Dowdin.

The warriors stood to the right, the women to the left. Vauren stood with the warriors; he had completed his walkabout the year before, and had spared no opportunity since then to impress his superior status on Nijon—or on Lai'iani.

Poai beamed proudly from amid the women. Lai'iani smiled nearby, giving Nijon a searing glance that promised much upon his return.

Chief Mo'ian stepped forward. "Right," he said, shaking the Staff of Office, shriveled snakes swinging with the motion. "Ho-ni-ha-ni-ho-ni-ho, and so forth and so on." He performed a few perfunctory dance steps.

Tsawen scowled beneath his mask.

"Naked you go into the wilderness," the chief intoned. "Naked you shall not return. You go as a boy; you shall not return as one. Yatata yatata. Off with you, then, lad." He turned to head back to the camp—and lunch.

"I protest!" cried Tsawen. "You must say the words!"

"Oh, bother," said Mo'ian. "He knows the words by heart. Don't you, Nijon?"

Nijon swallowed. "Ah—yes, Chief," he said, hoping to avoid a quarrel.

"That's not the point," said Tsawen petulantly. "It's more than a sequence of empty words. It's a ritual. Rituals have magic content, by the fact of being rituals. He won't return a man solely because we then call him one; he shall be transformed from boy to man, not only by experience, but by the ritual itself—"

"Really, Tsawen," grumbled Mo'ian. "You are a pain."

"Someone has to uphold tribal traditions," said Tsawen stiffly.

"All right, all right," Mo'ian muttered. He sighed and hopped into an arthritic dance, chanting: "Ho-ni-hah-ni-ho-ni-ho. . . ."

The dance slowed to a painful crawl. "Ho-(puff)-ni-(pant)-ha-(puff)-ni," chanted the chief. He paused and stood, hanging on his staff and panting.

Embarrassed, Nijon studied the tribe, avoiding Mo'ian's

eyes and wishing Tsawen had held his tongue. Dowdin and Vauren exchanged a glance, he saw; Dowdin rolled his eyes and Vauren smirked. They were amused by the old chief's incapacity. Nijon scowled at this disrespect.

At last, Mo'ian finished the dance. After regaining his breath, he stood painfully erect.

"Naked you go into the wilderness," Mo'ian said in a matter-of-fact tone. "Naked you shall not return. You go as a boy; you shall not return as one. For this is the manhood rite of the Clan of Naleu: that each boy child shall, unarmed, naked, without tools or aid or artifact, go forth onto the plain and, by his own wits, survive, prosper, and return.

"Forty days must you live apart; and forty nights. If you should starve or come to mishap, we shall know you are not fit to join us as a man. But if you survive and return, then shall you join our councils as a warrior, entitled to all the rights, benefits, liberties, chattels, cattles, wives, and other items of value of and pertaining thereto. So sayeth Ro-Mo'ian, Great Chieftain of the Va-Naleu."

Mo'ian shook his staff again. "Is that bloody formal enough for you?" he demanded of Tsawen.

"I have a question," said Nijon.

"What is it now?" asked Mo'ian testily.

"If I am to leave with nothing, why do I take a horse?" Nijon asked. "And an obsidian knife? And my mongoose talisman?"

The chief looked uneasily up at the sky. "The Laws of the Manhood Ritual," he said loudly, "are sacred to Dorij the Thunderer, may he smite somebody else! They must be obeyed, lest we suffer his wrath. All praise Dorij!"

Everybody shouted "Praise Dorij!" and eyed the sky worriedly. It remained as blue and cloud-free as before.

"Look," said Mo'ian softly. "We're bloody horse barbarians. The god can't possibly want you to leave without a *horse*. And anyway, a horse isn't an artifact. As for the other items. . . ." He seemed a little embarrassed. "Well, we tried sending the boys out with nothing but a horse, but too few survived. So—well, two objects seems like a reasonable compromise. Two, that's not too much to ask, is it?" He scanned the sky again.

"I see," said Nijon. "May I have my horse, then?"

"Right," said Mo'ian. "Get him his horse."

Somebody brought up Naenae. Nijon ran his hand down her neck. She was the first pony he had owned, a present from his parents on the occasion of his fourteenth birthday. He had grown considerably since then, and she looked barely big enough to carry the heavily muscled boy, but Nijon knew she was a sturdy little creature. Naenae would serve him far better than some skittish stallion.

Tsawen came forward, holding Nijon's mongoose's foot. The talisman was as familiar to Nijon as his horse; indeed, Tsawen had made it for him when he was yet an infant. "Here you are, boy," Tsawen said, his voice thick with emotion. "I enchanted it up proper for you. Just rub it for good luck, there's a good lad." The scrawny older man pulled brawny Nijon into an embrace; his spirit mask pressed uncomfortably into Nijon's shoulder. Tsawen shook with emotion. "Come back to us, boy," he whispered.

Then it was Poai's turn. She swaggered up to Nijon, handed him an obsidian knife, and slapped him resoundingly on the back. She was a big, beefy woman; Nijon suspected he inherited her strength, rather than that of—whomever his father might be. "Do us proud, there's a good lad," she bellowed. "Come back a man, or don't come back. Not that there's much danger of that, boy. You can handle yourself out there."

"Sure, Ma," Nijon said, grinning and ducking his head. "Easy as clubbing porcupines."

"That's my lad!" she crowed. "Go to, boy!"

Then it was the turn of the rest of the tribe. Each came

forward to wish Nijon well. Vauren, grasping Nijon's arm, bore down painfully, grinning nastily; Nijon squeezed back, and had the satisfaction of seeing Vauren wince. Nijon embraced Dowdin for his stepfather's sake; Nijon would have preferred to punch the apprentice in the nose, but Tsawen would have been offended.

At last, Lai'iani came forward, twisting a braid of hair. Nijon grinned, grabbed her, and kissed her soundly. There were whoops and hollers from the older boys and some of the young men.

After a while, Poai began to hum impatiently. Vauren scowled.

Long moments passed.

"Ahem," said the chief. "Ahem. *Ahem!* I say, boy, enough of that."

Nijon broke suction and staggered away. "Bye-bye," breathed Lai'iani.

Nijon gave Lai'iani an insouciant grin. And then he mounted his horse, kissed his mother and stepfather, saluted the chief, and rode, naked, off into the wild and vacant steppe.

He raced through the tall grass, blood thundering in his temples, the wind on his skin. A sense of eeriness overtook him: The ancestor spirits rode with him, he felt. He was marked out for great things.

2
▶▶▶

An animal coughed—not an antelope. Nijon skittered to a halt.

Ten feet distant, a lioness crouched on a boulder. One of her cubs peered from behind the rock.

A lioness alone on the steppe was no great danger; a lioness with cubs to protect—that was another matter.

Sweat pouring down his back, panting for breath, bearing only a handmade bow, a single arrows, and an obsidian knife, Nijon prepared to die.

It had been cool that morning. Wisps of cloud moved lazily across an azure sky. Waving grasses extended as far as the eye could see. Upwind, a herd of piva grazed—small antelopes, patterned in black and gray, the males boasting complexly curved horns. Nijon lay prone in a clump of briza, bow and arrow clutched in one hand. He wormed himself forward.

One of the antelopes raised its head. Nijon froze. It looked about, scanning the distance; nostrils flared, testing the breeze. Nijon knew the slightest movement would give him away; the briza in which he lay would rustle and sway. He permitted himself only shallow breaths. At last, the piv's head lowered, and it returned to grazing.

Nijon swallowed. He had not eaten well since leaving the tribe. Blood drained from the neck of his long-suffering horse; the flesh of a prairie chicken he'd killed with a well-thrown rock; that was all. He had fletched his arrows with the dead bird's feathers.

Nijon pulled himself forward. He wanted a quick kill. A hit in the eye was best, or a wound to one of the veins of the throat. He must get as close as possible; his improvised bow was far from accurate.

That one was close, now; a female, hornless. It could hardly be thirty feet distant. It pulled at the grass, then raised its head to chew contemplatively. The face and throat faced Nijon. He could not hope for a better shot.

He rolled onto his left side and nocked an arrow. It wasn't much of an arrow; a stick, its point hardened in fire. But a well-aimed shot would kill.

He rolled onto his back, drew the bowstring across his body, and released. . . .

At that instant, the piv lowered its head for the next mouthful of grass. The arrow hit not its eye, but its flank.

Instantly, the creature sprang into the air and fled, squealing. The ground about Nijon thundered with the beat of small hooves as the rest of the herd stampeded.

A male ran straight toward him. Nijon pulled up his legs protectively; but the male must have spotted him, for it leapt high, over Nijon's body, and away, across the plain.

Nijon cursed and sprang to his feet. He spotted the piv he had injured.

He had half-expected this. He ran after the wounded piv, not sprinting, but at a speed he knew he could maintain.

On horseback, it would be easy to catch the piv; ride it down, club it, kill it with the knife. But Naenae was back at the water hole, where he had left her. He could not possibly have crept close enough to the herd to make a kill, not with a horse; the pony was too large to hide.

The piv was wounded. Its wounds would tire it; it might well bleed to death, given time.

The piv could run faster than he, in brief spurts; but there is no prey, Nijon told himself, that a man cannot run down—in time.

But he might have to run for hours.

He would make a kill today, he told himself. He *would*. He would. He would. Under his breath, he repeated the words, like a chant. And he touched his talisman, for what good it might do him.

Hours later. Nijon ran. Ran on. Ran ever on. The wide world had narrowed down to three things: Nijon, running. The piv, running. The heat of the sun, beating down.

Sweat ran in rivulets down Nijon's back. His right hand was cramped from the effort of holding the bow, the knife, and his last remaining arrow. His legs were molten, hardly felt, down there beneath his body; his breath came in short pants.

Right, left, right, left, right, left. He was invincible; he could run forever. He was undone; he must collapse.

He ran, will driving body beyond its limits; empty stomach, dry throat, limbs awash in fatigue.

Ahead, the piv halted, head down, panting heavily, blood oozing from its wounds. Nijon slogged on.

He was down to a single arrow. The rest had been expended in the chase. Most were stuck in the earth, back there somewhere. But one protruded from the piv's flank, blood seeping around the shaft. The piv was weakening. But as long as it ran, Nijon must too. Run on. Run always.

As the piv rested, the distance between them closed. Nijon considered another shot, using his final arrow, but decided against it; the chase was coming to an end, he felt. It would be only minutes, now.

There was the piv, sides heaving with exhaustion and pain. Twenty feet. If he could get close enough to grab it, kill it at last with the obsidian knife, a quick stroke to the neck. . . . Fifteen feet. Ten.

With a snuffling sound expressive of despair, the piv began to move, trotting tiredly down a rocky slope into the gorge of a stream. Nijon followed grimly, slowing to avoid tripping on uneven ground.

In a burst of sudden speed amazing in so weary an animal, the antelope darted away at right angles, directly off downstream.

Almost before Nijon could wonder what had startled the piv, he heard the cough.

Not the cough of an antelope; still less the cough of a man.

A lioness. With cubs to protect.

She crouched . . .

And sprang.

He dived to the side and raised the bow, his only meager protection. The lioness hurtled toward him, claws extended. He had seen the great cats hunt before; she would knock him down, lie across him, rake with all four claws. . . .

The bow caught the lioness square in the chest. It bent under her weight, then splintered, but deflected her enough that she fell to Nijon's right. One claw caught him, gouging a deep furrow across his ribs; that and the glancing impact sent Nijon asprawl. He lost his grip on the knife as he hit earth; it skittered off. . . .

The lioness regained her footing first. Nijon rolled swiftly away downslope, panting for breath, stones smashing into already-injured ribs.

He sprang to his feet. Above, the lioness paced down into the gorge, eyes fixed on him, tail atwitch.

The bow was gone. The knife was gone. All he had left, Nijon realized with despair, was a pointed stick: his last remaining arrow.

The lioness leapt from a standing start. He tumbled to the left. She missed him, slid on the scree, and splashed into the stream.

Her back was to him. Instantly, Nijon flung himself on her, wrapping his arms about her neck, his legs about her flanks.

She roared, rolled in the stream, scrabbling with her paws and flinging her head from side to side. It was all Nijon could do to hang on. As long as he could, he was safe; but the instant he let go, she would be upon him.

She squirmed, trying to duck her head under his arm. Holding on with his left arm, legs clamped about her body, Nijon stabbed desperately toward her face with the arrow.

He felt the point crunch on skull. She rolled over, in the stream; Nijon choked on a mouthful of water, stabbing again, feeling his arrow skitter off a tooth, perhaps injuring the gum. He could feel her body twisting out from under his legs, and knew, with a sickening sensation, that his young life was ended—

And the point of the arrow found the socket of an eye. He felt it plunge, deep into the great cat's brain.

The lioness howled in agony. She bucked and writhed; Nijon kept his grip on her throat, but his legs were tossed to the side; in her death throes, the lioness raked deep into his calf.

And then she was still.

Half in the stream, Nijon lay panting, shivering in shock.

At last, he realized that the water was filled with red filigree: his own blood. It would not clot, so long as he was in the stream.

Groaning, he pulled himself up onto the scree.

Where he passed out.

"Wake up, son," said a voice.

Nijon peeled open an eye. It was night. A moon was out. His wounds had stiffened; he could barely move.

A furry face hung a few inches from his: small black eyes, protruding nose and whiskers. A mongoose.

"Shoo," said Nijon.

Mongooses did not eat carrion, and certainly never went after live prey as large as he; but in his current condition, Nijon felt, it was probably a bad idea to let any animal snuffle around him.

"Is that any way to talk to your pa?" asked the mongoose. It sat beside Nijon and began to groom itself, small tongue running over dense fur.

Pain came in waves. The air seemed curiously thick. Although it was night, Nijon felt hot. And a talking mongoose sat next to him, licking its tail. "Delirium," groaned Nijon. His wounds must be infected.

The mongoose peered at him. "Yes," it said. "True. But irrelevant. I brought you dinner." It nodded off to Nijon's left.

Nijon glanced there; to his surprise, a dead snake and two bird's eggs lay on the ground.

Cautiously, trying not to open the gouges on his chest, he reached over and grabbed one of the eggs. He tried to break it over his mouth, but fumbled. Afraid of losing it, he put the whole egg in his mouth, broke it with his teeth, sucked down the contents and a good part of the shell, and spat the remnants onto the ground.

The stars were out of focus, dancing strangely in the sky. Nijon wondered whether the infection would kill him. "Mongooses don't talk," he said through bits of shell, reaching for the other egg.

The mongoose sighed and curled up, tail touching its nose. "What is your patronymic?" it asked.

"None of your business," Nijon snarled.

The mongoose chuckled; a curious, chirring sound. "A sore point?"

"My mother's fault," Nijon said.

"For claiming your father was a god?" asked the mongoose.

"Aye, very credible," said Nijon sarcastically. "The tribe was greatly impressed. She could have kept quiet. No one would have known that it wasn't Tsawen who fathered me."

"He was off plundering Motraia with most of the Va-Naleu at the time," the mongoose pointed out.

"So?" demanded Nijon. "So she was diddling someone on the side. She needn't invent so daft a tale."

"I take it the tribe didn't accept the story at face value," said the mongoose.

"Hardly," said Nijon. "Can you really eat raw snake?"

"Can I? Certainly. I'm a mongoose, you notice. Can you? Why not? It's not poisonous; a grass snake. And you are my son, after all."

"Right," said Nijon skeptically.

He grabbed the snake and took a bite out of its side, scales and all.

Mongoose scurried off.

The sun was hot on his skin, hot; or was it his fever that was so hot? There, in the cloudless sky, hovered black things, huge black things; they must be vultures.

They were not vultures; someone stood over him, someone in buckskins, someone with a large, black knife, held awkwardly, but—

at his very neck—

Despite his wounds, Nijon struck upward with all his force. The figure and its knife went flying. There was a stinging at Nijon's throat; he took it for a scrape from the knife.

His leg in agony, Nijon propped himself up on an elbow and blinked. His throat was as scratchy as pumice. The world was filled with smoke; he had to squint to see anything, and what he could make out was shaky, shimmering like a heat mirage.

It was Dowdin. "You," grated Nijon, the words ripping his throat; he was dry, like the great desert, dry as bones.

Dowdin scurried to fetch his knife but did not respond. He stood up the slope of the gorge, shifting from foot to foot, uncertain as to what to do.

How had Dowdin found him on the plain? Nijon wondered. Dowdin was no great tracker. . . . Ah. At Dowdin's belt, Nijon saw a snakeskin, a piece of slate, a bag—shamanic objects. He had used magic. And perhaps he had intended to slay Nijon with magic, but seeing the boy injured, had reasoned that a knife would suffice.

"You tried to kill me," Nijon managed to whisper.

Dowdin curled a lip. "Why bother? You're dead anyway. Yes, you're dead," he said, as if trying to convince himself. "Infected wounds, exposed in the sun."

Nijon understood. The apprentice was brave enough to kill a comatose boy, but too cowardly to kill one awake, even one crippled with wounds and sickness. Dowdin was trying to make himself believe he could leave Nijon here, and let nature do his work.

There seemed nothing more to say, so Nijon said nothing, but kept a wary eye on Dowdin.

Gods knew he despised the little sneak; but why would Dowdin want to murder him? He mulled over the thought, but got nowhere with it. His brain felt like clotted blood. He put the puzzle aside for another time.

Despite exhaustion, despite his fever, despite a raging thirst, Nijon forced himself to stay awake, lest he feel the bite of Dowdin's knife.

Until he realized that the man was gone. Willy-nilly, Nijon slumped into unconsciousness once again.

3

A mind adrift . . . Sun . . . Thirst . . . Wavering light. . . .

A man crouched over Nijon. "Dowdin," croaked Nijon, and raised his arms to strike the apprentice again, but he was weaker now, too weak, helpless before the knife. . . .

"What?" said the man. It was not Dowdin. He was as naked as Nijon and bore a huge brown mustache, flopping over a skimpier beard.

His brown eyes were close-set; and there was, Nijon was startled to see, a line of hair running from his scalp down his back—not the hair that the back of any hirsute man might bear, but a thick pelt.

"Who are you?" Nijon rasped, brain fuzzy.

"I am Mongoose," said the man. "Here. Drink more." And he poured water from a gourd into Nijon's mouth. Nijon lapped at it greedily.

A god might appear in whatever guise he chose, Nijon supposed. And it was a relief to realize that his mother had almost certainly known Mongoose in this form—not as a furry creature.

"Enough," Mongoose said at last—and although Nijon's

thirst raged, he knew Mongoose was right. It was dangerous to drink too much at once, after great deprivation.

Mongoose scooped something from a pouch. It was a gooey substance, like butter but transparent; within were tiny globules, glowing lambent red. He smeared it on Nijon's leg. The globules danced within the substance. Almost immediately, the pain in Nijon's wound subsided.

"What is that?" Nijon asked.

"A healing salve," said Mongoose absently, rubbing it now onto Nijon's chest.

"You made it?" said Nijon.

Mongoose peered at him. "Made it?" he said. "No. Making things is a human trait. I stole it."

"From whom?"

Mongoose glanced at the sky. "I'd rather not say," he said.

Nervously, Nijon hoped Mongoose wasn't talking about one of the other gods.

"There's someone I want you to meet," said Mongoose, standing up.

"Who's that?" asked Nijon.

"Your brother," said Mongoose. Between his legs twined a golden-furred, whiskered form; in its mouth hung the limp body of a prairie dog. "He caught you supper," said Mongoose. "I thought you might like a mammal for a change."

"My brother?" said Nijon, nonplussed.

"Your half-brother," amended Mongoose. "I am his father, but"—Mongoose chuckled—"but Poai is assuredly not his mother."

The little creature came forward, dropped the prairie dog by Nijon's head, and circled him, sniffing. Apparently deciding the scent was to his liking, he gave Nijon's ear a lick, then settled down, leaning companionably against Nijon's side, and began to groom.

"What's his name?" asked Nijon.

Mongoose looked startled, as if the idea hadn't occurred to him. "He has no name," he said. "You may give him one, I suppose."

"I like him," Nijon decided.

"Good," said Mongoose. "He will stay with you."

Nijon blinked. "All right," he said. "But why?"

Mongoose smiled slightly. "Did I father you so that you might be but another man? Did I father him so that he might be but another mongoose? Your destinies are entwined."

Nijon and Mongoose looked at each other for a long moment.

"Your foot," said Mongoose, reaching over to touch Nijon's chest. "Your foster father's talisman. Where is it?"

Nijon reached for his neck, and realized that the mongoose foot was gone. There was a wild moment of panic; he had worn it since infancy, the gift of his foster father. It was his luck, a ward against the vengeful spirits of slain prey, protection from magical attack. He felt suddenly vulnerable.

Could he possibly have lost it in the tussle with the lioness? Then he remembered the sting at his throat when he had beaten Dowdin away. He had taken the pain for a scrape from Dowdin's knife; but it must have been the thong breaking.

"Dowdin," he said. "Dowdin must have it."

Mongoose frowned. "You must recover it," he said.

"I must," agreed Nijon.

"I should go," said Mongoose, a little reluctantly. "You eat your dinner, now."

Nijon looked at the prairie dog and grimaced. "It would help," he said, "if I had something to skin it with."

Mongoose looked at him again in that startled way. "Ah," he said. "I shall see if I can do something about that tomorrow."

And then he was gone.

A black-footed form scurried sinuously up the gorge.

It was not his idea of a feast, Nijon thought, spitting out bits of fur. But it beat starvation.

The next morning, there was no burning sun. Nijon awoke when Brother's cold nose nudged him insistently in the face. Thunder rolled across the prairie. A few fat drops of rain fell nearby.

Nijon's first thought was for shelter; was there a cleft between two boulders into which he might crawl? Then came another thought: Brooks such as this were prone to flash floods. He must get out of the gorge.

Surprising himself, he managed to stand shakily erect. He should not have been able to do so, not with wounds as bad as these; Mongoose's salve must have been preternaturally effective.

He gazed up the slope. The corpse of the lioness caught his eye.

The lioness. If the stream flooded, the body would be borne off by the waters.

"I killed a lioness with a pointed stick," he said—and grinned. Now, that was a truly heroic deed; that was something that would impress the tribe. To return, wearing a cloak made of the lioness' skin; that would be sweet indeed! Lai'iani would be impressed. He was not going to lose that skin, he decided.

He worked his way carefully down the loose stone of the gully, back to where the lioness lay. He wished, again, for a blade; any blade. He knew how to skin a cat; the skin would weigh far less than the animal as a whole. She must weigh more than a hundred pounds, he judged. And he was weak with his injuries—his injuries, and starvation.

Rain began to patter.

Brother cocked an eye at the sky and, glancing at Nijon apologetically, made off up the slope.

Nijon watched the mongoose go, then turned, bent over,

and painfully picked up the lioness. He took one step—and realized he could not bear this weight, not on his leg, not up this slope.

Nijon stood, cursing to himself, a hundredweight of lioness held defiantly in his arms.

He would not abandon the skin. He would *not*.

How could he possibly save it?

A boulder stood not far away, Nijon saw, up the slope from him. Its tip was higher than his head, and might remain dry even if the streambed flooded. Perhaps . . . He took a hesitant step toward the rock.

The ankle of his bad leg twisted. He fell headlong into the stream, the lioness splashing with him.

He came up coughing and choking, water in mouth and nose. The rain beat down steadily now; not yet a downpour, but quite wet enough.

There was blood in the water. His leg ached abominably; the wound had reopened.

He dragged himself to his feet. The injured leg protested, but he could still stagger forward, weight on the good leg as much of the time as possible. With determination, he heaved up the lioness.

He took a step; his bad leg crumpled; but he swept his good leg forward swiftly enough to take his weight again before he fell.

Again. And again. And he stood before the boulder.

If he were healthy, he judged, he would be able to swing the lioness high and deposit her on the rock; she was heavy, but he was strong. In his current state, he could not manage the feat.

He shifted his hands so they were flat underneath the lioness and lifted—strained—lifted. She rose an inch, two, six. His arms shook with the strain; but at last the lioness was high enough. He shoved her against the rock and held her there, not quite atop the peak, but high enough that the rock bore part of the weight. He waited until his arms stopped trembling, then rolled her onto the boulder's pinnacle.

He stood, leaning against the rock, rain running in rivulets down his face and into his beard. He was shivering, he realized; whether from strain, the cold of the water or the shock of a reopened wound it was hard to tell. But he must not stay here, one foot in the rising stream, rain pouring about him.

He stumbled away from the boulder and up the loose shale. He managed a dozen hard-won steps before, overcome with fatigue and trembling, he fell again.

Thunder crashed. Nijon curled himself into a ball, to retain as much heat as possible, and lay miserably in the storm.

He felt a snuffling at his arm; Brother had returned. The mongoose pushed Nijon's arm with a paw. "Sorry," Nijon said softly. "I don't think I can make it any farther."

4

Thunder still rolled across the steppe, but it was more distant now. Rain pattered down, but no longer in a downpour. It was dim, the gray of twilight. Strong arms carried Nijon.

He looked up. Mongoose bore him, up the scree, up to the rock where the lioness had crouched. Mongoose laid him down in the lee of the rock, partially protected by an overhang.

Brother was there already. He scurried over Nijon's chest and butted him affectionately.

"Thank you," Nijon said to Mongoose.

"What do you think you were doing?" Mongoose asked, annoyed. "Your wound has reopened."

Nijon sighed. It seemed so foolish now. He told Mongoose of his desire to save the lioness' skin.

"Whatever for?" demanded Mongoose.

Nijon tried to tell him of the prestige he would gain by the skin, and by the tale of how he had slain the beast, naked, with a sharpened stick; that without the skin for proof the tale was worthless. Mongoose listened, but seemed not to understand. At last, the god sighed. "A human thing," he said, as if that explained all unexplainables. "Here." He pushed something toward Nijon with his foot.

Nijon looked; it was a bronze spearhead, verdigrised with corrosion, no shaft in its socket. Nijon picked it up; the edge was dull, but that was easily fixed. No doubt he could find an appropriate stone, down in the streambed, with which to sharpen it. "Thank you," he said. "Where did you get it?"

Mongoose gave a fluid shrug. "At an old battle site. Not far from here."

Nijon frowned. He'd never heard of a battle in these parts.

Mongoose crouched down in the shelter of the rock. "I must go soon," he said. "It may be that we will not meet again; not, perhaps, for some time."

"Is it so?" said Nijon sadly.

Mongoose sighed. "I have responsibilities," he said. "And you have your destiny."

"What is that?" asked Nijon.

Mongoose stared out over the plain. "There, northward; there is another world. A strange world, where men do not roam, but till the earth. A world of—of cities," Mongoose said, as if the word were strange. "Of kings and priests and odder gods."

"Of dragons," said Nijon, "of headless men, elves, monsters; of adventure."

Mongoose gave him a startled and skeptical look, then smiled.

"Yes," he said, "quite so. There lies the future; the future of mankind. This prairie, this wide land; I fear one day it will be transformed."

It was Nijon's turn to be skeptical; the steppe was vast, eternal. He could not imagine it transformed. Transformed into what?

"You must go there," said Mongoose. "There, to the north; to the cities of men."

"I—I had hoped," said Nijon, a little apologetically, "to become one day a chieftain; a great warrior, to bring honor to your name, my father. And to take a wife; to—"

Mongoose made a chirring sound. "You will be a great warrior," he said, "and a chieftain. You will lead your people into a glorious future. But there is more to the world than the plains, more to life than pillaging villages and counting coup on rival clans and whelping another generation of humanity. Go you; experience all you can in your brief life; learn all you can learn; do great deeds; and your name shall be remembered for—a generation or two, at any event."

Nijon could see it: magics beyond comprehension, gold and bronze, sumptuous fabrics, delicacies none of his tribe had ever tasted; exotic women, intrigue, warfare, bloodshed, triumph. Heroic lays and eldritch stories came to him, tales told to children over the communal fire. "Yes," he said, with rising excitement. "Yes, Father; I shall go north."

Mongoose nodded once. "Take your brother," he said. "He will aid you. I would give you other gifts if I could; but making things is not in my nature. From me you have, at least, the gift of inheritance: sharper senses than natural, resistance to poison, a sense of magic forces at play—and," he said, leaning closer and smiling slightly, "also this: You need never fear a serpent, for it is in your nature to slay all of that kind."

Nijon received this news wide-eyed, for he had never suspected that his keen eyesight and keener sense of smell were anything more than natural.

Mongoose turned his gaze to Brother and, without further word to Nijon, transformed into a mongoose himself.

The two creatures touched noses, and a golden spark seemed to pass from Mongoose to his child.

And then, the god was gone.

Far away, thunder rolled over the steppe.

Raindrops made staccato rhythm on the earth about the rock.

Nijon sighed. His stomach was empty still; Mongoose had not brought dinner, this night.

Where had Brother gone? he wondered, noticing the absence; the question was answered at once, for the golden mongoose returned into view, a dead prairie chicken in its jaws. It dragged the bird to Nijon's feet, dropped it, and waited, apparently to be praised.

Nijon was delighted; even raw, this was a far more appetizing repast than he had eaten of late. Feathers could be plucked, where fur or scales could not. And those feathers would fletch new arrows.

Nijon woke, dry again, stomach empty; groaning, he sat up, then gingerly rose to his feet. His wounds were stiff; walking was painful, but he managed to clamber down the gorge and slake his thirst at the stream, Brother drinking alongside. Despite the pain, Nijon concluded he was healing well.

The day boded heat. The sun shimmered a hand above the eastern horizon; the wind was desultory, barely enough to stir the still-cool air. Nijon sighed, then fished a smooth, black stone out of the stream and set about sharpening his spearhead. Once the edge was keen, he pulled the lioness off her perch atop the boulder and began to skin her, doing his best to ignore the developing smell. He washed the skin and set it out to dry. It ought to be properly cured, but he had neither the skills nor the supplies to cure it; dried, it should last through his walkabout, if he kept it supple with animal fats.

Nijon cut himself a sapling, trimmed it, and pegged the shaft into the spearhead. As he worked, an aardwolf appeared. It eyed Nijon worriedly, but was brave enough to dart in and rip a chunk of meat from the lioness' corpse.

Brother studied the creature, whiskers set at an angle indicating clear contempt for eaters of carrion.

Nijon hefted his spear. Experimentally, he hurled it at the aardwolf, which fled, yipping angrily. The butt end of the spear lagged as the spear flew, Nijon saw; it was next to useless as a missile weapon, though it might kill a rabbit at close range. But the shaft was sturdy enough, and Nijon had no doubt it would be quite effective against, say, a charging warthog; on the whole, it was a more effective weapon than his obsidian knife.

Thinking of the knife, Nijon began to search the gully for it. It had skittered off during his fight with the lioness; surely, it must be lying somewhere about. But Nijon could not find it; perhaps Dowdin had stolen it, he finally concluded.

By the time Nijon was finished, it was midday and hot indeed. He folded up the lioness pelt and, leaning on his spear shaft for support, began to limp across the plain, northerly, toward the water hole where he had left Naenae. Brother came with him, batting at butterflies and scurrying off to chase rodents.

Toward evening, Nijon trudged up a low rise, leaning wearily on his spear. His wounds were a constant ache, and Nijon knew they would become more painful still when at last he could rest. Still, he had been days apart from his pony. What had been a few hours' absence to hunt had turned into nearly a week, laid up with injuries.

He paused to rest atop the rise. His shelter was down there, bundled grasses leaning against a rock; and down there, too, was his mare, tied to a tree within reach of water. Naenae would be snorting with frustration, he thought; frustration and hunger. By now, she must have cropped all the vegetation within reach of her tree.

He began to descend. There was the water hole, brown

liquid glistening in the morning sun. Birdsong sounded from the trees about the water. But where was . . . ?

A scent reached Nijon's nostrils; a low shape was huddled on the ground. He halted in dismay: It was Naenae's corpse.

As Nijon approached, a cloud of flies took flight.

He crouched and, sadly, turned the animal over. She had been disemboweled. Ragged claw marks, black blood clotting in the sun, ran up her flanks. A predator had killed her: by the claw marks, a cat. Nijon ran a hand forlornly down her neck, as he had so many times before.

Predators drank at the water hole. He must have been gone long enough for the man-scent to wear off the pony. And tied as she was to a tree, she could not possibly have escaped.

He crouched over the body for a long and miserable moment. It was as if the god Dorij had purposefully stripped him of each of the items that he had taken from the tribe: knife, talisman, pony. Even his bow, made using the knife, was gone.

The thought made Nijon feel faintly better: His ill luck was not the result of his own stupidity; it was, perhaps, divine will.

And now he was free of it. The terms of Dorij's charge were satisfied; if he had not gone wholly naked into the wilderness, he had been sundered from the few objects that sheltered him from nakedness. True, he now had the lion skin and the spear, but the lioness he had killed himself, using only a fire-hardened stick, and the spear had not been taken from the tribe; it had been acquired during his manhood rite, a gift of the gods, or a god, at any rate. Surely his tribulations were over now. Yet he had thirty days to survive before he might return to his tribe—

More than survive, he thought. "Survive, prosper, and return," went the ritual chant; and surely no tribesman would consider one who lost his horse to have prospered.

To lose one's horse; what could be more shameful, to a people who lived by the horse?

He turned and scanned the area around the hole. This much was true: If he was not to return in shame, he must find another mount.

There were no unclaimed mounts on the steppe. He must steal one. He must find another tribe, out here on the plain; find them, and steal from them.

Horse theft was an honored crime, a crime of the brave. To steal a horse from another tribe was to prove the superiority of your own clan. Yet it was not a crime viewed lightly. A captured horse thief was accorded the highest honor an enemy might receive: He was tortured to death, so that he might prove his bravery by refraining from displaying any pain.

Nijon preferred to demonstrate his bravery in less dramatic ways.

The trail was fresh; there were horses ahead. But Nijon was puzzled.

Deep ruts cut the sod. The Vai commonly pulled goods on travois, poles with nets strung between them, hitched to horses or steers. A travois would leave ruts like these. But the furrows were deep; Nijon wondered how any animal could pull a burden so heavy.

There were the hoofprints of cattle, but of only a few animals—and of uncommonly large ones. And there were horses, too—the marks of horseshoes.

The Vai did not shoe their horses; metal was too precious. But the people of the northern cities did, sometimes. Shod hooves had better traction in mud, and were less likely to split or lodge a stone.

The tracks must have been left by northerners.

The caravan passed upwind. Nijon studied it, crouching in the grass alongside Brother.

Two wagons—large, four-wheeled carts, covered with cloth—were each pulled by six oxen. That explained the ruts: The wagons left deep ruts because they were far heavier than a Vai travois. And the cattle were larger because they were northern draft animals, not the smaller grazing beasts kept by the Vai.

The horses were ridden by men. They were not wearing armor—no sane man would, on a hot summer day, with no enemy in sight—but each had a bronzen axe at his belt and a lance on his saddle. A few bore bows and quivers of arrows.

A pack of dogs darted about the caravan, barking and playing. Nijon frowned; if he were to try to steal a horse, they would sound the alarm.

That must, he realized, be the main reason the caravan traveled with dogs. Not the only reason, though; dogs could be eaten. They were an alarm—and a self-mobile larder.

The men were armed, but obviously not raiders. Raiders travel light, and quickly. Oxen are too slow, far slower than horses; raiders would not bring them.

An army would. The heavy neck bones of oxen make them ideal draft animals, far better than horses, which would choke when pulling heavy loads. And an army would need to carry supplies.

But this was no army: two wagons, perhaps a dozen soldiers. They were too small a force to stand up to any sizable tribe. They must be traders.

Northern traders sometimes braved the steppe, bringing metal goods and ornamental items the Vai could not craft for themselves. In return, they sought mastodon ivory, pelts, sometimes gems or gold panned from the streams. And also, they bought booty: goods reaved from the northern cities by the Vai in their raids. A merchant lacking scruples could make a ready profit by buying back the goods of his own murdered people.

Traders were unlikely to slay him out of hand, Nijon told himself. And if he could stay with them—the opportunity to steal a mount might present itself.

He stood up, and walked nonchalantly forward.

One of the soldiers caught sight of Nijon and shouted something Nijon did not catch, wheeling to face the boy, unslinging his bow and drawing an arrow from the quiver attached to his saddle.

Hooves thundered as the other guards rounded the caravan to face Nijon in a ragged line, lances and bows at the ready.

Nijon stood alone, facing the weapons of a dozen men.

5

There were shouts of "Ho!" and the bawls of oxen and the creak of leather as the wagons came slowly to a halt. The soldiers tensed in their saddles, weapons at the ready, horses dancing nervously, facing a single, naked savage armed only with a spear. But where one savage was visible, they knew, a hundred might lie in ambush.

Nijon stood nervously, ready to flee, ready to bring his spear to bear if they should charge.

The caravaneers scanned the horizon and consulted one another.

One man was evidently in charge: The others looked to him. He wore a dun tunic and a torque of gold, with something red—a garnet? a ruby?—at its center. After a moment of indecision, he ordered another man forward.

The other wore buckskins and leggings, clothing a Vai might wear, but he was no tribesman. He dismounted and walked out toward Nijon, empty-handed, swaggering a bit—perhaps to deny fear, perhaps to impress his companions. He held up a palm in peaceful greeting.

"Mika Oonashram," he said through a luxuriant, blond mustache: Mika, son of Nashram. The "oo-" of the Vai tongue—"son of"—sounded odd connected to such un-Vai names.

"Nijon Ootsawen," said Nijon, claiming to be the son of his foster father; eyebrows might be raised if he were to claim kinship with a god.

"You here to parley," Mika asked, "or are you here on your own tick?"

"I'm on my own," said Nijon.

Mika looked a little closer. "Hmm," he said. "You look like you could use a meal."

Nijon gave a wry grin, remembering his most recent repast: raw prairie chicken. "Yeah, I could," he admitted.

"Good," said Mika. "We could use a scout. What do you say?"

Perfect, Nijon thought. This gave him an excuse to stick around—until he might steal a horse. "Maybe," he said. "Eat first, talk later."

"Fair enough," Mika said. "Stick with me and keep that spear out of anyone's stomach. I'll get you something to eat." He turned and led the way toward the soldiers. "He is no danger," he shouted in Agondan.

All male children of the Va-Naleu learn the northern tongue, for use in war and trade; but they also learn the usefulness of pretending not to know it. Nijon gave no sign he understood.

The northerners were ahorse, heavily armed, in a rough circle about Nijon. Their leader, the man with the torque of gold, studied Nijon distrustfully.

Their Leader (*in the Agondan tongue*): "How is he called?"

Mika (*in the same language*): "He is named Nijon."

Leader (*in badly accented Vai*): "Son of tribe?"

Nijon (*in Vai, of course*): "What?"

Mika (*in Vai*): "He means, 'What is your tribe?' "

Nijon (*lying*): "Va-Tsalu."

Mika *(in Agondan)*: "Fela, O prince among merchants, leave the translation of his rude animal snarls to your servant. He is of the tribe of Tsalu."

Fela *(frowning, in Agondan)*: "Have you heard of this clan ere now?"

Mika: "I have. It is a large tribe, possessing thousands of head of cattle. They joined with the army of Dikon Khan, two decades past."

(Nijon bit back a grin. The Va-Tsalu numbered fewer than a score. They came from the western steppe and had probably never even heard of Dikon Khan.)

Fela: "Are the Tsalu in these parts?"

Mika *(to Nijon, in Vai)*: "You married?"

Nijon *(surprised at the non sequitur)*: "No."

Mika: "Got a girlfriend?"

Nijon *(grinning)*: "Well, yes."

Mika *(turning to Fela, in Agondan)*: "He says not. He asserts they are a hundred leagues distant or more."

(True, Nijon thought—though Mika couldn't possibly have known it.)

Fela *(frowning)*: "Does he know of the Mammoth Graveyard, and where it may lie?"

Mika *(to Nijon, in Vai)*: "You any good as a hunter?"

Nijon *(surprised; what tribesman would admit to being a poor one?)*: "Why yes. I have slain all manner of beasts, from the lowly porcupine to the mightiest of mastodons. See you the skin I bear on my back? It is the pelt of a lioness, the fiercest and most dangerous animal in all creation. I slew her myself, with no weapon but a fire-hardened stick less than three hands in length. I was naked at the time, and had run seven leagues. Picture the scene, if you will: Nijon Ootsawen, pouring sweat, exhausted by his run—"

Mika: "Yes, yes, fine. You're the mightiest hunter in all the south."

Nijon: "Verily, it is so."

Mika *(turning to Fela, in Agondan)*: "He is excited. He claims he knows the Graveyard well, and that it lies no farther than a dozen leagues from here."

(Nijon blinked; he'd never heard of a Mammoth Graveyard. And then he realized: Mika had known that any tribesman could boast for hours about his own hunting prowess. He had wanted Nijon to babble for a pass, to give Fela the notion that important information was being transmitted.)

Fela: "Excellent, good Nashram! This is most welcome news. Can he be induced to guide us to the site?"

Mika *(in Vai, to Nijon)*: "You want food now?"

Nijon: "I could use a bite."

Mika *(in Agondan, to Fela)*: "He demands that we feed him first."

Fela: *(Snorts.)* "See that he is fed." *(To soldiers)*: "Ho! We shall make camp here. You, there—unhitch and hobble the oxen. You—"

This, thought Nijon, as he walked toward a wagon and the prospect of food, looks as though it might be entertaining.

The food was horrible. The caravan's only fresh meat was dog. The rest of the meal was some kind of biscuit— Nijon didn't know what, exactly, since his tribe rarely baked, ovens being the possession of sedentary peoples. The biscuit was so hard he nearly broke a tooth on it. The only way he could break it was along the lines left by the weevils that infested it.

Mika showed him how to eat it; you dipped it in the stewpot, apparently, and the liquid softened it enough for

you to choke it down. Hideous stuff, but Nijon was hungry
enough not to care.

"What tribes are around here right now?" Mika asked.

Nijon shrugged, masticating a biscuit. He wished he
knew. "Just the Va-Naleu," he said. "You don't want to go
near them."

"Why not?" asked Mika.

Nijon gave a theatrical shudder. "Very bad medicine, the
Va-Naleu. Their shaman, he is of the undead. They eat
children and slay all strangers out of hand."

Mika grunted skeptically. "Look here," he said. "When
you're through eating, we'll speak with Fela. The fellow
with the gold torque, right?"

Nijon nodded.

"When I ask you to, I want you to stand up, point
southeast, and say something. Doesn't matter what. 'There,
there, there it is,' something like that."

"Why?" asked Nijon, interested.

"Ah—it's rather complicated," said Mika. "I'll give you
these if you do." He held out a handful of beads. "Have we
got a deal?"

Nijon picked a bead up and examined it. Trade beads,
moderate quality. They might make a nice necklace for
Lai'iani.

"Sure," he said, dropping the bead back into Mika's
palm. "Is there dinner in it?"

"All right," said Mika.

"Can I hang around for a couple of days?" asked Nijon.

Mika's eyes narrowed, wondering what Nijon was up to.
"Yes, fine," he said at last.

The sun was an orange orb on the horizon. The earth still
breathed the warmth of the day, though the slight breeze
was already chill. The men of the caravan busied themselves with the preparation of the evening's repast. Oxen
and horses grazed calmly, hobbled by lengths of rope.

Nijon, Mika, Fela, and the soldiers' captain stood out on the plain, a few yards away from the wagons.

Fela: "The savage is agreed to guide us, then? He shall take us to the fabled Mammoths' Grave?"

Mika: "Yes. He is happy to do so, in exchange for a few sequins."

Fela (*eyes narrowing*): "How many?"

Mika: "Six."

Fela: "Four."

Mika: "Good Fela, surely some modest magnanimity is in order. Six sequins is a pittance, a derisory sum—"

Fela: "Four."

Mika (*sighs; then, to Nijon, in Vai*): "Are you ready?"

Nijon: "For what?"

Mika: "To point and jabber, remember?"

Nijon (*shrugs*): "Sure."

Mika (*in Agondan, to Fela*): "He agrees."

Fela: "Well enough. Therefore ask him where the Grave-yard lies."

Mika (*in Vai*): "Folderol Mammoth gabble gabble. Do it now."

Nijon: "Huh?"

Mika (*still in Vai*): "Now, boy, now!"

Nijon (*jumping up and giving an aardwolf howl*): "There!" (*Points to southeast.*) "There it lies! Verily, it is true, so sayeth Nijon of the Va-Tsalu, and may the Thunderer strike down all those who gainsay me! What is it that lies there, by the way, Mika, Nashram's son?"

Mika (*in Vai*): "Never mind, Nijon. You've earned your beads."

And what about my silver? Nijon thought, knowing quite well that Mika would pocket the coins.

After dinner, Nijon prowled around the encampment in the shirt and leggings Mika had given him, the air filled with the sound of locusts.

He regarded the camp with a critical eye. The two wagons were drawn up parallel to one another, with a wide space between them. The campfire burned in the center of this space, and the cook's equipment was set up by it. The horses and oxen were tied to stakes nearby. Men had already unrolled blankets by the fire.

It appeared the soldiers had at least some sense of military order. Two men were on watch on opposite sides of the camp, sheltered from the light of the fire by the bulk of the wagons, peering out into the dark and walking back and forth. This, Nijon knew, would avail them little; any warrior of the Vai could spot this group miles away, its campfire shining beaconlike into the night. Creeping closer, the warrior would see the guards silhouetted against the light. A war party could overwhelm the guards and be among the northerners before they grew alert.

But the setup was quite adequate protection against Nijon's own plans. He did not fancy his chances of unstaking a horse from amid sleeping men, then escaping past waiting guards.

Sighing, Nijon sat cross-legged in the grass and studied the rising moon. A small head butted his leg. Brother, who had disappeared when Nijon approached the caravan, had come to visit. Nijon scratched the little mongoose behind the ears.

The moon was full, or nearly so, east and a bit to the north. The soft, blue-tinted glow revealed the vastness of the plain, stretching untrammeled for. . . .

There was a pillar of smoke in the distance, off toward the moon. Nijon rose to his feet and peered that way until his eyes burned.

A pillar of smoke on the prairie. There were several possible meanings. First, war: a summoning to the clans. No, not that; there would have been messages to and fro all summer, hurried conferences among the elders and the

Women's Council; and it was late in the year for such a summoning.

Second, a grassfire, sweeping across the plain, endangering all before it. But that would be a line of smoke, not a pillar; and the wind would drive the scent of the fire before it. Too, the summer had been a wet one; it had rained only days before. A grassfire was unlikely.

Third, an encampment raided, put to the torch. But that would be an irregular mass of smoke, not the regular puffs Nijon could discern.

The fire could only mean one thing: the death of a chieftain. Lesser mortals were buried in shallow graves. Wood was scarce on the prairie; bonfires were burned only rarely. But a chieftain was burned with his possessions.

Ro-Mo'ian is dead, Nijon thought, and as he thought it, realized it must be true. The Va-Naleu were there, off that way; it must be they who burned that fire.

Nijon fretted. What was going on? The chief had seemed in good enough health, the tribe satisfied with his rule. True, by ancient tradition, any warrior might challenge the chief, slay him in honorable combat, and assume the chieftain's bonnet; and true, Mo'ian was a dodderer, unlikely to triumph in any such contest. But that was tradition, and not reality: The Women's Council was happy with Mo'ian's rule. If some upstart were to challenge and kill him, they would urge their husbands and sons to challenge the usurper, again and again, until at last he fell to some young warrior's blade. Without political support within the tribe, it was suicide to challenge the chief.

Nijon itched to return to the tribe. He was concerned for his mother and foster father; a sorcerer's position in the tribe depended closely on his relations with the chief.

Nijon rose and strode uneasily about, Brother watching him with worried eyes. There was nothing he could do, he concluded. His period of wandering was not yet ended; and he might not return until it was.

It took some minutes, until the moon was full in the sky, for Nijon to master himself. At last, he sighed, and made his way back toward the wagons.

Brother scurried on ahead, rustling the grass. "What was that?" said a voice—and Nijon instantly halted. He had not sensed anyone before him.

"Just an animal," said another voice.

Noiselessly, Nijon slid prone into the briza. Peering carefully, he made out two figures in the moonlight: a grizzled veteran, whom Nijon had taken for the captain of the guard; and a younger man, of whom Nijon had not previously taken note. "We've been out here for over a month, Captain," the younger said.

"I know," said the older. "Patience, Dana. It will not be long now."

"So Fela seems to think," said the younger. "But—that Mika is a slippery one. And the story sounds too good to be true: a place where mammoths go to die, the graveyard of their kind, where ivory lies all about and one may load a fortune in an afternoon—bah. If so, why haven't the savages picked it clean?"

The older one sighed. "The men are uneasy, I take it," he said.

"Yes," said Dana.

"Counsel them to patience," said the captain. "What have we to fear? The tale will prove true, in which case we wait till the ivory is loaded before we strike; or it will prove false, in which case we strike regardless, and at least gain the merchant's money."

"What have we to fear?" said Dana. "Who knows when some barbarian will take it into his head to butcher us. Best we kill the merchant now, and leave for the north expeditiously."

The older man grunted. "We have waited thus far," he said. "A few days more will tell."

Dana sighed. "I suppose you're right," he said.

"Your watch is up, Dana," said the captain. "Get some rest."

"Aye," said the younger man, and headed back to the camp, Nijon drifting after.

6

The mighty sun lanced the doe of night; her grume of rose and gold clotted on the horizon. Somewhat to his surprise, Nijon was not the first awake; the cook bustled about the campfire, preparing the morning meal. Nijon rose and helped the man pour water from a huge clay pot kept in one of the wagons. The cook offered Nijon a bit of smoked meat by way of thank-you.

Nijon accepted it; it was extremely tough, becoming palatable only after minutes of chewing. Its taste, however, was not unpleasant.

The sentries wandered in, yawning and rubbing their eyes, to scoop a bit of soup out of the stewpot and watch the cook scuttle about. At last he was ready, found a pot and a utensil, and set about banging the two together, shouting, "Ahoy! Roust ye, slugabeds! Chow!"

With grumbles, moans, and unhappy faces, the caravaneers stumbled to their feet, fumbled with belts and clasps, and wandered off onto the plain to make water. Soon, they were lining up for ladles of soup and bits of weevilly biscuit.

"Eat lively, boys," said Fela. "I want to be on the move before the sun is clear of the world's edge."

The order was not well yeeived; and in truth, the wagons

did not begin to move behind straining oxen until at least two hands stood between the sun and the horizon. Still, the merchant did not seem displeased; apparently, this was rapid progress enough for one morning's work.

As the day wore on to hotter noon, the wagon train moved at slow oxen-speed across the plain. From time to time, soldiers would scout off on horseback. Nijon forbore from pointing out the uselessness of this: A mounted party could be seen miles away, while warriors could crouch unseen within the tall grass, invisible lest a rider should stumble across them by some mischance.

But this gave him a notion. "I would like to scout, too," he told Mika. "Could I have a horse?"

Mika studied the young man gravely, then burst into a wide grin. "Nice try," he said, "but I think not."

Nijon could only grin wryly back. To lend a Vai a horse; Mika could hardly fail to realize that meant to lose a horse forever.

Still, Nijon walked out, some distance from the caravan, pacing it as it sailed across the grass. The oxen moved slowly, slowly enough that Nijon could wander back and forth without risk of being left behind. After some hours, he stumbled across a trail.

A herd of animals had passed this way; recently, for the grasses had not yet sprung aloft. Judging by the dung, they were aurochs.

Prime game, Nijon thought. The huge, wild cattle were superb eating; equally, they were dangerous creatures to hunt. An adult bull aurochs could reach seven feet at the shoulder; enraged, horns tossing, it was a fearsome creature.

Following the caravan, but casting farther afield, Nijon found also what he had half-expected to find: the imprints of unshod hooves.

Vai tribesmen were following this herd of aurochs—preparing a hunt?

Va-Naleu? Nijon wondered—but the tracks led south; his tribe was northeast of here. The trail was probably of a different tribe.

Nijon scowled at the prints. Should he tell Mika?

He chewed over that. No, he thought at last. Why help the northerners? They were headed southeast, anyway, and would probably miss the tribe.

Nijon wandered back toward the caravan.

A soldier galloped toward the wagons, shouting something Nijon didn't catch. The merchant, Fela, bellowed orders, and the wagons creaked to a halt. With most of the men, Nijon went forward, to see what caused this commotion.

A great gash sundered the earth: a canyon, perhaps fifty cubits across. The grass of the plains went almost to its lip.

Down on the canyon floor was a talus of dirt and sand, washed over the edge by periodic rains. Down the canyon's center ran a clear stream. River gullies were not uncommon on the plain; but one with so steep a drop was rare.

Down there, on the streambed, in the canyon, were heaps of bones, white-bleached in the sun.

With excitement, Fela turned to Nijon. "Is this it?" he demanded in Agondan. "The Mammoths' Grave? Is this it?"

Nijon returned a gaze of bland incomprehension.

"There is a trail, downstream," Mika said. "Wide enough for us to take the wagons down."

And how, wondered Nijon, do you know that?

"How far?" Fela demanded.

"A league or so," said Mika.

"Let's go," shouted Fela, and turned back to belabor the caravaneers. There was excitement in the air now, everyone feeling their trek was nearly over; even the oxen seemed to step in a livelier way.

The trail into the canyon led down over tumbled talus; the canyon had collapsed here, leaving a broad ramp descending toward the stream, which, partially dammed by the rubble, bubbled into a pond.

It was not too steep for the oxen, but the footing was uneven. The men scurried about, shoving planks beneath wheels to ensure that the wagons were not trapped in cracks between the rocks. Other men guided the oxen carefully, sometimes going so far as to grab an animal's leg and guide it to a safe position.

It was dusk before they made the canyon floor.

"Camp here?" the soldiers' captain asked.

"No, no," the merchant said, excitement burbling through the fatigue on his face; "it is but a league back up the canyon. Come, we are so close."

And so in gathering darkness, the tired oxen labored up the stream, tired men and panting dogs trudging alongside, until Fela, walking ahead, gave a crow of victory.

Nijon went to see what he had found, and was astonished to see, rising from the canyon bed, a pair of huge mammoth tusks, arranged to form an arch.

"So," said the captain behind Nijon, "it is true. The fabled Mammoth Graveyard."

Fela was running about like a man possessed, darting hither and yon, stooping to pick up fragments of bone.

Nijon examined one the merchant discarded, and saw that it, too, was mammoth ivory; a chip, a fragment.

Could it possibly be that all the bones they had seen from the canyon lip were ivory? Could this truly be the place where weary mammoths came to die? Nijon had seen aged, starving members of the species; their teeth eventually rotted in their jaws, as the teeth of many humans did, and they became unable to feed themselves. Might there not be some special place, holy to the mammoth kind, where they might go to seek a final rest? And would not a fortune in ivory lie there, as the northerners seemed to believe?

It seemed incredible. And yet, there were chips and chips of ivory, scattered about the ground; and behind them stood those mammoth tusks. The bulk of the Graveyard was up the canyon yet, but. . . .

Nijon's finger caught an unevenness in the surface of the ivory. He brought it close to his eyes, then turned so that his body would not block the light from the fire the cook was building.

It was hard to make out in the dim light, but he believed he saw faint toolmarks on the bone.

Now, if this were the secret resting place of dying beasts, why would their ivory bear toolmarks?

The oxen dozed in their traces; the caravaneers had not bothered to unhitch them. In celebration of their arrival, Fela had ordered up a feast, or as close to one as the cook's limited supplies might allow. Casks of ale had been broached, and most of the men were drunk.

Nijon lay near the fire, a bowl of ale in his hands. The slightly bitter northern brew was quite unlike the kumiss of his own people, but not unpleasant in its way. Earlier, there had been songs and rude jests, but now men were drifting off to sleep, some drunk enough that they simply made their rest on the rocks of the canyon floor.

Nijon himself felt a powerful languor creep over him. He yawned and found a more comfortable position, putting his ale aside.

There was a curious smell in the air, a metallic smell. It was the odor, Nijon sleepily thought, of—

Of his stepfather's tent, as Tsawen performed a spell.

The thought was disturbing enough to drag Nijon back from the brink of sleep. He forced open his eyes and surveyed the camp.

The northerners were sleeping, every one of them—

Except for Mika Nashram, who threw a pinch of powder into the fire. There was a brief green flash—and Nijon's eyes grew heavier again. Aware of the threat of enchantment, the shaman's son was able to force them open once more.

Nashram surveyed the sleeping bodies, then confidently turned and made his way up the canyon, toward the heart of the Mammoth Graveyard.

Nijon rose, first to hands and knees, then woozily erect, and followed.

Some distance from the campfire, the sleepiness departed. Nijon felt tired still, as one ought to feel after a long, hard day—but no longer on the brink of passing out. Had he left the area affected by Mika Nashram's spell?

Stealthily, he followed Nashram, wondering at the man's unsuspected talent.

They passed the tusks, the scattered ivory chips.

Past a rough heap of broken tusks, more ivory . . .

To a great heap of bone.

Nashram continued up the canyon, but Nijon paused to examine the pile. It was aurochs bone.

Ribs, collarbones, thighs—most hacked with crude blade marks, the kind of mark a tribesman's axe would make when he butchered an aurochs corpse.

Nijon peered up at the canyon rim, faintly visible as a lack of stars against the starry skies, and realized what he was looking at. He had heard of places such as this, but had never seen one.

Aurochs were dangerous animals to hunt: large, fierce, willing to fight to protect their young; too large, really, to hunt, save for the glory of the kill. But they stampeded as easily as any other animal that gathered in herds. A party of warriors, on horseback, with hoots and hollers, could herd them on, stampede them toward—toward a canyon such as this.

Whereupon the animals would fall to their death.

And afterward, the hunters could descend and butcher their prey.

Nijon hunted around, and found what he expected: wood frames, and charcoal circles where fires had burned, though not in recent months. There would be too much meat to eat at once, in such a kill; the tribesmen would smoke and dry the meat, to preserve it for future use.

No mammoth graveyard this, Nijon thought, although he expected there was probably a mammoth skeleton or two among this jumble.

As he hastened to catch up with Nashram, he pondered the conundrum. Why the chips, the tusks downstream? Suppose one wanted to persuade others that this was the legendary Mammoths' Grave; what better way than to plant a few tusks, some random bits of ivory. . . .

Still, Nijon wondered; on the morrow, Fela and the others would explore the canyon more thoroughly, and make the discovery that he had just made: There was little ivory here. How did Mika hope to profit from this deception?

Ahead, Nashram paused, then began to climb the canyon wall. There was a path, Nijon saw, and the canyon lip was considerably lower here.

He waited until he saw Nashram's head silhouetted against the starlight, then followed.

The path was narrow; at times, Nijon was forced to scramble ahead on hands and knees; but at last he came to the canyon lip.

Perhaps two dozen feet away, a fire burned. Near it stood a wagon. Its high wooden sides were elaborately carved, with gaily painted friezes of monsters, demons, kings and paupers, creatures of legend. Along the roof ran letters in the Agondan script, which Nijon could not read.

About the fire, men and women stood or lounged; a dozen, perhaps, more men than women. Their clothing was unlike any Nijon had seen before: extravagant, ornate, of varied and brilliant hue. They were northerners, clearly, but not soldiers, not traders, not peasants or artisans; Nijon could not even hazard a guess as to their profession, or their intentions here.

They welcomed Mika with glad cries; a buzz of conversation ensued. To his regret, Nijon was unable to make out what they were saying. Alas, he dared not venture any closer, especially since there might be dogs about. Since he could not overhear Mika and the others, there was little point in tarrying, and no little danger of discovery. So, reluctantly, Nijon descended the canyon wall and paced thoughtfully back, through the jumbled bones, the arched tusks, the rocky streambed, back to the campsite of the caravaneers.

That oppressive sleepiness pervaded the camp still. This time, though, Nijon was happy to let it carry him off into the land of dreams.

7

There was a high, high howl; high in tone, and high above. It echoed off the walls of the canyon. Nijon came groggily awake in the gray dawn. About him, soldiers leapt to their feet and lunged comically for weapons.

That strange noise sounded again. It was something like the call of a jackal, but not too much like it; a tribesman would imitate the animal better, Nijon thought.

A bass drum beat: BOOM BOOM. BOOM BOOM. It, too, resounded off the canyon walls.

Along the rim of the canyon stood men; at least a dozen. Impassive men, proud men, men bearing spears.

Vai tribesmen.

Or were they? Nijon wondered. That silhouette, there, on the western rim: That looked a little pudgy for a warrior of the Vai. And that: That was definitely a woman.

No woman would be with a war party.

Nijon darted under one of the wagons. That was the safest place to be, if arrows began to fly.

The space was already tenanted. Fela was there, on hands and knees, terror on his face.

Outside, legs ran to and fro across the canyon floor. The soldiers' captain bellowed orders.

Not ten cubits away, a man struggled wildly, a bronze

breastplate held with one hand to his chest while the other reached behind his back and tried to grab the leather thong that would allow him to secure the armor.

A pair of buskin-clad legs scritched to the wagon's other side and halted. "Fela?" Mika's voice said. "Are you there?"

"Y-yes," Fela said.

"What shall we do?"

"Give them—give them whatever they want," quavered the merchant.

Mika chuckled. "There do seem to be rather a lot of them," he said. "Shall I see if they'll parley?"

"Yes," said Fela.

Nijon scuttled over to watch Mika, who strode away from the wagon, cupped hands, and shouted, in the language of the Vai, "Parley! Parley!"

Immediately, that drum began to beat again: BOOM BOOM. BOOM BOOM. BOOM BOOM. A man appeared at the lip of the canyon. A huge man, a fat man; a man who weighed what two others might. He was clad as a chieftain might be clad: feathers in hair, heavy gold armbands, a vest of richest byssus—reaved, no doubt, from a northern city—and a staff in one hand, a staff adorned with the mummified heads of small animals.

He gestured peremptorily. Several tribesmen bustled about, there atop the cliff. They hung what looked like a net over the side. Gingerly, the chieftain stepped into the net and held on to two ropes. It was a kind of rope seat, Nijon saw.

As the drums continued their bass chant, the tribesmen began to lower the chief, pulleys creaking, into the canyon. BOOM BOOM. BOOM BOOM. BOOM BOOM.

Nijon struggled to contain laughter. Any lingering thought that these clowns might be Vai was gone.

The entrance was dramatic, to be sure. But—who in his right mind would send his chief into the camp of the enemy, to serve as their hostage? No, they should have demanded that the northerners send up their own leader to parley; and, failing that, agreed to meet on neutral ground.

Nijon didn't know what their game was, but he doubted it involved battle. He crawled out from under the wagon, stood up, and strolled toward Mika.

BOOM BOOM. The rope chair approached the ground. BOOM BOOM. The chief's feet touched soil. BOOM-boomboomboom, the drumbeat tailed off; and the chief toppled over, no longer supported by the ropes.

Mika offered a hand and, pulling mightily, hefted the chief to his feet.

The chief turned and waved to the men at the top of the cliff. They raised the rope seat.

The chief stood impassive, chin jutting out over massive belly, arms folded. One of the caravaneers came running up, waving an axe; the chief faced him without flinching.

"No!" Mika shouted at the axe-wielder. "Kill him and we're dead men!"

"Mosha, you twit!" bellowed the captain of the guard. "Get back!"

The captain pushed and pulled men into position: archers behind the wagons, men with axes and spears in a semicircle before the chief. Nijon edged away from Mosha, who stared wildly about and waved his axe in a disconcerting way.

"Gods," said the chief to Mika in Vai. "Where did you get such clods?"

"I didn't hire them," Mika said.

"Ah," said the chief. He eyed Nijon, perhaps wondering where the young man had come from.

Nijon studied the chief. The man was a northerner; one made up with greasepaint to resemble a chieftain of the Vai. His accent was terrible. Had there been a fat man among the folk at the top of the canyon last night? He didn't remember seeing one, but it was certainly possible.

"Who's the kid?" the chief asked.

"Don't worry about him."

The rope chair was now back at the lip of the canyon. Two warriors jumped into it and began the descent to the canyon floor.

"What's the deal, Mika?" Nijon asked.

Mika eyed the boy. "Look," he said. "Just play along, all right? There's money in it for you."

Nijon grinned. "How much?"

"We'll talk about it later," said Mika.

"Mika?" asked the captain of the guards in Agondan. "What the hell is going on?"

"They want to parley," Mika said.

"Where bossman?" asked the chief in Vai. "Hard to pull con without mark."

"Cowering under the wagon," said Mika. He turned to the captain, switching to Agondan. "Would you get Fela? The chief will only negotiate with our headman."

The soldier grunted. He beckoned toward one of the archers, and the two moved off. They both bent over to peer under the wagon, the archer with an arrow nocked. "Get out of there, you dog," the soldier told Fela, "and talk to the barbarian, or you will have more feathers protruding from your bosom than has an eagle." The archer waved his bow and grinned.

"You—you talk to him," came Fela's voice from beneath the wagon.

"*Get out of there, you swine!*" shouted the captain, his neck reddening, "*or I will save the savages the trouble of gutting you from crotch to gizzard!*"

Fela shot out from under the wagon like a rabbit in flight. He steadied, and trotted toward the chief, giving the captain a wide berth.

"How," said the chief.

"Chief Mo'aloo offers greetings," said Mika.

"Uh—greetings," said Fela.

"Thanks for getting here on time," Mika said to the chief.

The chief shrugged. "You made such a point of it last night," he said. "The company isn't used to farmers' hours, you know."

Mika nodded and turned to the merchant. "Chief Mo'aloo says, 'You have violated our holy of holies.'"

"What?" said Fela, backing away a little.

"Heap big bad thing," the chief said, in pidgin. Then, in Vai, "Big crack in ground sacred to all Vai peoples. City folk get lost, or we butcher."

This was news to Nijon. Why should a canyon be holy? He hadn't seen any evidence of the gods around here. They lived on the clouds, anyway, or so legend said.

In Agondan, Mika said, "Chief Mo'aloo says, 'Canyon of Mohae is holy of holies. Very bad medicine for anyone not of the valiant Vai race to be here. You have defiled this place, and must leave at once, or face the wrath of the Va-Jiwa.'"

Fela turned white. "But Mika," he said. "The mammoth ivory . . . We can't just leave it here."

Mika spoke in Vai again. "Now we get to it," he told the chief.

The chief drew himself up and put on a thunderous expression. "Bones of god!" he shouted. "Must stay undisturbed!"

The Vai warriors reached the canyon floor and stepped from the net. One, Nijon noted, had blond hair, darkened with grease and soot.

The warriors on the canyon rim all shook their spears and shouted in approval of their chieftain's words.

Mo'aloo—if that was truly his name—folded his arms and jutted his chin once more.

"I'll—I'll give you money," Fela blurted, facing the chief but speaking in Agondan.

"Ah, the words I long to hear," Mika said in Vai.

"How much?" said the chief, also in Vai.

"Not yet," said Mika. "Play him out a bit." He turned to Fela and switched to Agondan. "Money cannot restore the honor of our god! You must prostrate yourself!"

Instantly, Fela fell to his face, moaning. Dana and some of the other soldiers snickered. "Woe!" moaned Fela. "Woe is me! Please accept my profound apologies. See? I rend my raiment to indicate my grief and abject contrition." He reached up, face still in the dirt, and made a neat and rather small tear in his tunic.

"Ask him how much money now," said the chief.

"All right," said Mika. And in Agondan: "The chief asks, 'How much money?'"

Fela's head popped up. He eyed the chief and then sat up, in obvious relief. "To—assuage the anger of the gods," Fela said craftily, "one might be willing to offer—a crown of gold? Would that sound like a lot to a barbarian, Mika?"

Nijon's eyes grew wide. A lot? Ye gods, it was a bloody fortune. . . .

"Better say three," said Mika, to Nijon's astonishment.

"All right," said Fela, "but also—this is important, Mika—also, I'll offer another *ten* crowns if he'll let us take the ivory. No, make that, if he and his tribe will help us *load* the ivory."

Nijon felt faint at the sum.

Mika turned to Mo'aloo. "Jabber jabbity gold gold, three something-orother nixty ten. What do you think?"

"How much has he got?" asked the chief.

"He's hidden his treasure chest, damn him," said Mika. "I haven't been able to find it."

The chief grunted. "Well," he said, "I'd be a fool to take a first offer. Tell him fifteen crowns to make the gods sweet, and a hundred for the ivory, and we absolutely won't help him an inch, as we'd be banned from paradise if we did."

Mika translated Mo'aloo's statement, more or less unadorned.

"He's mad," complained Fela, getting to his feet, obviously feeling much better. "Tell him I am a poor man, driven by desperation to trade in this horrid place, and I cannot possibly afford even a tenth of the sum he mentions. Tell him that I offer my fortune entire: five crowns for the gods, fifteen for the ivory."

"How is Dozita?" Mika asked the chief in Vai.

"Still mad at you," grinned the chieftain. "I can't imagine why you're so sweet on her."

"Some of us don't like our women to look like cows," Mika said.

"I wish you luck," said the chief, "but Horja would probably sever your oysters if you succeeded."

"How do you want to respond?"

"Tell him I'm a generous man but becoming impatient. You think I would accept eight crowns for the gods, twenty for the ivory, but don't want to make that as a counteroffer, because that would then become our new negotiating position. If he can put up that much, fine. If not, no deal, and we butcher the lot of you."

Mika shook his head, grinning. "I never knew that the actor's life demanded such negotiating skill," he said.

"You've obviously never tried to rent a theater," said the chief.

Mika translated Mo'aloo's offer.

Fela moaned like a man condemned. He dithered a bit, but at last gasped, "Agreed." And he strode purposefully toward one of the wagons.

The rest of the party watched, but none went to follow. A long moment passed.

Nijon cocked his head. He heard a sound; a faint sound. A bass sound. He couldn't place it; it sounded distant, yet pervasive, as if it resounded from the walls of the canyon themselves. He frowned, trying to divine the noise; no one else seemed to notice.

Fela returned with a chest: a little casket, perhaps one

hand wide and three hands long, studded with rubies and cabochons. Mika's lips pursed in a silent whistle; the casket alone was worth a small fortune.

The chief's two warriors exchanged a glance. The chief licked his lips.

The sound was louder now. Nijon noticed that two or three of the soldiers were looking about, as if they, too, heard the noise.

"No!" shouted Mosha, turning to his captain and waving the axe. "No, Captain! You can't let him do it!"

"Shut up, Mosha," said the captain dangerously.

"But—if he gives it to the savage, we'll never see the money! You can't let him!"

Mika gave the captain a worried glance; obviously, this was not an expected development.

"You want to die, Mosha?" grated the captain. "You think we can fight off these barbarians? With them atop a cliff and loaded with arrows?"

The noise was thunderous, now, but no one seemed to pay attention, intent on the scene within the canyon.

No one except the "warriors" on the western canyon rim, Nijon noticed. Two had dropped their spears and were running madly. Others were shouting down into the canyon.

Nijon's eyes went wide in sudden understanding.

"No!" shouted Mosha. He flung his axe directly into the blond warrior's stomach. The young actor went down, pain and surprise writ on his face. The chief backed away, swallowing, stomach jiggling.

There was a sudden wild melee, men swarming forward toward the "Vai," the chief and his sole remaining warrior backing away in dismay.

Nijon sprinted toward the wagons and dived for cover—

And at that very moment, something fell atop Fela, smashing the merchant into a boneless, crimson mass.

There was a stunned silence, as everyone took in the

sight: the corpse of a massive animal, sprawling on the ground, dead from the impact, horns in the dust; and the gore of Fela leaking out from beneath.

From above, there was the thunder of many hooves and the exuberant "yipyipyip" of genuine Vai warriors. . . .

And suddenly, it was hailing aurochs.

8
▶▶▶

Horror, fear, and bemused laughter burbled up through Nijon. Horror: the screams of dying men, dying horses, dying aurochs; gore splattering across the canyon as bodies piled atop bodies, an entire herd of huge beasts plummeting to their deaths. Fear: The wagon served to shelter Nijon, but an aurochs landing on it might well crush him. Bemusement: at the men, running hither and yon in fright, astonished at a phenomenon for which they could have no explanation. Fool northerners, Nijon thought, almost fondly.

A fat man wedged himself under the wagon near Nijon; it was "Chief Mo'aloo." He clasped his hands over his head and moaned in fear.

At last, like a storm diminishing, the thunder of aurochs smashing into the earth became merely an occasional crash—and then there was silence, or at least comparative silence. Wounded beasts bellowed in fear and pain.

Hesitantly, Nijon crept out into daylight. At the western rim stood a number of figures: Vai on horseback, pointing into the canyon and conferring. They were, no doubt, puzzled by the existence of a caravan amid their slain prey.

The canyon was chaos. Nijon had been lucky in his choice of wagons; the other one lay smashed, a dead bull aurochs draped over its center. Only one horse remained alive, eyes rolling in fear, prancing about, nostrils flaring with the scent of blood; it would have fled long since if it had not been tied to a stake.

There was a grunt and a rustle nearby. Nijon turned. Mika was wrestling with a dead aurochs, grunting as he shoved it to one side. The aurochs had killed the merchant, Fela. And beneath it . . .

Mika scooped up the casket. Rubies glinted in the light; he sprinted for the last remaining horse.

"Mo'aloo" had by now staggered to his feet, and a number of the surviving guards were peeking hesitantly from whatever shelter they had found. Simultaneously, Nijon and the "chief" divined Mika's intention.

Nijon sprinted after Mika. "Mika Nashram!" the chief bellowed. "Halt, you mountebank, you palter!"

Mika sawed through the horse's rope with a knife and hurtled atop it. The horse, startled, galloped off up the canyon, toward the "graveyard," at a speed that threatened a broken leg. Mika clutched its mane for dear life.

Nijon slowed to a walk, then stopped. He could not catch a horse at full gallop, not soon.

The chief leaned against the wagon, cursing Mika bitterly. Nijon listened with interest, widening his knowledge of foul Agondan.

Hooves sounded; there was the ululating cry of the successful Vai hunter. Trotting up the canyon was a ragged line of Vai warriors, lances at the ready, arrows nocked.

The guards dithered, uncertain whether to stand, to surrender, or to flee.

Before the guards could react, the Vai were among them. The leader, a young man with a braided blond beard, shouted in Agondan, "Resist and die—surrender and live," and, to prove the point, killed a guard who did not drop his weapons with sufficient speed.

Vai ahorse moved among the caravaneers, collecting weapons and herding them into a circle.

"And who are you?" the Vai leader asked Nijon, leaning down from his perch atop a roan pony.

"Nijon Oonitsaupivia, of the Va-Naleu."

The hunter raised an eyebrow but withheld comment at the claim to be the son of a god. "Va-Naleu, eh?" he said. "We're Va-Daloa. Your chief is dead, had you heard?"

Nijon frowned. "I saw the funeral smoke."

"What are these outlanders after?" the hunter asked.

Nijon could only grin. "Someone told them that all the bones hereabout were mammoth ivory, just lying there for the taking."

The hunter threw back his head and laughed. "And who told them this?" he asked.

Nijon hesitated a moment; he had no wish to tell the hunters of Mika, and of the casket he had stolen. They would hunt down the northerner, and Nijon intended the wealth for himself. "It was this one," Nijon said, pointing to "Chief Mo'aloo."

The hunter rode in a wide circle around the captives. In Agondan, he spoke sardonically to the "chief": "So, tribesman. What do you do among these outlanders?"

The actor was at a loss.

"And what shall we do with them?" the leader asked his warriors, still in Agondan.

"Hold them for ransom," suggested one, in the same tongue.

"Enslave them to the women," said another.

"Ah, we have not eaten mansflesh in months," said a third, alluding to the northerners' erroneous belief that the Vai practiced cannibalism.

Several caravaneers began to babble in fear, promising rich ransoms if only their kin were contacted.

The leader laughed again, his beard braids flying.

"No," he said at last, "soldiers for slaves? Too dangerous. Ransom? I doubt these louts can raise a copper among them. And as for mansflesh"—he jabbed toward one grizzled veteran with his lance—"they look too gamy for my taste. No, see here, foreigners. About you are many feasts of aurochs meat. It must be skinned, gutted, butchered; dried and smoked. All will eat well, but we must preserve it, to bring it back to our tribe. We can use every hand available. And when we are done, we shall free you."

"How are we to trust you?" asked a guardsman with suspicion.

The hunter shrugged. "Trust or not, as you wish," he said. "You will work or die. Freedom is no great thing; I doubt any of you will survive long on these plains, without your wagons, your horses, your supplies."

The caravaneers grumbled; but there was no better offer on the table, and freedom was more than they had expected. All set about the task of preparing the aurochs.

After a pass, Nijon approached the hunters' leader. He was busy scooping tripe from an aurochs's belly. "I am on my walkabout," Nijon said. "May I go?"

The leader eyed Nijon. "If you help us," he said, "you shall have your share of meat."

"I have—a task to perform," Nijon said, a little shiftily.

The blond man shrugged. "Go then, if you will," he said. "Stay away from the horses, mind, or your back will be missing its skin."

"No doubt," said Nijon.

"Here," said the hunter, and handed Nijon the liver, raw and still warm.

Nijon was touched at the gesture: The liver, lights, and kidneys were prized, the hunter's own reward for a job well done. Organ meats could not be preserved, and must be eaten at the kill site. "Thank you," he said, with feeling.

"It's nothing," said the warrior, waving a gore-smeared arm and returning to his work.

Nijon strolled up the canyon, in the direction Mika had

taken, munching the gooey substance in the warm sun. Soon, Brother appeared. The little mongoose sniffed suspiciously at the liver, but condescended to partake of a bite or two.

Nijon followed the horse's trail. It had left spoor in the canyon; and damaged bushes showed where it had struggled its way up a narrow path to the canyon lip. Once on the plain, Nijon adopted a brisk walk. Belly full, he did not want to risk cramps by running; but even at a quick walk, he guessed he might catch up with Mika, unless the man was driving his horse beyond endurance.

The guess proved well founded. The horse had been tired by its fright, its flight, and the struggle up the canyon side. By dusk, Nijon spotted a horse alone on the plain, eating its fill of the briza. He went to ground and waited. He expected to see the yellow flicker of a campfire, out where Mika must be; but when no flame appeared, Nijon comprehended why. Mika would not wish to give away his position.

The doe of night, with her sparkling coat of stars, crept forth as the sun, that mighty hunter, went to his rest. The air grew cold, but Nijon was inured to such hardship. He sat for a long time with only his thoughts and Brother for company.

The stars wheeled. If Mika was being as wary as the absence of a fire suggested, he might not be asleep. He must suspect that someone was on his tail.

There would be plenty of people who might pursue the northerner: the actors whom he had defrauded, the guards who had their own eyes set on that treasure, even the Vai hunters, who might have learned of it from their captives.

Yet it would be necessary to rest; not for Mika so much as his horse. Three hundred miles from the nearest city, his best hope of reaching safety lay with that horse. It would not do to tire the beast excessively, so early in the journey.

But Mika might drive himself to stay awake; he had no others to watch for danger.

At last, Nijon decided to move forward. Even if Mika had decided to stay awake all night, he might have drifted off by now; and there was the possibility that he had been unwary.

Mouth dry, Nijon crept stealthily toward the spot where he had seen the horse. This could be the start of a death struggle. This was no animal he was hunting, but an armed and wary man. Nijon did not underestimate his opponent's potential.

He was nearby. He heard the horse snort; and he felt—he *smelled*—something more. Something—

It smelled like magic, again that metallic tang.

Nijon crept to the right until he came to a stick; a simple stick, shaven of bark, stuck into the ground. Willow wood, Nijon thought. There was power in it.

He continued, circling Mika's camp. There was a second stick. And a third.

Nijon realized there were four in all, arranged in a square about the camp. He could sense lines of force connecting them.

After a moment, he understood. It was not a magic he had seen before, but it was obvious enough; the sticks were wards. Mika must be asleep, depending on his wards to awaken him should someone penetrate the space the wards marked out.

Nijon sat and thought for long moments. Then he reached awkwardly out with his magic-sense, to see if he could feel a force *above* the wards.

He could not. They protected the sleeper against one who might blunder through the ward-marked space, but . . .

Nijon stepped back, ran, and vaulted on his spear above the lines of magic.

He fell with a crash into a bush, realizing that he awoke Mika quite effectively thus.

He ran full tilt toward a rousing shape on the plain. Mika rolled away as Nijon thrust a spearpoint into dirt.

The northerner was afoot and had his bronze knife out. Mika shifted, dancing; and must have adjudged his chances poor, a knife against spear-armed Nijon. His stance shifted—Nijon dived to one side—and the blade came fluttering through space, where Nijon had been moments before.

Mika cursed at being uselessly disarmed, turned, and fled toward the horse. Nijon sprinted after.

Mika dived to the ground, rolled, came up as Nijon ran past—he had another knife in his hand, smaller, perhaps pulled from his boot. Nijon felt a scrape in his arm before he could react; nothing worse, he noted thankfully.

Nijon came to a sudden stop, swung instantly with the spear, no time for finesse—there was a crack as the spear butt met Mika's skull.

Mika tumbled to the sod.

Nijon danced on the balls of his feet, half-expecting Mika to rise. He considered killing the northerner, but had no stomach for slaying an unconscious man.

Almost, he poked Mika with the spear to see if he was truly unconscious—then realized that, if the man were indeed faking, he might grab the spear and try to yank it from Nijon's grasp.

What to do?

Was that a fluttering eyelid?

Ah! Nijon swiftly darted forward—and rapped the shaft of his spear smartly against the man's skull.

There; that sprawled body; that looked more convincing.

Nijon searched the northerner's clothes, spear held at his throat, one hand patting. The casket was in a bag, hanging from Mika's belt. Nijon swiftly cut the bag free and backed away.

Mika lay still.

Nijon soothed the horse, unhobbled it, mounted up, and rode away—leaving Mika's knives where they lay.

It would have been wiser to kill the northerner, he knew, and to take Mika's knives. But he liked the man, and so granted him a meager chance of survival.

Nijon Oonitsaupivia rode through the silent hours before the dawn, well-pleased with himself. He had a horse, again; he had a fortune in gold. But a week of his manhood rite remained; who now could deny that he would survive, prosper, and return to his kin?

Nijon counted himself a man.

9

▶▶▶

How different Nijon felt: fed instead of starving, clean instead of filthy, hale instead of mad with fever. His horse, northern-trained, had been skittish at the feel of a bareback rider; but a week had served to build a certain bond of trust between the two. With his spear, a lance he laboriously carved with the sharpened spearhead, and a newly made bow, Nijon found it easy enough to bring down prey; and the bronze spearhead sufficed to cut branches to build a fire. From being a beast at the mercy of luck and weather, Nijon had, he felt, become a king of the prairie, master of his destiny.

Tsawen, he knew, would have shaken his head at the thought. Sarcastically, Nijon mouthed Tsawen's words to himself: "All men are at the mercy of their weird; all freedom is delusion." How many times had his father said that? He loathed the sentiment.

Still, with lance, bow, and spear, the pelt of a lioness on his back, his belly full and a casket containing inconceivable riches at his belt, Nijon felt half a god. As he was, he reflected; he was half a god, if his memory of Mongoose was not a fever dream.

Alongside, Brother loped, as if to say, "It was no dream."

Exuberantly, Nijon heeled his horse into a gallop, out-pacing Brother. Nijon relished the wind in his hair.

There were riders, ahead; six or so. Quickly, Nijon reined in the horse, dismounted, and guided her into a kneel, a maneuver he and she had practiced.

On this broad plain, a man on horseback was visible; but tall grass made it hard to spot a kneeling horse and man. Thus might one avoid detection, if one acted quickly.

Nijon raised a hand to shade his eyes, and peered. He could make out a travois, trailing from one horse; by the way the horse moved, it bore a heavy load.

It was probably a hunting party, returning with a kill. They would probably not leave their kill to chase a stranger.

Brother gamboled up. Nijon gave him an absent pat, then clucked to the mare. She rose to her feet and Nijon re-mounted.

Brother gave a chirring sound, as if to warn of danger. Nijon cocked his head, but disregarded the warning. Boldly, he approached the party, leaving the mongoose behind.

They had indeed been hunting; the sledge bore a bison, not yet butchered. They turned and spread out, as any group might, approached by a stranger, weapons at the ready.

Nijon recognized them: Va-Naleu, his tribesmen. He whooped and broke into a gallop, conscious of the lioness' skin fluttering from his back, the gallant figure he cut.

"Dihaen!" he called. "Jutson! Well met!"

They conferred, conversation passing swiftly among them, Nijon yet at a distance that he could not hear. Unex-pectedly, they did not relax as he closed, weapons remain-ing poised.

He whirled to a halt, a showy sideways turn with his horse, bits of sod scattering through the air.

"I have returned!" he said excitedly. "See? I bear—"

"Drop that lance, boyo," Dihaen advised. "And keep your hand from your bow."

Nijon gaped in astonishment. "What means this?" he demanded.

"Now!" shouted Jutson, rage on his face. "Do as you are told!"

Numbly, Nijon let the lance fall.

"Off the horse," Dihaen said, his arrow drawn full back to his shoulder. Nijon dithered for a moment, then complied.

"Let us slay him now, Dihaen," Jutson said, "and take back his head for trophy."

"Wait!" Nijon said.

Dihaen shook his head. "No, Jutson," he said. "We have no right to give him justice."

"What am I supposed to have done?" asked Nijon.

Angry beyond measure, Jutson swung his spear butt at Nijon. Nijon dodged the blow and glared.

"Chief Mo'ian was slain, with a blade of obsidian," said Dihaen, studying Nijon carefully, "asleep, in his tent."

Shock hit Nijon like cold water. "Mo'ian? I saw the funeral fire, but I . . . I would never. . . ."

"Was not your talisman found clutched in his stiff fingers, the cord broken as he ripped it from your neck, struggling to the last against your treachery?" shouted Jutson.

"Talisman?" said Nijon. He touched his throat, where his mongoose foot had hung. "Dowdin stole it," he said softly—but the sneak would never dare to kill Mo'ian; it must have fallen into someone else's hands.

"Dowdin?" said Dihaen.

"Yes," said Nijon. "I was wounded and feverish, and Dowdin came across me; he tried to kill me, I believe, but managed only to steal the talisman."

Jutson spat. "Lies," he said. "What else from a murderer?"

Dihaen looked uncertain. "He approached us openly,"
he said. "Why would he do so if he were guilty?"

"He did not know we knew of his guilt," said Jutson.

"Perhaps," said Dihaen. "Still, it is for the next chief to
determine his fate. You, Nijon; you must come with us for
decision."

Nijon dropped his remaining weapons and stepped away
from them, keeping the leather pouch and the jeweled casket it contained, glad now he had not mentioned the contents. "Very well," he said. "Who will the next chief be?"

One of the hunters bound Nijon's hands, and they set
him atop his horse once more, tethering it to Dihaen's
saddle, that he might lead the captive. "That is not yet
decided," said Dihaen. "Some favor Vauren."

Nijon's heart sank, mistrusting the quality of his rival's
justice.

The tribe had moved since Nijon's departure; that was not
surprising, over a period of forty days. The cattle would
have eaten the best pasturage about the old campsite. Nijon
recognized where they were going: toward a water hole
where the tribe had camped many times before. While they
were still leagues distant from the camp, Nijon's nostrils
began to twitch.

"What is that smell?" he asked.

Dihaen turned, looked at him, then tilted his head and
tested the air. "I smell nothing," he said, and turned forward once more.

Nijon sniffed, probing the air. The smell reminded him
of blood, a brazen tang. A flash of poppy, a tinge of sweat;
it made no sense.

Again came that feeling of his stepfather's tent: There
was magic on the air. "Magic," he said softly. The others
paid no heed.

Suddenly, above them in the sky, Nijon glimpsed two birds, locked in combat; a goshawk and a golden eagle, wings battering, beaks darting toward eyes, claws extended, and a *"Screee. . . ."* Nijon shouted wordlessly in astonishment. . . .

The image was gone. Jutson had his spear at Nijon's back; Dihaen had whirled. "What is it?" Dihaen shouted, reaching for weapons.

Nijon, shaking, could only say, "Did you not see it? The eagle, the . . ." His eyes burning with the afterimage, he waved to the place in the sky where he had seen them—but there was only the sun.

Warily, the other men kept a closer eye on him, uncertain what to make of this; they continued onward.

The horses were at a walk; they could not lug the bison at faster speed. The riders sat with long familiarity, able to endure this pace for weeks, if need be. But Nijon began to feel a buzz in his head, a buzz as if he were drunk, or fevered. He squinted; the world wavered, as if the sun were so hot it sent up waves of heat from parched earth—but the breeze was cool.

Did the others notice?

Dihaen had his bow across his horse, and was peering about, as if he sensed something awry; Jutson, too, looked faintly uneasy—but neither seemed as affected as Nijon felt.

The buzz in his head took on tangible form; a hum. Nijon shook his head, trying to drive the noise from his brain, but—"Look there!" shouted one of the hunters, pointing behind them and to the right.

A cloud hung low over the prairie, not far distant. Nijon had never seen its like. The sky above was blue; the cloud was vaguely transparent, as though a thin patch of mist; but it was tan or brown, not the white a mist would be. And no mist would long survive this sunny glare.

The noise was not in his head, Nijon realized; it came from the cloud.

"Locusts," said Jutson, revulsion in his voice. Nijon understood; he had never seen a plague of the insects, but he had heard of them. Every so often, the locusts, normally sedentary and few, would band together in great armies and pillage the plain, stripping it of all vegetation; tribesmen feared such plagues, for cattle would grow lean in the aftermath. And a plague of locusts looked just so—a cloud of insects, moving at considerable speed across the prairie, flittering through the sky, landing to devour, launching to flit again. It was said an army of locusts could move faster than a running man.

The brazen tang of magic was everywhere about.

Almost before the party could react, the locusts were all about them. The horses went insane, bucking and trembling at the buzzing noise, the feel of insects crawling everywhere. Arms still bound, Nijon was hard-pressed to retain his seat. He lay against his horse's neck and whispered words in her ear, or tried to; there were thumb-sized locusts in his hair, his eyes, crawling into his mouth.

He spat them out and managed somehow to gentle the horse, though he was having difficulty breathing. He fought panic himself, chitinous forms crawling over his body, insects within his clothes, his eyes firmly shut to keep them out. It was hard to breathe, the creatures were so thick; hard to speak, for fear they would crawl into his mouth. It was almost as if the creatures were trying to smother him, to . . .

Dihaen brushed Nijon's face clean and tied a cloth loosely over nose and mouth. Mouth open wide, Nijon panted, straining air through cloth, his eyes tightly shut, gasping words of comfort to his still-trembling horse.

And then, the locusts were gone. They had not moved on; they were simply gone, as if snuffed from existence. The air about them was sweet.

"What are you doing here?" said an annoyed voice. "Return to the camp until the duel is ended!"

A man in a spirit mask stood before them. Nijon had never seen the mask before—a sorcerer does not make one until ready to assume the shaman's mantle—but he recognized the voice: It was Dowdin's.

"Duel?" said Dihaen, startled.

Nijon gave a wordless snarl and tested his bonds, but to no avail. He was securely bound.

"Well, well," said Dowdin, pushing back his mask. "Nijon lives. Come home to face justice, I suppose." He gave a short, barking laugh.

"What do you mean, duel?" asked Dihaen, a little sharply.

"I have challenged Tsawen for the post of shaman," Dowdin said.

"You repulsive . . ." choked Nijon. How like Dowdin to turn on his teacher. Still, thought Nijon, Dowdin was unlikely to win; Tsawen ought to be able to master his own student handily.

"I suggest you leave this place," said Dowdin, "lest you be caught in our next exchange of magic. I can't let myself be weakened by the need to protect people who stray into the duel site. This is no place for the powerless."

"Indeed," said Dihaen nervously. "Which way?"

"North," said Dowdin, pulling down his spirit mask.

"Leave the bison," Dihaen told the other hunters.

"What?" replied one hunter. "No! We—"

"We have blundered into danger," said Dihaen. "Leave it. Perhaps it will still be here afterward."

"And mayhap otherwise!"

While the hunters argued, Nijon warily studied Dowdin. The apprentice was chanting now, evidently preparing some spell; Nijon could sense the power drawing about him. Dowdin took a medicine bundle from his belt, opened it, and drew forth several eagle feathers tied with a string—

With a sudden chill, Nijon recognized those feathers. They came from *Tsawen*'s medicine bundle; he used them frequently in his own enchantments. How had they fallen into Dowdin's hands?

For the first time, Nijon began to fear for his foster father's sake. Half or more of Tsawen's power lay in his medicine bundle; if Dowdin had somehow stolen it—Dowdin would control that power. That might well be enough to tip the scales.

"Enough," said Dihaen at last, cutting short the protests of the hunters. He slashed the travois's traces, mounted, and led the party northward at a gallop. Nijon was hard-put to stay balanced without a saddle, his arms bound.

Behind them came a sudden roar, like a forest taking flame in an instant; Nijon glanced over his shoulder, and his eyes were seared with a glimpse of cyan, an avalanche of light across the plain—did Tsawen stand there? Was this Dowdin's attack? The light was so bright that Nijon blinked for minutes afterward, trying to lose the impression in his eyes. He muttered prayers to every god and spirit he could think of.

10
▶▶▶

They galloped until Dihaen thought it safe, then continued at a fast trot, giving the duelists wide berth, and headed into camp.

Nijon could not get the odor of magic entirely from his nostrils, though as they approached the camp, he was met by earthier scents: fires burning, horse dung in the sun, leather curing, even the green smell of the water hole itself.

But one faint scent leapt forth, as a familiar voice in a babble can leap forth, though it might be one of the faintest: a cold smell, a quiet smell. He could not place it, but it somehow bothered him.

The camp was a picture of halfhearted activity. A few fires burned desultorily, smoking fish or firing pots of the clay that could be found nearby. No one wanted to waste the day entirely, so men were carving fishhooks of bone or sharpening weapons, women were drying herbs or working leather. But all anxiously awaited the victor of the shaman's duel. As soon as the party came in, they were assaulted with a babble of questions.

Nijon scarcely noticed, casting about, looking for the source of that bothersome smell—for he had at last identified the odor: venom. Snake venom. Tsawen sometimes extracted it for magical use, and Nijon had smelled it before. But where did it come from? How had he smelled it at such a distance from the encampment?

"So, son," bellowed Poai over the babble. "Are you now a man?"

Nijon grinned; he did not look like the newly minted warrior returning in triumph from his walkabout—not bound, a prisoner, stripped of his weapons. Still. "Aye, Ma, that I am," he said. "I have survived, I have returned, and I have prospered."

The crowd murmured uneasily. "Man you may be," snarled Jutson. "Man enough to die for your crime."

"Where is Father's medicine bundle?" Nijon asked Poai.

She looked at him curiously. "With him, I have no doubt."

"No," said Nijon, sniffing the air again. "I don't believe so." Poai looked stricken; she knew as well as he that the bundle stored half, more than half, of Tsawen's power: enchantments cast long ago, talismans, powders, and herbs.

The smell of venom wafted toward Nijon from the left; thin tendrils of smoke rose toward the sky, there, from the smoke hole of one tent.

Why, Nijon wondered, would one build a fire within a tent on so warm a day? It was common enough in winter, when the need for warmth outweighed the discomfort of choking smoke; in warm weather, cooking could as easily be done at a fire outdoors.

Waving his bound hands over his head to balance himself, Nijon jerked a leg over his mount and tumbled heavily to the earth, landing on his knee. He was up and sprinting for the tents before his captors could react.

"Hoy!" Jutson shouted, kicked his horse's ribs, and maneuvered her through the crowd, cursing at obstructions, till he reached clear ground and could canter. Dihaen followed Jutson with the other hunters; and soon a rabble of tribefolk on foot joined the chase, shouting, "Murderer! He seeks to escape! Catch him!"

Nijon heard hooves behind him, glanced back; there was naught but fury in Jutson's face, his spear leveled. Jutson would kill him, Nijon thought; an attempt at escape gave Jutson excuse, and he was convinced of Nijon's guilt.

Nijon dodged around a tent. Jutson cursed, reined his horse, wheeled to follow.

Nijon simply charged through another tent, knocking down its pole and uprooting its stakes. He weaved through space, with Jutson never far behind.

That smell of snake; that cold and silent smell. There was the tent, smoke rising from its roof. And on the smoke was borne the scent of poison.

Nijon ripped open the flap and dodged within.

Eyes accustomed to the sun, at first all Nijon saw was a low fire, two forearms, and the blur of a face reflecting red flames. The smoke made Nijon's eyes sting.

Gradually, Nijon's eyes made sense of the image: Vauren, standing over the fire, a medicine bundle in the coals, smoking but not yet burning, protected by enchantment—Vauren, holding a snake, slit open from mouth to anus, his hands squeezing the poison sack so that drops of venom would land, steaming, on the medicine bundle.

Jutson stood openmouthed in the entrance, lance raised to strike bound Nijon; but he did not strike. Behind him crowded tribefolk.

"Sympathetic magic," Nijon said, almost distantly. "He poisons Tsawen's medicine bundle; he poisons Tsawen. Tsawen is weakened not only by the loss of his magic token, but by its corruption."

"This is foul beyond imagining," said Jutson.

"It . . . I . . ." Vauren sputtered, the snake dropping from his hands: the snake, like Vauren's ambitions, falling into ashes.

Surely, Nijon puzzled, untutored in magic, Vauren

would not have conceived of this spell by himself. And then he nearly gasped with the realization of Vauren and Dowdin's audacity. Dowdin stole Nijon's talisman; Vauren slew Chief Mo'ian, planting the talisman so that Nijon would be blamed. Dowdin challenged Tsawen; Vauren was aiding Dowdin in the duel, by stealing and poisoning the medicine bundle. Vauren would be chief, Dowdin would be shaman; together they would rule the clan. And Nijon—Nijon would be dead, or at the very least would become an outcast, as befit a murderer.

There was a stir from another quarter of the tent. Nijon glanced that way.

It was Lai'iani.

"Come," said Vauren to her, grabbed her hand, and with his other hand took a knife from his belt. He slashed a slit in the tent and pushed her through it.

Nijon, stunned, could not react.

Vauren ducked through the slit, stumbled—and fell, half within the tent, half through the slit. Jutson's lance protruded from his back. Vauren thrashed like a slaughtered animal. Lai'iani wailed.

"You stew!" Nijon shouted at her.

"His betrothed," said Dihaen. Nijon snarled; much had happened in his absence, it was clear.

Through the slit, Nijon could see Lai'iani's kin converging on her, offering support to the weeping girl.

Savagely, Nijon thrust both hands into the fire and snatched out the medicine bundle. It burned, raising blisters on his palms.

He turned and took two steps toward the horse Jutson had dismounted—then halted. How could he mount, his arms still bound, his hands filled? "I must take this to Tsawen," he said.

"That is only just," said Dihaen.

"He will escape," complained Jutson.

"Why should I?" said Nijon. "I didn't kill Mo'ian—

Vauren must have! He and Dowdin conspired—Dowdin stole my talisman—I—''

"So you say," said Jutson.

"Someone must go with him," said Dihaen, "to see that he does not escape."

Jutson snorted. "Are you volunteering?"

"No," said Dihaen, a little distantly. "I'm not going back into that. Since you're so keen on dragging the boy to justice, I thought you might go."

"Man," said Poai. "He is a man."

Dihaen waved a hand, as if to say it was of no account.

"Very well," said Jutson grimly, "I shall." He yanked his lance from Vauren's now-still body and waved its crimson point under Nijon's nose. "This lance has tasted one traitor's blood; see that it does not taste yours."

So they rode. Nijon's hands were in his horse's mane, to provide the balance his bound arms could not; the bundle was at his belt, with the casket he dared not leave behind, still in its pouch. Behind rode Jutson, lance at the ready, spear held in a loop on his saddle, bow strung and at Nijon's back; his temper was foul.

Again, Nijon nudged his horse into a gallop; the roan was tired from the morning's exertion, but still she responded, flying over the briza with dispatch. Jutson cursed, but followed.

The smell of bronze came again to Nijon. The air seemed cooler than before—cool enough to raise goose bumps and send a shiver down his back.

They galloped over a rise. Nijon clucked, sitting back on his mare, bringing her to a stop. Before them was a hollow, a dip in the ground; and it was filled to the brim, as a kettle might be filled, with—a mist of blue.

The sun shone down with noontime brilliance; what mist could be here now? And its color was strange, the color of turquoise. At its center, it silently boiled, as if huge bubbles of mist were rising to the surface and there collapsing.

Jutson gave an intake of breath: He saw it too.

Nijon dismounted.

"Where do you go?" asked Jutson.

"Into that," said Nijon.

"I was afraid of that," said Jutson, dismounting himself.

"Hold your breath," said Nijon—and waded into the blue. As he strode down the slope, it came up to his knees—his waist—and finally, over his head.

Whatever the mist might be, it rasped the skin, like sand under clothing. Nijon's eyes watered; he took to keeping them closed, blinking briefly from time to time to fix his whereabouts.

His vision extended no more than six cubits, through the blue dimness; but the light seemed to darken no further as he descended. He had no way to determine where Dowdin or Tsawen might be—but strode downhill, on the supposition that they must be at the center of this strangeness.

Nijon's pulse thundered in his temples.

His air was running out; his diaphragm quivered with the need to breathe. Cautiously, he took blue mist into his mouth, not breathing it down into the lungs; it stung a bit, as it stung his skin, but no more than that. He took a breath—and nearly gagged. The smell was foul, his lungs ached with it—but it was no worse than breathing smoke from a fire. Coughing a bit, Nijon continued onward.

Jutson was with him still.

Ahead, two figures loomed into view: Dowdin, spirit-masked; and some creature the like of which Nijon had never seen. It hung in the air, higher than a man stands: a bulbous hemisphere, seeming somehow to blend into the mist. From it hung innumerable tendrils.

Beneath the monster lay a supine body: Tsawen. The older man's lungs labored. His eyes were blank, his limbs asprawl. Tendrils played almost tenderly over his form.

"Dowdin," choked Nijon through blueness.

The mask turned. "Nijon," said Dowdin easily, as though unaffected by the mist.

Nijon tossed the medicine bundle to his stepfather. It touched one arm—but Tsawen made no motion toward it. He choked on the mist, water flowed from his eyes; Nijon saw that he was far gone.

Dowdin saw the bundle and started in fright. "Where did you—"

"Vauren is dead," said Jutson.

Behind Dowdin, Tsawen stirred, eyes focusing, at last, on the medicine bundle beside him.

Dowdin dithered for a moment, then came to some decision. He began to keen, a song or chant in a language Nijon could not place. Power drew about him.

Fingers shaking, Tsawen fumbled open the medicine bundle's mouth. He reached inside and withdrew an irregular ball of dried mud.

Dowdin shouted his spell, a blob of light expanding from his mouth. . . .

Tsawen lobbed the ball of mud at Dowdin. It hit the apprentice in the temple; he fell silent in surprise. The ball fell to his feet and bounced twice.

Dowdin began to shrink. He was four feet tall, three feet; he was the size of a baby. . . . His spirit mask tumbled to the side.

Tsawen crawled painfully. He reached over, picked up the dung beetle Dowdin had become, popped the insect into his medicine bundle, and pulled the string.

It was bright day; the choking mist was gone, and with it, Dowdin's monstrosity.

"Good day, son," Tsawen said mildly. "Are you now a man?"

"A man—and a murderer," rasped Jutson.

11

They tarried in the sunlit hollow to give Tsawen some time to recover. Nijon found his stepfather some water, and Jutson lent a stick of jerky. Tsawen sucked at both greedily, but seemed to draw as much strength from the presence of his bundle as from the food.

Not long after the mist lifted, Brother appeared, and went to gambol in Nijon's lap.

Jutson seemed startled, but accepted that Nijon had somehow tamed the mongoose during his walkabout. Tsawen could not avoid a smile at the little creature's antics.

"You should leave the tribe," Tsawen advised Nijon. "Sentiment is much against you. Another clan will be glad to adopt a strong warrior—"

"He shall return to face justice," grated Jutson.

"And if he does not?" asked Tsawen.

"He shall die," said Jutson.

Seated, masticating jerky, the tired old man eyed the warrior on his mount. "Having seen a shamans' duel, do you doubt I could prevent that?"

Jutson blinked. "No," he said slowly. "But it is my duty to ensure his return."

"I did not kill Mo'ian," Nijon said. "They can't—"

"Of course you didn't kill Mo'ian," said Tsawen irritably. "That's not the point. The point is whether the chief, whoever he will be, believes you did or not."

Nijon was a little shocked at the notion that the justice of his tribe might be less than perfect. "But—"

"You should go," said Tsawen.

After a silence, Nijon said, "I shall not go until my name is cleared."

"Until justice is done," said Jutson, still doubting that justice involved clearing Nijon's name.

With a sigh, Tsawen rose, and mounted up behind Nijon. Brother hesitated, then leapt in a fluid motion to clutch at the horse blanket before Nijon. The mongoose perched as if he, too, had sat a horse virtually from birth; both sorcerer and son could not contain a laugh.

Nijon presented the tribe with a problem; he must be guarded, yet every man of the tribe wished to be present at the folkmoot. The women of the Council were there, too, for they must give their assent; but the other women were not.

The solution was to bind Nijon, and leave him with women as guards. They could wield a knife, if need be—or run to fetch warriors.

Nijon scowled, his stomach grumbling; no one had eaten, for it was traditional to fast before a moot. Brother kept close by, nosing Nijon's bonds worriedly. "There is no help for it, little one," murmured Nijon.

"How long do you think he will last?" asked a granddaughter of the murdered chief, toying with a blade.

"Long and long," said a sister of Lai'iani. "He is strong. He will last long, before he dies."

"Good," said the granddaughter viciously—and proceeded to describe her plans for him. Nijon blanched, and knew more deeply what all in his tribe knew: The lion might be stronger, but the lioness was the more cruel. For that reason, murderers were turned over to the victim's female relatives, to exact whatever justice they might please.

Lai'iani's sister smiled and nodded at her companion's plans. "Why are you so dead against me?" Nijon asked.

She virtually spat at him. " 'Twas you who slew Lai'iani's love."

Nijon blinked. "It was Jutson!" he protested.

"Jutson wielded the lance; but had you not been there, Vauren would be alive."

"And my father dead," said Nijon.

"One old man against a future chief," spat the woman.

Nijon tasted bile, but forbore to speak. When family sentiment was involved, what use to argue? He wished Poai were present. She would shut these two up, but she was at the moot.

Nijon was vastly relieved when at last footsteps approached. It was Dihaen. "So," said Nijon. "Who is chief?"

"Jutson," said Dihaen.

Mo'ian's granddaughter crowed in delight as Nijon's hopes evaporated.

Dihaen removed Nijon's bonds, then led him to the moot. Jutson sat on the chieftain's stool, the stick of office with its mummified heads in his hand, the chieftain's bonnet on his head. The fire had been built high; its yellow flames reflected from the faces of the tribe.

"Nijon Oonitsaupivia," said Jutson. "You stand accused of murdering Mo'ian, our chief."

"I did not do the deed," said Nijon. "Who makes this accusation?"

Mo'ian's wife rose painfully, and hobbled forward. "I," she said. "We found this by his body."

Jutson took the mongoose foot and the broken leather thong from her hands. "Is this not yours?" he asked Nijon.

"Yes," said Nijon. "It is. But it was stolen from me, by Dowdin."

"Do you maintain Dowdin murdered the chief?" asked Jutson. There was mild laughter; if the apprentice had wanted to slay, he would have chosen sorcery. Everyone knew he had neither the strength nor courage to cut a man's throat.

"No," said Nijon. "Vauren did."

There was a stir. "Lies!" shouted Vauren's mother. "You seek to blacken—"

"His name is already black!" shouted Poai. "He—"

"Enough!" roared Jutson. "Neither Vauren nor Dowdin is here to face your claims."

"A moment," said Tsawen. Jutson looked at the shaman askance, as if he had not expected this. Tsawen came forth, in his shaman's garb, his spirit mask in place. He stood within the circle for a long moment, holding out a clenched fist—

Tsawen unclenched his fist. Something tumbled from it, hit the ground, scurried—and Dowdin was there, on all fours, naked, looking up in fright and surprise. A murmur of awe went through the tribe.

"Give him a cloak," ordered Jutson. When the apprentice had hid his nakedness, the chief asked, "Did you steal Nijon's talisman?"

Dowdin's glance darted here and there, as if he were uncertain of his footing. "No," he said. "Certainly not."

Jutson frowned. "Nijon said you did."

"Let him prove it," said Dowdin.

"You conspired with Vauren!" shouted Nijon. "He would be chief, and you shaman; you aided him to smear me, he aided you to overthrow my stepfather. You—"

"I'll grant you Vauren poisoned Tsawen's medicine bundle, aiding me against the shaman," said Dowdin, now almost smiling, "but as for the rest—mere fantasy! I sought to defeat Tsawen in honorable battle—"

"Honorable!" Nijon choked.

"—But to slay a man asleep? That would be vile. If Vauren sought to kill Chief Mo'ian, why not challenge him to single combat? The chief was a dodderer."

Mo'ian's kin hissed at hearing the patriarch so described.

"Because," said Nijon, "if Vauren slew Mo'ian, even honorably, the Women's Council would not countenance his chiefhood. By murdering the chief and planting my talisman, he not only removed the chief without endangering himself, but also removed me, his rival for the affections of—a woman," he said bitterly, not wanting to speak Lai'iani's name.

"Supposition." Dowdin fleered.

"Why would I want to kill Mo'ian?" demanded Nijon.

"You, too, were spoken of as a future chief," Dowdin said. "You planned to remove Mo'ian—then return from your walkabout in triumph—with a drove of cattle, perhaps, or golden treasure, well placed to claim the bonnet. But your scheme did not go as you had planned; in his death throes, Mo'ian grasped your talisman—and you did not notice its absence until too late."

Nijon fought hard to contain his anger. Dowdin merely smiled in mockery.

"One of them lies," said Jutson. "Tsawen, can you not compel the truth?"

The shaman sighed. "Not from Dowdin," he said. "He is sufficiently skilled to deflect a truth enchantment. And would you trust the efficacy of a spell I cast on my own stepson?"

"No," said Jutson. "I would not."

"Enough with this charade," bellowed Vauren's father. "The talisman is proof sufficient! This tale of planted evidence is far too smooth. The murderer must die!"

"Aye, aye!" shouted the families of Mo'ian, Vauren, and Lai'iani.

"We know Vauren and Dowdin schemed against

Tsawen," said Dihaen loudly. "Why seize the shaman's post, and not the chief's? Of course they sought Mo'ian's death as well! Has Nijon ever acted but honorably?"

Dihaen's family, and Poai's extended clan, shouted their approval. Nijon was grateful for Dihaen's unexpected support.

"Honorably?" said a woman. "Was it honorable when Nijon stole my stewpot?"

"And what about the time my daughter and he—"

"And the beating he gave my boy!"

"Youthful indiscretions," bellowed Poai. "What one might expect from any spirited lad."

Nijon blushed; he had been a hell-raiser, no doubt about it. Under normal circumstances, the tribe would have been faintly proud of his transgressions—but they did not aid his case, not now.

Jutson sat on the chieftain's stool, obvious dismay on his face; but still he did not speak.

"He killed! He must die!"

"But Vauren—"

"Pah! Your family has always envied ours. You seek only—"

"Envied! Did not your uncle abandon my grandfather to the Guard of Gray when they raided Kaisham?"

"He retreated when faced with certain death!"

"And your mother, she called my father coward—to his face!"

Nijon looked about the fire; the entire tribe was on its feet, shouting, red-faced, gesticulating. The tribe was divided; and old disputes, anger at past injuries long forgotten in the interests of tribal harmony, broke forth with the division. Men and women were dividing into small groups, shaking fists, bellowing imprecations; Nijon expected fights to break out at any moment.

"The cattle you stole—"

"Stole! What mean you?"

"The spoils that were rightfully mine—"

"How you mistreated my daughter, you lecherous—"

Jutson sat his stool in uncertainty and confusion. Nijon saw the wisdom of the rule forbidding weapons at a moot; if there had been weapons, there might already have been bloodshed. This, he realized, is how tribes die. If Jutson dithered much longer, the tribe would splinter.

Jutson rose at last. "Hear me!" he shouted.

The babble of angry voices died gradually away.

"Nijon Oonitsaupivia," he said, once he had the tribe's attention, "you stand accused of a grave crime; but the accusation can neither be proved nor disproved. Yet for you to remain with us would cause dissension. You are banished from the Va-Naleu, but may take your rightful possessions with you when you go.

"Dowdin Oolaejen, your fate is in Tsawen's hands, for he has defeated you. But if he permits you to live, you, too, are banished from the tribe.

"So says Ro-Jutson-a-Va-Naleu."

And Jutson turned to enter his tent.

For a moment, there was silence; then, a murmur of conversation arose.

The tribe would survive, Nijon saw; the anger was largely gone. He wondered whether Jutson would likewise survive. Only if the wisdom of his decree was generally accepted would he be secure.

Dowdin faced Tsawen across the communal fire. "Well?" he demanded.

Tsawen sighed. "You are free to go," he said. "But I place this geas on you: Never will you marry, and never will you find a tribe."

Dowdin scowled. "I will find a way to break your curse."

"I doubt it," said Tsawen. "Come, Nijon, Poai; let us go home."

* * *

Under a canopy of stars, the three stood silently together. "Well," said Poai at last, "it could have been worse."

"I had planned to travel north anyhow," said Nijon. "I promised Mongoose I would."

"Mongoose?" said Tsawen, a look of faint skepticism on his face.

Epiphany washed over Nijon. Tsawen, like most of the tribe, must never have believed Poai's tale—but he loved her enough to feign belief. And she, Nijon realized, would have known that—and never pressed the issue.

"You have seen him, then?" asked Poai, with satisfaction.

"Yes," said Nijon. "He came to me on the plain when I was wounded and feverish."

"Feverish, or deprived of food or water, sleepless, or with the Sacred Mushroom in your belly," said Tsawen slowly. "Yes, that is when the gods reveal themselves."

"What did he say?" Poai asked.

"He—he gave me Brother as my companion," said Nijon, stroking the creature's golden fur.

"Brother?" asked Poai.

"Ah—" Nijon was a little embarrassed. "So I call him. Mongoose said he was my brother—my *half*-brother. I mean, he had a different mother."

Both Tsawen and Poai broke out laughing.

"And," said Nijon, "he said I would be a great warrior. And a chieftain. And I would lead my people into a glorious future."

"Then," said Poai, "you will return, and the tribe will accept you."

"Perhaps," muttered Tsawen.

"Perhaps?" said Poai sharply.

"Perhaps," said Tsawen firmly. "Mongoose is the Trickster, after all."

"True," said Poai thoughtfully.

Tsawen sighed. "I have something for you," he said, and

disappeared into their tent. Moments later, he returned, with a long bundle, wrapped in leather and bound with thongs; longer than Nijon's arm.

He began to unwrap it. The smell of suet met Nijon's nose; the bundle was coated with rendered fat. It was—a knife, far longer than any knife Nijon had ever seen. Tsawen placed it in Nijon's hands.

"What is it?" Nijon asked.

"It is a weapon," said Tsawen. "It was my brother's, before he died in the service of Dikon Khan. The northerners call it a sword."

Nijon hefted it; it was oddly heavy. "Won't it bend?" he said. So long and thin a blade of bronze would indeed bend or shatter in combat; that was why axes were the weapon of choice.

"No," said Tsawen. "It is not bronze."

"What is it, then?" asked Nijon, running his thumb along the edge.

"Star-metal. It fell from the heavens, in a molten lump. The substance is rare, very rare; few smiths know how to work it. It will hold an edge far better than bronze, and smash through any armor."

Nijon stared at his thumb; blood welled up. He had exerted hardly any pressure. It was, indeed, far sharper than bronze.

"But it has a flaw; it corrodes, bubbling up in blisters of brown. You must keep it oiled always, and keep it from water."

Nijon nodded; so must a composite bow be kept.

He gave his parents much of the caravan's treasure. They talked late into the night. Bleary-eyed, Nijon saddled up with the dawn.

The sinuous form of Brother danced alongside as Nijon and his roan plodded north.

12

From the far wall, a slow trickle of water dripped onto the great bronze plate above the hypocaustum, where it billowed into steam.

The calidarium was dim, though it was broad daylight without. There were few windows, and they far up on the walls of the chamber, covered with stretched skins to contain the heat while admitting light. The walls were yellow-flecked marble. About them stood statues of many kinds: gods and goddesses, heroes and queens, monsters, and children at play. They lent a touch of levity to the otherwise somber room. The bath was a center of public life, and notables often vied to endow them with the grandest, or noblest, or most entertaining statuary. This, the Baths of the Chamites, was neither the least nor the greatest of the baths of Purasham.

"Shall I take your peplos, O Exalted?" murmured the bath-servant.

"Please," said Nlavi. She reached to her shoulder, unclasped the amethyst brooch, and let the brilliantine cloth fall into the servant's arms.

Nimble fingers untied Nlavi's cincture; another servant carefully took and folded her chiton of alizarine blue, interwoven with thread of gold.

From her ears hung polished spinel, clad in intricately wrought gold; her toes bore rings set with tiny cabochons. After the custom of her people, her nose was pierced, and a stone of aquamarine jade set therein. She forbore to shuck her bijoux; though these servants were her own, still the likelihood of theft at the baths was legendary.

Clad only in her jewelry and her bandeau, she padded across the warm marble, through the steam, to the table of her waiting masseuse.

Nlavi stood by the table as a servant poured amphorae of water over her head: first hot, then warm, then tepid, as was customary. The sweat washed away and left her skin receptive to the unguents that would follow.

She gave a little sigh of contentment as she lay down on the slab of marble. The masseuse began her work, firm hands pressing into flesh. Nlavi closed her eyes, abandoning herself to the rhythm of the massage.

Ah, Mesech, Mesech; a strong name, a manly name. The foreignness of it only added allure. He would come, the swarthy Motraian; a prince among his own people; her prince, her own. Nlavi could see him in her mind's eye, handling a stallion of gray with the ease of long familiarity. His bronze breastplate is burnished to a brilliant sheen, the Motraian vulture in raised relief on its surface. The handle of his war-axe is well worn, befitting his many conquests. Behind him, in serried ranks, stand his valiant men: Motraian soldiers all, bearing spears and the square shield of their nation. The prince waves his arm and grins; his blue eyes flash, a shocking blue in so dark a man; his curly beard—no. Nlavi edited the image in her mind: his clean-shaven face. Unlike the men of Purasham, the Motraians shave. The oddness of the custom gave her a tingle.

Ah, he would come, did come, came now. He would march up the Royal Avenue, his high-laced sandals crunching on the black sand of the street, his men behind him: the conquering warrior. He would come, and present his sigil to her father, the king. She would stand beside, and their eyes would meet; a flash would run between them, a flash of understanding. And they would know. . . .

The masseuse began to anoint her with oil of cloves.

Nlavi imagined them, together, amid the gardens of Kerem, pomegranates growing between the paths, lilies. . . .

The masseuse began to dot her neck, her thighs, the small of her back with attar of roses.

Not lilies—roses, emitting their intoxicating scent. He wears a yellow tunic, belted with green; she, her gown of aubergine. They talk, not of wars nor matters of state, but of the classic writers, of fine ale, of the color of the flowers: persiflage. He is charming.

They come to a bower, an arched trellis with roses twining up it; from blossom to blossom flit the bees. He looks at her, and takes her in his strong arms; the smell of roses is all about them, birdsong, and the bombilation of the bees; his lips thirst for hers and she abandons herself to his passion.

"I am done, Exalted," said the masseuse.

With a sigh, Nlavi sat up, and suffered the servants to clothe her once more. She led the way down the stairs to the apodyterium, where waited a throng of noblewomen, banned from the baths until their princess might finish her toilet. Some greeted her, requesting audience, or offered gifts; Nlavi accepted a cup of barley ale with a gracious nod, then reclined in her litter, sipping the liquid.

The eunuchs hefted the litter, and bore her through the streets.

Behind, smoke poured from the baths' brick chimney. From the rear of the massive building rang bangs, cracks, and curses: A dozen slaves labored, sawing wood, splitting it into burnable logs. Other slaves carried the wood to the voracious hypocaustum.

Nearby, a patient team of oxen labored always in circles, turning a vast wheel that pumped water from the well up to the higher floor, to feed the pools and chambers of the baths.

The hypocaustum was hellish, red-lit by fires roaring in baked-clay hearths. Soot-blackened slaves scuttled about, feeding the fires, tending the flames and the machinery that fed the baths above.

The slaves sweated rivers; it was a hot summer day, and with the heat of the fires, the temperature was nearly unbearable. From time to time, a slave would collapse; overseers would carry him out, to awaken him with a bucket of cold water.

Six oxen and thirty men labored for the delectation of a few.

"Where the devil is Poran?" said King Manoos. He sat in the audience chamber atop his jeweled bench; two servants fussed with his manteau and tunic, while another fanned him with a palm frond and a third stood by with a cup of honeyed yoghurt.

"He is in his chambers, Father," said Nlavi.

"Thank you, Nobby, dear," said Manoos. "Miserable excuse for a son." He snatched the yoghurt cup, gulped at it, smearing his mustache with white, and shoved the cup back into the hands of the waiting servant, sloshing most of the remaining liquid onto the palace floor. The servant immediately fell to his belly, moaned, "A thousand pardons, O Lord," and began to mop up the spill with his chiton. Another servant dabbed at the king's mustache.

Poran entered through the side door, handsome as usual in himation, a crimson sash, and sandals. "There you are, you laggard," bellowed the king. "How you expect to become autarch when you can never be prompt is beyond me. I take it as an insult to your sister."

Poran sighed. "Yes, my lord," he said soothingly, approaching the dais.

"And look at your clothes! Motraia is a warrior-state, boy; yet you're wearing nary so much as a boot knife."

"I had understood this was a state audience, not—"

"Never mind, never mind," muttered the king. "What of the rats?" he asked Vakhan, the grand vizier.

That worthy, a painfully thin graybeard in begemmed felt cap and cloth-of-gold blouse, started at the unexpected change of subject.

"Rats, sire? Ah, rats. Yes, the rat problem. Ahem." He leaned over and whispered with a younger noble for a moment. "Ah . . . the problem worsens, Lord. The granaries are overrun. The harvest has been good, however, so we do not expect a repetition of last year's riots—"

"Dragon season coming up," said the king.

"Ah? Yes, sire."

"I want another century of infantry within the city walls. And keep an eye on the satrap's guard; don't want them making trouble."

Prince Poran sat down next to Nlavi—like all the chairs in the room, theirs were considerably lower than the king's bench—and gave her hand a squeeze.

Irritably, the king kicked at one of the servants fussing with his clothes. The servant fell off the dais with a crash, and cried, "I beg abject forgiveness for my clumsiness, Highness."

"Any *man*," said King Manoos, "would gird his loins and seek out a dragon. An enormous hoard of treasure; the thanks of every maiden in the kingdom—methinks that should be motivation enough. For a *man*."

Prince Poran whistled tunelessly and studied the enormous statue of Sak, the hippopotamus-headed god, that stood at the far end of the room. Though Poran had no doubt a dragon would enjoy *croquette de prince flambé*, he had no desire to become such himself.

"Your Highness," said the chancellor, "Satrap Mesech is displaying a certain impatience."

"Yes, yes," said the king, waving his hand. "We've let him stew long enough. Admit my future son-in-law."

A corps of musicians began to play; the audience doors were thrown wide; and a herald announced the Most Puissant Mesech, Motraian Satrap of Noshen. Six Motraian soldiers marched into the room, then wheeled to line the satrap's route.

Eagerly, Nlavi craned for a glance of the man to whom she had been betrothed; Mesech, conqueror of Noshen, Mesech the Valiant, of a valiant race.

The satrap strode forward into the room, smiling broadly. Behind him came a boy in a felt cap, bearing a jeweled casket that must contain a gift for Manoos.

Why, the man is a house, Nlavi thought.

His raiment was notable not only for its richness, but also for the sheer yardage of cloth it must contain. Nlavi had seen an elephant only once, with a troupe of visiting Nyanzan soldiery, but Mesech's ponderous gait reminded her of the creature.

His piggish little eyes met hers, and a chill of revulsion swept down her spine.

From overhead hung gaily colored cloth; all about, the pipes of musicians and the cymbals of dancers sounded. On the floor's center lay a huge platter of gold, heaped with barley pilaf, roast lamb, whole chickens, dates, almonds, all perfumed with cinnamon. The diners sat surrounding it, each on a cushion, holding a loaf of lavash.

Nlavi reached forward with her right hand—never the left; that would be a grievous violation of etiquette—and scooped up lamb and pilaf, dumping it on her flatbread. Then, rather daintily, she transferred bits of food to her mouth, wiping her hand on a cloth after each bite. At her right stood a goblet of xanthous ale, which servants refilled the moment the level dropped.

Mesech guffawed at some witticism of her father's; grains of pilaf spattered from his mouth, some flying back onto the golden tray. Nlavi felt faintly sick.

Tipsily, King Manoos stood. "Ho!" he bellowed. "A toast!" There was instant silence, as the pipers and dancers halted and the other diners ceased all conversation in deference to the king.

"To friendship and peace, between Motraia and Purasham! To wedded bliss and the joy that children bring!" He quaffed a goblet of the ale, and everyone cheered, then quaffed their own.

Mesech gave an imperious beckon to two of his guardsmen, the wan flesh of his upper arm jiggling with the wave. The soldiers approached. Each took one of Mesech's arms. Together they heaved, straining to haul him to his feet. Mesech pointed, and one soldier lifted the satrap's goblet and handed it to him. Mesech waved the goblet: "Thank you, good king!" he shouted. "Thank you all for your kindness. Here's to brotherhood and friendship among our peoples, between our own empire and your kingdom. As I think of you as my father, good Manoos, so, I hope and trust, will Purasham come to think of Motraia as a parent, to be revered and trusted."

"Hear, hear," shouted the king, and everyone cheered and drank.

But the king scowled, Nlavi noticed; he had not liked that bit about revering Motraia as a parent. The reason for this marriage, Nlavi knew, was that Motraia had overrun half the independent cities of the River Uk—and the king hoped thus to ward off a similar fate for Purasham.

Laboriously, the satrap seated himself once more. With gusto, he leaned forward, thrust his arm half into the pilaf, pulled forth a massive gob of food, and crammed it into his mouth. Still masticating the food, he turned to Nlavi, put a grease-smeared paw on her leg, and bellowed, "How fares my poppet?"

Since she had not the slightest idea how to respond, Nlavi took the easy way out. She faked a faint.

13

Behold Nijon, mighty warrior, approaching Pura-sham.

He sits his horse lightly, the jaws of a lioness his head-dress, her pelt his cloak. At his back, wrapped in protective skins, he bears a great sword of iron, gift of his stepfather; balancing on the horn of his saddle sits a golden-furred mongoose. In his pack lies a casket dotted with fabulous gems, its contents a fortune in gold.

Two hours ago, he had entered the city, marveling at the height of the houses—some three stories tall!—and the labor that had gone into their solid adobe. There had been so many folk, bustling about, so many horses, carts, stalls. . . .

They laughed at the bumptious barbarian; no, no, this was not Purasham, certainly not. Why, Purasham was a great city; this was merely Kholem, an outlying market village.

Now Nijon stood atop a low hill, the road stretching down it to the floodplain of the Uk. The river ran in broad meanders, upstream and down, out of sight, flanked on both sides by neat fields and irrigation trenches. And on the hither bank was—some great congeries of structures, chaotic, odd; at first Nijon could make no sense of it.

At length, he began to realize that the long, irregular line he saw was a wall, enclosing the central part of the city; a wall, he realized with astonishment, higher than a man standing on a saddle; a wall that must run for miles. How many men had worked for how long to build such a thing? Spilling out, on the near side, was building after building. Some buildings leaned up against the wall itself, a warren of irregular streets among them. To Nijon's eyes, they appeared grand houses, far roomier than a nomad's tent.

Down the road ahead of him labored oxcarts, men under burdens, the occasional horse with a rider. This stretch of road alone held more people than constituted his entire tribe.

Up and down the river passed lateen-rigged craft with gaily patterned sails, decks groaning with cargo. The plain was dotted with villages, and here and there groups of people could be seen, working in the fields, or feeding the irrigation trenches with buckets of water drawn up with counterweighted levers.

Within the walls, he glimpsed structures of truly monstrous size: temples and palaces. Why, he thought, they were mountains: mountains built by men. From the city rose the smoke of so many fires that a pall hung over the walls.

A thousand folk must live yonder, Nijon thought with amazement; in truth, some twenty thousand did. It was a vast metropolis.

Inwardly, Nijon quailed. Yet his visage remained stern; he would not betray the tumult within.

He clucked, and began the descent.

Entering the city fringe, Nijon noticed the stench first; many fires, people living close together, cooking, waste, things rotting unattended in the street. In truth, Purasham was clean, as such places go; the honey carts came around daily, collecting waste to be used as fertilizer in the fields without, and garbage could readily be disposed of in the River Uk. But to one used to the steppe's sweet air, it was almost overwhelming.

Nearing the wall, Nijon grew nervous; surely, these folk would not let a Vagon, a savage barbarian, within their defenses? Yet it was so; there seemed no guard at the gate, and a steady stream of people passed through.

His dress went unremarked, too—puzzling, until he realized how jaded Purasham must be, with traders of all lands congregating here.

"Hail, son of the steppe," shouted an urchin, running with Nijon's horse. "What do you wish of Purasham? Lodging? Food? I know where glasswork of great rarity may be had, where sacrifices are made to seventeen gods, where scented courtesans seek to fulfill every whim, every desire. May—"

Nijon slowed his horse and peered down at the grubby girl. "An inn," he said.

"I know just the place," said the urchin, rapid-fire. "A veritable palace of—"

"No palace," said Nijon. "Simple lodgings."

She grimaced. "Very well, simple lodgings. Not far from here is the Barkers' Inn, a homely but wholesome place where—"

"Fine," said Nijon. "Lead on."

"Ah, princely one, forgive my crude temerity, yet there is the minor question of recompense for my hard-won knowledge."

Nijon sighed. "How much?"

"A crown," said the girl.

He blinked. Were prices so high? "One sequin," he offered—a far smaller sum.

They settled on three. Nijon fumbled open his pouch and withdrew his casket. The girl's eyes grew round. Nijon noted her reaction; evidently, it was unwise to flaunt so much wealth. He removed several coins.

She accepted the money, kissing his foot, and ran ahead.

They came to an adobe structure, enormous to Nijon's eyes. Outside, men lolled on benches, quaffing ale. The girl stood with a fat man in an apron of coarse cloth.

"This kingly Vagon warrior seeks shelter," she said. "He—"

The innkeeper sniffed deeply. "Not without a bath," he said.

Nijon was puzzled. "What?"

"Bad enough to cater to barbarians," grumbled the innkeeper. "You drink too much and brawl. But I shall not lodge so foul-smelling a creature; a bath, I say."

"Foul-smelling?" said Nijon, taken aback. "Honest man-scent is all, unlike the foulness that reeks in these gutters."

"O mighty king," said the urchin, "it is the fashion in our city to immerse oneself in water, thereby cleansing the skin."

Nijon scowled. "Unhealthy habit," he said.

"For a modest additional stipend, I will usher you to a sumptuous bathing-place, where you may wash away the dust of the road."

"Very well," said Nijon.

"Good," said the innkeeper. "One crown a night."

They haggled a bit; Nijon advanced one night's rent, and the innkeeper called a boy to take Nijon's horse to the stable.

"You should tip him," said the girl.

"Why?" asked Nijon. Gods, these people demanded money at every turn.

"Would you have your horse well cared for?" asked the urchin.

He saw her point, and gave the lad a few coins. The boy babbled thanks. Nijon took his leather pouch and skin-wrapped sword from the saddle, thinking it unwise to leave them behind.

"You stay with Nialo," he told Brother; so had he named

the mare. "See that she does not come to harm." The mongoose chittered in apparent agreement, and twined through the horse's hooves as the hostler led her away. Nijon turned to go with the girl.

They wandered through the streets, turning this way and that; Nijon quickly lost the path, and fervently hoped his guide would not lead him astray. Nervously, he touched his sword, hoping he would be able to unwrap it quickly, if need be; his only other weapon was the knife up his sleeve.

There were so many people; how could there be so many people? They hustled everywhere, each on his own mission. Some carried enormous bundles of goods on their backs. Others stretched out their hands and beseeched alms. Here and there, a litter fought its way through the mob, guards clearing a path ahead of the bearers, striking with clubs at those who did not scurry away quickly enough.

There were vendors crying wares, and canopied stalls stacked with goods and presided over by women suspiciously eyeing those who stopped to finger the merchandise. There were buildings of brick, of stucco, of adobe; shanties of wood; small temples and shrines interspersed among the other structures. The streets were a maze, alleys and avenues built apparently as whim struck, intersecting at haphazard angles. Nijon was unable to stop himself from gaping all about.

"Here we are, Master," said the girl, tugging at his arm. They had halted before a large building, carven sphinges flanking the entrance.

"I may not enter," she said; "these baths are for men."

"What must I do?" he asked.

"You pay at the entrance—two sequins—then proceed to the apodyterium, where you disrobe. From there"—she shrugged—"perhaps to the frigidarium, for a dip in cold water; or to the calidarium, where slaves will poor warm water over you.''

Nijon sighed; if he must, he must.

He paid at the door, then turned left, as others seemed to be doing. Behind, he saw the urchin conferring with the doorman. Inside the apodyterium, a host of men removed their clothes. A Vagon in full tribal dress attracted some attention, but none approached as he disrobed.

He stored his things in a bank of compartments apparently provided for this purpose.

The apodyterium alone inspired awe: It was the largest room he had ever seen. The frigidarium was even more impressive: The pool was elaborately tiled, the walls a montage of murals. After a moment of discomfort, Nijon began to enjoy himself.

He had frolicked in streams as a child, and found it relaxing to loll about as the other bathers did. He explored each of the rooms of the baths in turn, concluding that there was something to be said for civilization.

At last, he returned to the apodyterium to secure his garb. He reached into the compartment: There was his sword, still wrapped in skins, but where . . . ?

No tunic, no leggings, no lioness pelt; no leather bag. The wrappings to his sword were half undone; apparently, someone had examined it and, unfamiliar with iron, had left it as too heavy to steal.

Nijon's eyes darted about the room. Could the thief be here? No, not likely. What was he to do? Alone in a strange city, ignorant of the customs, far from his inn—and, apparently, penniless.

Penniless, and naked. His thoughts tumbled wildly. At last, he swallowed, and thrust his hand into another compartment. A rectangle of rough cloth was there, and a pin of bronze. He pulled them out, and surveyed the room. No one paid him any attention; the owner of this garment must still be in the baths.

Nijon watched another man dress, then imitated his motions, draping the cloth as he had seen the man do, and pinning it at the shoulder. The form of dress felt strange, and Nijon feared he had done a clumsy job—but no one batted an eye as he strode from the room.

There was a different doorman, now. And the urchin was nowhere to be seen.

Nijon berated himself for an idiot. Of course: The bint had seen the jeweled casket. She had known he would leave it in the apodyterium. Women might be barred from the baths; but she had made some arrangement with the door-keeper—and the two had stolen his wealth, then fled. No doubt a doorman's pay was a tiny fraction of the gold the casket contained.

He hoped the doorman would beat the urchin, and steal her share. That would serve her right.

Behold Nijon, mighty warrior. Clad in a crude himation, awkwardly draped, he wanders barefoot, forlorn in Pura-sham's filthy streets. He holds his skin-wrapped sword, feeling it unwise to wander about with a naked blade. He is jostled by people who run to and fro—and suffers the blow of a club to the shoulder, as a litter approaches and a guard seeks to beat him from its path.

Nijon fought down anger; slaying the guard would be satisfying, but would do nothing to improve his lot.

Daylight turned to dusk, and still Nijon wandered, desperately seeking his inn. He passed a charcoal brazier, where a vendor cooked meat on skewers; Nijon's stomach rumbled, but he had no coin.

A young beggar tugged insistently at Nijon's garb, begging for a sequin. Nijon's temper rose, and he began to shout that he had none—then thought better of it, and took a firm grip on the boy's ear. "Take me to the Barkers' Inn," said Nijon, "or I shall beat you until your very flesh cries out."

The boy whimpered and shouted, but none came to his aid; at last, he headed down the street, protesting Nijon's still-firm grip.

The inn was no more than three blocks away; but Nijon could not have navigated the twisting streets unassisted.

He let the boy go. The whelp hurled abuse at him, but Nijon was too tired to care. He went to check on Brother and Nialo; they were well, and the hostler had evidently combed and curried the mare. Nijon picked up the mongoose and carried him into the inn.

The innkeeper scowled at the animal, but said nothing, only pointing Nijon to his room. Two others were already there, sprawling on the straw mattress; Nijon almost turned to protest, but realized it was probably customary to put several customers in the same bed. Sighing, he lay down on the floor; he had spent many a night on the steppe's cold ground. The planks of the floor were soft by comparison.

His stomach growled. He salivated, thinking of the room below, where a lamb roasted on a spit; but he had no money to spend, and dinner was not included.

There was a squeak; Nijon opened an eye, to see Brother biting the head off a rat. At least someone would eat tonight, he thought—and drifted off to sleep.

14

Nijon gave a contented belch. He had devoured two bowls of pottage, a mass of chicken livers, a portion of leftover lamb, and nearly a quart of small beer. The innkeeper's wife totted up his bill, her lips moving as she counted on her fingers. "Twelve sequins, love," she said.

Nijon waved a hand, rising hastily and grabbing Brother. "Ah, I shall pay with tonight's lodging," he said, and legged toward the door.

The innkeeper appeared, his apron bloodied, holding a meat cleaver. "You'll pay now," he said, "if you hope to find lodging tonight."

Nijon swallowed, wondering whether he should unwrap his sword; but it would not do to kill the man, not if he wished to stay in the city. "Ah . . . as to that. . . ."

The innkeeper lowered his cleaver, cursing. "You're broke," he accused.

"Ah, yes," said Nijon. "But tonight, I'll—"

The innkeeper turned and shouted, "Kalon! Bar the stable door!"

Nijon hesitated.

"You'd best find the money," the innkeeper advised, "if you hope to see your horse again."

Nijon scowled; but he had to admit the justice of this.

* * *

The stout man stood on a box. "Strong men!" he bellowed. "Hefty men! I need a dozen, two; twenty sequins for a day's work."

A crowd gathered round; Nijon wandered over. "How long is a day's work?" shouted one onlooker.

"Till sundown," said the man.

"I'm your man," said the one. The stout man motioned, and the speaker went to stand behind the box.

Another offered to work, but the stout man refused. "I need strong men," quoth he, "not graybeards."

"What manner of work is this?" asked Nijon—to curious glances; apparently, the crowd already knew.

The stout man surveyed Nijon, obviously liking his size and strength. "A cargo of betel must be unloaded."

"Lifting and hauling," said Nijon.

"Aye."

"Work fit for slaves," said Nijon. There were angry mutters from the crowd.

The stout man flushed. "Slaves don't get paid," he protested.

"Does money ennoble the labor?" asked Nijon. "Rather, payment demeans the recipient."

The stout man laughed uproariously.

"Fear not, barbarian," he said, "I shall not demean you; you will receive no pay. What ho! Are there others without such scruples? Twenty sequins for one day's work! Strong men, hefty men!"

Scowling, Nijon turned away.

Nijon sat in the shade of a building, wrapped sword across his knees, Brother casting about in the street and sniffing suspiciously at pieces of trash. The air was filled with murmured conversation and the shouts of vendors: "Fresh carp! Lovely persimmons! Delectable brochettes!" Nijon's stomach was rumbling once again.

"Master, I beg of you," said a voice from the street. "I am a soldier, crippled in the service of King Manoos, reduced to penury in the gutters of Purasham." Nijon looked up; the voice belonged to a man with matted beard and hair, one-legged, clutching a crutch. A man in a well-draped himation stood by, facing away, embarrassed; he fumbled a few coins out of the pouch and gave them to the beggar.

"Bless you," said the beggar, lifting the man's garment to his lips.

Once his target was gone, the beggar ducked into a little alley at the side of Nijon's building. Curious, Nijon went over and peered round the corner; the man had unlaced his "bad leg," and was massaging the limb. He had doubled it up and bound it, to give the impression of deformity.

Spotting Nijon, he snarled, "Get lost, pal," grabbed his crutch, and waved it threateningly.

Nijon lifted a lip, and sat back down in the shade. A little while later, the beggar hobbled forth from the alley, his leg again bound, and made his way down the street, looking for another mark.

Nijon sat scowling. How could he honorably earn the money he needed?

He was a skilled hunter, tracker, horseman; what value did Purasham put on that? And he would not sweat in the sun like a slave; he was the son of a god, a king of the steppe, not some peasant scrabbling for coin in the filth of the city. He—

A sequin fell in the dust. Nijon reached over and picked up the silver coin, then looked up; a woman with a ewer of ale on her head bustled away. She had cast the coin.

Shame flushed across Nijon's face. He had been sitting here, obviously miserable; she had taken pity, and tossed him a coin. He snarled and lunged to his feet; he *would* not be an object for pity!

He whistled at Brother and stamped away.

* * *

Nijon studied passersby with new eyes: The cut of that chiton was too ragged, that one was obviously poor. This one's garb was rich, but he fingered a lightweight pouch, judiciously considering the price of a roasted chicken—evidently down on his luck. There, a litter was borne down the street; great wealth, but well protected.

Ah, that might do; a portly woman made her way down the street, followed by a boy with a little wagon. She stopped to buy fruit, some fish, a bundle of herbs, paying from a purse at each stop, loading the purchases onto the wagon. Nijon sidled after her, stopping at nearby booths and faking an interest in the merchandise, while keeping an eye on her. Brother rode on his shoulder.

This went on for quite some time, until the matron came to a door in a long courtyard wall. She opened it and passed through; Nijon glimpsed fountain and fruit trees, and then the door was shut and bolted. Nijon cursed.

He wandered, muttering, down the street. A man in a rich cloak strode ahead, then turned into a narrow alley.

There were many alleys in Purasham; wheeled traffic was rare, so a lane wide enough for two men to pass was adequate for most purposes. On an impulse, Nijon turned down that alley, too, and adopted the silent crouch of a Vai hunter. Brother adopted a stalking gait in imitation. The alley was cool, sheltered by the buildings to either side, but rank, with an open gutter down its middle.

The man in the cloak whirled. "Wherefore do you follow me?" he demanded. His hands were back behind his head, each holding the blade of a throwing knife. Nijon had no doubt the man could plant at least one of the knives in Nijon's brisket before Nijon could lunge with his own unwieldy sword.

"Err . . ." he said, then turned and fled, leaping back and forth over the gutter to present a less stable target—but no knives came.

In a fouler mood than ever, he wandered on, Brother

sometimes following, sometimes carried. "Hola, sweet-ling," said a low voice from a doorway; a bekohled woman was there, beckoning to him. Even had he the inclination, Nijon thought, he did not have the coin, and passed on.

He heard her call behind him, and turned his head to see a young man stop to converse with the stew.

The young man's clothes were simple, but the pin holding his himation was jeweled; with interest, Nijon drifted to the side of the street. After a moment, the man and the woman turned, to walk down an alley.

Nijon paused, then followed slowly. From down the alley, he heard a thump; in the dimness, Nijon saw the stew and two men with clubs, standing over the unconscious form of their "customer."

Nijon scowled and withdrew, his own plans thus preempted.

Gloomily, Nijon wandered onward. Half-despairing, he lifted his eyes from the dust of the street—to spy at last the answer to his prayers.

An older man was leaning on a cane; his chlamys betrayed knobby knees, but the cloth was fringed with purple dye, very expensive. The fibula, too, was set with cabochons, and he wore a purse about his neck. Under his right arm was a heavy book.

Nijon followed, hardly daring to hope for an opportunity. The man turned in to an open door; beyond it was a foyer, with two stairways to either side, and another door, into a courtyard. Nijon peered in; the old man was studying a list of names, impressed into the stucco of one wall. There would be no observers.

Nijon loosened the skins around his sword and let them fall. Then, he rushed in and swung the flat of his blade.

The man half-turned at Nijon's rush, taking the blow across the jaw instead of the temple. He fell sprawling, the book fluttering to the stone floor. "Villainy!" he shouted. "I am beset!"

"Be quiet if you wish to live," said Nijon urgently, and made to bash the supine man again. The old man deflected his blow with his cane.

"No, you scoundrel," he shouted. "While I breathe, you shall not. . . ."

Nijon kicked the man in the head, yanked the purse away, breaking its strap, and tumbled out the door, scooping up Brother, who had viewed the struggle with interest.

Nijon dashed off down the street, trying to juggle his sword, the purse, and the mongoose, all at once.

Behind him, the old man struggled to the door, and shouted, "Thief! Palter! Stop him!"

No one moved to intercept Nijon, but heads swiveled as he ran past.

He darted down a narrow street, doubled back, then adopted a rapid walk—less noticeable, he hoped—and doubled back again.

He was thoroughly lost, and only hoped he had also lost whatever pursuit might follow.

The innkeeper took Nijon's money without comment; Nijon prepaid a week's lodging, as well as the price of his breakfast. It was getting on to dusk and he was tired; he sat heavily down on a bench in the taproom.

"Ho! Woman!" he bellowed to the innkeeper's wife. "Meat and drink!"

She scowled at this abruptness, and looked to her husband.

The innkeeper gave her a weary nod, and drew Nijon a bowl of chestnut ale, while she shaved slices of meat from the lamb carcass over the flames of the hearth, draping them onto a round of flatbread heaped with bulgur.

While Nijon noisily sated his hunger—with both hands, to the disgust of others in the room—he fed bits of lamb to Brother.

Soon after he had polished off the meal, a thin voice rang out across the inn: "There he is!"

The girl who had guided him here stood in the doorway, grimy as ever; and behind her, at least three soldiers, bearing spears.

Nijon started up, grabbing his sword and tipping over the table—then hung for an instant, caught between the desire to murder his defrauder and the need to flee.

He scooped up Brother, then hurtled across the room, knocking over the innkeeper's wife. He darted out the rear door, into the filth of the alley beyond.

Down the alley. A glint of moonlight off breastplate revealed soldiers at the alley mouth, spears at the ready.

Nijon was fairly sure they had spotted him, coming through the door, silhouetted by lamplight from the inn; as he neared, he hurled Brother into the face of one. The mongoose squealed and the soldier fell back, clawing at the little creature. The other soldier was distracted long enough for Nijon to bash him aside with the sword. He felt the blade slice through bronze; the man was wounded.

Not, Nijon hoped, mortally; he had no objection to slaying foes, but had no wish to be named a murderer again.

Out into the silent street. Brother skittered behind, chattering; Nijon paused to pick him up, then darted on. Occasional dim light glinted from a house where a lamp was lit; overhead, a thin sliver of moon and a pageant of stars gave meager light.

Nijon ran on, keeping to one side of the street, doubling back—

There was the slap of sandals behind him; several men pursued. There were whistles in the night; some from the right, some behind. They were signaling to one another. He was at a disadvantage, Nijon feared; he was on the enemy's home ground.

He found a doorway, slipped within, put his back to the wall and tried to breathe shallowly. Sandals neared. . . .

15

Sandals slapped past; four men, axes ready. No, three with axes, the fourth bearing some dim blue light. . . .

Nijon gave a silent prayer of thanks—then the sound of sandals faltered. There was low conversation, then two piercing whistles—then nothing. Nijon peered out the doorway.

The blue light hung in the air, suspended above one man's outstretched palm, blueness falling in highlights and shadows on the folds of the man's himation. He studied the glow and walked, as if led onward by the light; the axe-wielders followed. Nijon felt the sudden tang of magic; that blue light was somehow tracking him.

Then he was lost. Was he not?

Perhaps not; the spell might have a limited range of effect. If he could outdistance it—but crouching here was obviously not the way to freedom.

Out into the street again. Nijon felt lumbered, one hand holding the sword, the other Brother; it was less the weight that bothered him than the awkwardness.

Back, double back, round the corner, straight on for several blocks; Nijon heard no runners behind him, but there were whistles not far off. Suddenly, one side of the street was open space; a low fence ran the length of it. Nijon leaned over it, dropped both mongoose and sword, and vaulted. He picked up his sword, leaned down and said, "Run, now, Brother; you at least may escape."

The creature cocked its head, as if saying, "Do you mean this?" Nijon ran; Brother did not follow.

He ran through scrub—weeds, shrubs, grasses, none higher than his ankles, as if the vegetation had been scythed in recent weeks. The land sloped down; stench assaulted his nostrils. The smell was intense, but he could not place it; it was many smells combined, and the overwhelming scent a strange one.

He stumbled into a pile of—something that rustled as he fell. He lay in a rick of dried seed pods, each the length of his arm. From the fence came a shout: "Hola! He is in the tanyard!"

So that's where I am, thought Nijon. Were the seed pods used to tan leather? He rose and ran over a flat place, paved with stones, crunching flakes of a vegetable substance beneath his sandals.

He skirted a pit that smelled of rotting flesh—and suddenly was ankle deep in water. He stood in the River Uk; a gentle breeze came off the far shore. The water reflected the stars, but the breeze raised waves that chopped starlight into chaos. Nijon could not swim, and doubted he could wade the mighty Uk; with Nialo, he might have risked the crossing, but his mare was at the Barkers' Inn.

He realized the tip of his sword was in water; that would not do.

There was torchlight behind, by the pit he had skirted—then, a harshly whispered order: "Put out that light, you idiot; he'll see us." The torch tumbled end-over-end into the pit.

Nijon waded back to the shore, slowly to avoid a splash; then ran, on a hunter's silent feet, upstream.

Another pit was before him; he halted only just in time. A harsh, acidic stench came from it; over it ran trimmed tree branches. Things were hanging from the branches, soaking in the odiferous liquid below.

Nijon skirted the pit; adjoining it was another, separated from the first by a narrow spit of land. Behind, Nijon heard a muttered curse, and faint splashes. Immediately, he darted out down the spit.

The spit ended in wood; Nijon halted to examine it, uncertain of his footing. Earth ended, a sort of wooden hatch began; there were handles inset in the wood. One might yank them, raising a wooden sluice gate, Nijon surmised; thus might the liquid contents of one pit be drained into the adjoining one. Beyond the gate the spit continued; Nijon danced across the wood, and darted on.

There was the flare of another torch behind him. In the sudden light, Nijon saw that he ran between the first of three pairs of pits; six in all, separated by narrow spits of land and wooden gates. All bore poles, from which things—hides?—depended. The liquid in every pit was brown; some pits held a deeper brown than others.

Behind, holding the torch on high, was a soldier of Purasham; bronze breastplate, spear, axe at his belt. Three others stood nearby.

To the right, two soldiers ran alongside the pits, running to cut Nijon off, that he might not escape down his spit of land, past that final pair of pits.

Nijon came to an intersection; about him lay four pits now.

He might continue forward to the north, return, or dart left or right. To the right was the river, behind were soldiers, and more were running to block the route ahead; he turned left.

A shouted order sent two of the soldiers behind sprinting to block the leftward path. Nijon halted, and returned to the intersection.

The man with the light of blue above his palm came up;

he spoke a quiet word, and the light died away. "Ho!
Vagon," he shouted. "Surrender, now; it is hopeless."

"Why do you pursue?" asked Nijon.

"You have been charged with theft," said the man.

"And . . . what is the punishment for theft?" asked
Nijon.

"To return treble the value of your theft to your victim."

"And if I cannot?"

"Then your hand will be struck off."

Wonderful. Nijon considered; seven soldiers, three
routes of escape. Seven might overwhelm him, but against
two he had a chance.

He turned back to the left and charged down the spit
toward the soldiers waiting there.

Other Purashamians ran to circle the pits, but they had
farther to travel than he. The soldiers backed away, axes at
the ready; Nijon leapt over the corner of a pit, dodged a
blow, and, awkwardly swinging his heavy sword one-
handed, managed a cut to the soldier's calf.

Then, away. Pursuit followed—but he was free of the
trap! Free! He would—

He would run forward, feel his sandal sink, and pitch
forward into a muck, a foul-smelling muck. He had fallen
into another pit, containing some sort of paste. A warm
paste, body-heat. A rank paste. A gray paste. It was . . .

Nijon gagged; it was some sort of dung. He was wading
in dung. Another rod hung over this pit, hides hanging
from it; the dung must be used in some stage of tanning.

Wild with revulsion, Nijon lunged for the rod, then
pulled himself up the pole toward the edge of the pit.

Sharp pain. Blackness.

The soldier stepped back from the man he had bashed
unconscious with the flat of the axe. "Ye gods!" he said.
"What is that?"

"The droppings of hens," said another soldier. "It is
used to bate the hides."

"Excellent," said the first soldier. "You know so much about it, you pull him out."

"Ech," said the first. "Not I. You captured him; the honor is yours."

Nijon awoke to chattering teeth and aching pate. His himation clung wetly to his skin. He was half-standing, half-crouching in a hole only slightly larger around than he. Its dirt walls had kept him upright while unconscious.

There were several inches of water in the bottom of the hole, but that wasn't why he was wet; someone must have thrown a bucket of water over him, to wash off the dung.

Above him, a good twenty hands above his head, was a circular opening; he could see faint gray sky. It was dawn of an overcast day. He was alone, save for dirt, water, a patch of sky—and a thundermug. He was grateful for the thundermug.

He soon realized that he could not sit—nor did he particularly want to, not in several inches of chilly water. But standing was wearing. He leapt up and down, hoping the exercise would warm him—but his head rang with pain each time he landed. At last, he wedged himself against the walls in an uncomfortable squat, and hugged himself to still the shivers.

He wondered if he could escape. He could dig hand- and footholds in the earth, pull himself aloft—but there must be guards out there, against just such an eventuality.

There was a trill; Nijon looked up to behold a familiar bewhiskered face. Brother dropped a dead rat into the hole. Nijon picked it up, considered it, and clawed out a little shelf in the dirt of the wall to hold the body. "I appreciate the thought," he told Brother, "but I'll have to get a lot hungrier before I'll eat rat." Brother scrubbed his face with his paws, chittered as if to say, "Suit yourself," and left.

It was full light out there now, but between the overcast sky and the depth of Nijon's hole, the sun did little to warm him. Nijon wondered when they would get around to him, not sure whether he should look forward to getting out of this hole or fear having his hand excised.

"Ahoy," said a grating voice from above. Nijon looked up, and made out a bearded face. "I shall drop you a rope ladder," said the man. "You will climb it, and submit to having your hands bound. Three armed men are with me. If you resist or attempt to escape, you shall be slain."

"Yes, all right," said Nijon. The ladder tumbled down, slapping him in the face; he grabbed it, and scrambled up it—too fast, perhaps, for his pulse quickened, and with it the pounding in his head.

He stood on a field of some twenty pits like the one he had vacated; someone in one of the holes was singing, his voice resounding hollowly. The area was fenced, and two guards with bows stood on a platform in its center.

"Is this how you punish criminals?" Nijon asked as they bound his hands.

"No," said the man who had spoken to him first. "The king has no desire to provide food and shelter for scum. Captives are held here, until they are given justice: death, mutilation, the lash. Along with you, now." He shoved Nijon, hard, in the middle of the back; Nijon staggered forward, toward the gate.

In an intricately woven cloak, Prince Poran lounged in the audience chamber. Patterned tapestries flanked his throne of ebony and gold.

Nijon's guards hustled him into the back of the room. It was a large chamber, but plainly appointed; a dozen people sat or stood around its sides. On a gaily colored rug before the prince stood two men.

"Complaint dismissed," said Poran, a little intemperately. "Take both parties out and give them six lashes for their temerity in bringing such a minor matter before the court. What's next, bailiff?"

"The Merchant Desha versus Maazila, his daughter, O Exalted."

"Bring them forth." A man and a woman came forward, and threw themselves onto their bellies before the prince. Desha was a balding, walleyed little man, evidently in his fifties. His daughter was dressed in the manner of a courtesan; she struck Nijon as quite beautiful. She had been crying. They stood up and faced Poran. "Your complaint, good merchant?"

"O Exalted," began Desha, "this conniving wench has cheated me of her bride-price. At great expense and heartache, her mother and I raised her from infancy, only to be betrayed—"

"How did she manage that?" asked the Prince. "Is it not customary for the husband to pay the bride-price directly to the father?"

"Y-yes, Exalted. She is not married."

"Betrothed, then?"

"No, Exalted."

"I fail to see—"

"She is no longer—a maiden, Exalted. She has shamelessly thrust herself upon—"

"I see," said the prince. "So no man would pay you a bride-price now."

"You have it, Exalted."

"Still," said the prince, "though moral laxness among the young is shameful, it is not criminal. Wherefore do you approach the court?"

"I demand recompense!" said the merchant.

The prince blinked. Unwed women normally owned no property. "How do you expect her to pay you?"

"She has—her own source of income," spat the merchant with distaste, "into which I do not care to inquire."

The prince chuckled. "What have you to say?" he asked of Maazila.

"Sire," said the woman tearfully, "the dragon season

approaches. Fierce beasts shall flit from the mountains, to seize young lasses and bear them—"

"Yes," said the prince. "So?"

"The dragons capture only maidens," said the woman. "Therefore, I divested myself of my maidenhead."

"I see," said the prince. "Clever, if perhaps immoral."

"And my father cast me out!" she wailed. "He called me trollop, and drove me from the hearth with blows! What else was I to do but become what he had called me? I have a source of income, yes, I rent my body, as I must to survive. And now my brute of a parent, not content with my ruination, seeks to steal from me my meager earnings—"

"Enough," said Poran. "Complaint dismissed."

"What!?" shouted Desha with outrage.

"Good sir," said Poran contemptuously, "if you cannot control your own daughter, you deserve the loss of her bride-price. And if you will not support her, you deserve no share of her earnings. Depart, before I hold you in contempt."

The merchant seemed mad enough to burst, but looked sidelong at the guards. Not wishing to risk a flogging himself, he stamped from the chamber. Maazila threw herself at Poran's feet; the prince, embarrassed, motioned to the soldiers to remove her. He sighed. "And now what?" he asked the bailiff wearily.

"Scholar Hamen versus a violent Vagon vagabond, your sublime highness."

"Very well. Is the scholar here?"

The old man whom Nijon had robbed came forth, and arthritically levered himself down to perform a kowtow. "I am present, O Light of Purasham," he said, kissing the prince's foot.

"And is this foreign brute present?"

Nijon's guards propelled him forward. "On your belly before the prince!" one bellowed, clubbing Nijon on the back of his neck. Another swept Nijon's feet from beneath him, so that, willy-nilly, he found himself flat on his face before Poran. Growling, he leapt to his feet, dodged another blow, butted the guard who had clubbed him in the stomach with his head—and regretted the action as his multiply injured head banged into bronze breastplate. He staggered to his knees with the pain. Guards kicked him to the floor again.

"Enough of that," said the prince. "Well, good Hamen; what has this creature done?"

"O Exalted," said Hamen, speaking into the stone floor of the chamber, "this vicious animal assaulted me in a building foyer, beating me to the ground and violently seizing my purse. Not content with my wealth alone, he proceeded to kick and beat me with vicious abandon, until I all but expired from—"

"That's a lie!" said Nijon.

"Silence!" shouted a guard, kicking him.

"May I not speak in my own defense?" asked Nijon, offended.

"No," said Poran coolly. "If you are guilty, there is no need to listen to your self-serving lies."

Nijon dared a glance at the prince. "And if I am innocent?"

"Then," said the prince, smiling, "there is no need to subject you to the unpleasantness of interrogation."

Nijon had nothing to say to this ineluctable logic.

"So, good scholar," said the prince, "you charge him with assault and theft; he has been multiply assaulted by his captors already. Do his bruises satisfy that aspect of your charge?"

Hamen got up and examined Nijon, still prone. He gave Nijon a vicious kick of his own, and said, "Yes, Your Serenity."

"And how much was stolen from you?"

"Ten crowns," said the scholar.

The purse had held no more than seven. Nijon began to protest—and received another blow to the ribs.

"Very well," said the prince. "By our law, he therefore owes you thirty. Had he any coin on his person when captured?"

One of the soldiers cleared his throat. "No, O Exalted. He was innocent of wealth."

Nijon began to speak—but noticed a soldier raising a club, and thought better of it. He had carried the scholar's purse; one of the soldiers must have pocketed it. Nijon scowled.

"Cut off his hand," said the scholar, "cut it off! Thus are criminals served!"

"Stand him up," said Poran. Soldiers yanked Nijon to his feet. The prince got off his throne and circled Nijon, examining him. "Are you weapons-trained?" he inquired.

Nijon blinked. "Aye," he said. "With bow, lance, and sword, I am unmatched on all the Vagon plain. All manner of beast and men have I slain, in ways beyond counting. With the great bow, that few of your puny race may draw, I can strike the eye of an antelope at fifty cubits—"

"Yes, yes," laughed Poran. "All know the boastfulness of Vagon men. You are well muscled. That sword with which you were captured; it is a rare weapon."

"It is," agreed Nijon.

"I am looking for men for the palace guard," said Poran. "The pay is one crown a week. Will you take it?"

Do I look like a drooling fool? thought Nijon. When the alternative was to lose a hand? At least it was honorable employment. "Yes," he said.

"Yes, O Exalted," said Poran, a little mockingly.

With the best grace he could muster, Nijon said, "Yes, O Exalted."

"Very well," said Poran, and turned to Hamen, who looked uneasy. "Pay the scholar thirty crowns; I shall withhold half the barbarian's salary until he repays the debt. Take him to the palace. And return his sword."

The captain of the soldiers gulped. "His—sword, O Exalted?"

"Yes, yes," said Poran absently, returning to his throne. "His sword. Bailiff—the next case, please."

Soldiers escorted Nijon out. "N-no hard feelings, Vagon?" said one.

Nijon gave the man his best lion snarl. The soldiers all edged away.

"You cut his bonds," said one.

"No," said another. "You clubbed him—*you* cut his bonds."

"I'm not getting that close."

Nijon smiled.

16

$\blacktriangleright\blacktriangleright\blacktriangleright$

Nijon sat idly in the barracks room, watching other guardsmen dice. He himself preferred to husband his half a salary, at least until he had figured out the game.

Brother appeared, dragging the still-twitching body of a rat. "That weasel eats better than we," joked one of the soldiers, looking up from his game.

"Keeps the rats down," grunted another.

"Something needs to," said a third. Recently, there had been panic-buying of bread and grain; rumors that the king's granaries were nearly empty swept the city. Nijon wondered if the rumors were true.

The captain looked up from the game and studied the windows and the angle of the afternoon light. "Change of watch," he announced.

Nijon sighed; it was his watch. He pulled on his cuirass and headed off to Princess Nlavi's chambers.

Detros stood before the door to Nlavi's antechamber, looking half-asleep. Nijon was not surprised; Detros drank ale at every meal. "I'm your relief," Nijon said.

"Thank Ptemesh," said Detros, shaking his head as if dislodging cobwebs. "I've been standing here for a mortal age."

"Anything to tell me?"

"If anything happened, I didn't notice it," said Detros, sidling down the corridor, toward the barracks—and, no doubt, another ale.

Nijon took his place, doing his best to look professional. The soldier's life was not what he'd expected; he had yet to see a domestic brawl, let alone a battle, and if Purasham had any conception of military discipline, Nijon had yet to note any evidence of it. Detros complained of the unrelenting tedium; Nijon was reasonably content to pay off his debt and eat three square meals every day.

No matter how bad the grain situation got, Nijon suspected, the palace wouldn't suffer any lack of provisions.

The antechamber door crashed open. Princess Nlavi stood in the doorway in little more than her bandeau. "I won't have it!" she shrieked.

A bevy of servants followed, murmuring soothing words: "Come, O Exalted, see this chiton, is not the color lovely? The king commands your presence, and your betrothed—"

"He is a fat, disgusting slug," shouted Nlavi, stamping around the chamber. She stood before a stuffed aurochs head and glared at it. "I shall not—"

"It will be but for an afternoon, an hour. Come, don this raiment, that we may—"

She stood before Nijon and spoke directly to him. "You!" she said. "Soldier. What is your name?"

"Nijon," said Nijon. A moment passed before he remembered to add—"O Exalted."

"You're Vagon, aren't you," she said, with slight contempt.

"I am of the Va-Naleu," he said with pride.

"Fine. I command you, carry me off to the rude tents of your savage tribe, where I shall rule in primitive splendor as your queen."

Nijon blinked. "Yes, O Exalted. At once, O Exalted. But

I shall have to consult with my captain. And there is the question of supplies for such an expedition."

Nlavi turned away. "Bah!" she said. "Captains! Supplies! It is always so; nothing can ever be done. The captain must be consulted. It is under consideration. The vizier has referred the question to expert opinion. Don't bother your pretty head with such questions," Nlavi shouted, "your brains will overheat—I am tired of hearing it."

She whirled on Nijon once again. "If you were a *man*," she said, "you'd gather me up with strong arms, gallop away to the boundless prairie on a steed of fire, and make passionate love to me under the wheeling stars."

Nlavi departed, pursued by anxious servants, one of whom gently closed the door behind her.

I'm a man, all right, Nijon reflected. I'm just not so much a fool as to get involved with *that*.

Less than an hour later, carefully coiffed and bejeweled in ebony and gold, Nlavi was disgorged by the doors once again. Scowling, she trotted down the corridor, servants following at a discreet distance.

The servants had had their way, Nijon saw: She was off to meet Mesech, her betrothed—in accordance with the wishes of the king.

Brother carefully arranged the dead rats; there were three now, all lying on the limestone floor, all arranged with heads pointing toward the wall. Brother sat back and examined them with the air of the satisfied craftsman, then disappeared into a cleft.

"Three in one night?" said Detros.

"I believe he's going to hunt another," said Nijon.

"Big animals for him to hunt," said Detros.

Nijon gave him a dangerous smile. "Of course," he said. "He has the courage and strength of all plains dwellers. Never would we be daunted by the size of a foe. Why I myself slew a lioness, while naked, with nothing but a fire-hardened stick. I had run seven—"

Detros laughed. "Yes, yes, your heroism is unquestioned. Tell you what; I'll wager six sequins your weasel will not be back before Poran finishes his ale."

Nijon looked to the prince, who was looking back, his attention drawn by the mention of his name. He sometimes caroused with the guards; he had been assigned personal responsibility for them by the king, and took it seriously.

Nijon studied the prince's bowl; it was nearly full. Nijon doubted that Poran would finish it soon. "Done," he said.

"What is this?" asked the prince, wandering over to examine the rats.

"Why, Nijon here is a man of unexpected depths," said Detros. "He is a magician, no doubt of it; and he has a weasel as his familiar, a vicious little brute that delights in the torment of rats."

Poran raised a skeptical eyebrow.

"Not a weasel," Nijon said, "but a—mongoose." He had to use the Vai word, for he knew none in Agondan. "An animal of the Vagon plain. Neither he nor I is magical."

"I see," said the prince. "And what was this bet?"

"Why, Great Prince," said Detros, "I bet that you would finish your ale before the weasel returned with another rat."

"And you, Nijon, that I would not?" said Poran, grinning. Nijon nodded. "Then," said Poran, "how much will each of you bid to have me quaff my ale at once—or leave it untouched?"

Before Nijon and Detros could respond, Brother returned. A fourth rat hung from his mouth.

"Astounding," said Poran. "Are there many such animals on the plain?"

Nijon considered. "A sufficiency," he said. "They do not darken the plains like antelope, but they are not uncommon."

"And they can be tamed," considered Poran. "And they like to kill rats."

Nijon cleared his throat. "This is the only tame one I know of," he said. "And rats are not common on the plain."

"Nonetheless," said Poran, and wandered off, obviously in thought.

"You owe me six sequins," Nijon said.

Detros reluctantly nodded, then went to find his purse.

Astonishing how one's viewpoint changes, Nijon thought as he gave a gleeful whack to a fishwife who failed to scurry from his way in time. Not a week before, he had cursed the forerunner of a palanquin who struck him with a club to clear the path; and now he was similarly cursed. Two other forerunners were with him, shouting at the crowd to make way.

Behind, Nlavi rode, her curtains drawn back, though it was day and the female nobility normally sought to maintain an attractive and indolent pallor. Mesech drove a chariot alongside, pulled by three hefty geldings. Nijon wondered how so huge a man ever sat a horse; perhaps he did not, though it was hard to see how a Motraian satrap might visit the cities of his domain except ahorse.

"Beautiful day, is it not, my poppet?" Mesech bellowed. He was sweating heavily in the noontime sun. A contingent of Motraian soldiers followed behind, eyeing the crowd warily.

"Gorgeous," said Nlavi with notable lack of enthusiasm. The crowd was thinning out now; they were out of the streets, and onto the plaza of the temple complex.

Beholding the pyramid, Nijon apprehended at once why Nlavi had brought Mesech here.

"Here we are, beloved," she trilled, swinging out of her litter and condescending to dirty her feet with the dust of the street. "The famed hanging gardens of Purasham."

Nijon stared at it with awe; he had seen this structure from outside the city, but its vastness was more apparent at close approach. It was at least a hundred cubits tall; small, perhaps, as mountains go, but by far the hugest man-made object he had ever seen. From the corners hung dragons, gargoyles, monsters, and gods, carved in intricate relief; up the sides ran steps, and from every step hung luxurious growth: vines, flowers, fruit trees trained on trellises. From the top ran an artificial stream, cascading down the steps.

"Come," said Nlavi, and took Mesech's hand—the closest familiarity between the two Nijon had observed. She began to climb.

The steps were so steep and narrow that one could not climb them face-on; one stood facing to the side, and climbed crabwise, the right leg taking each step.

Mesech's face was a study in dismay.

"Come," said Nlavi, "there is a garden at the peak, where only the finest ale is served; the view is breathtaking. There shall we make merry."

Mesech was panting already. "Yes, my sweet," he gasped.

Others were moving up and down the pyramid. Not a few simply sat on steps, contemplating the greenery. Here and there, men in the robes of priests were pruning, weeding, and watering. Nijon went on ahead, his task essentially unchanged: to divert folk diagonally across the pyramid, to clear a path for the princess and her party.

After some moments, he looked back; Mesech was wheezing like a winded mastodon, struggling up one step at a time. Nijon had to grin. He was quite glad he wasn't with the Motraian soldiers, several steps below the satrap; if the man were to fall. . . .

Some time later, Nijon reached the top.

Couches, tables, a small kitchen, and an enormous altar were set amid further lush greenery. A line of suppliants wended its way to the altar; some in the queue carried goats or lambs, which priests slew in sacrifice. Hearts were burned in a brazier, but the flesh was cooked in the kitchen and served. Other visitors lolled on the couches, quaffing ale and eating bits of lamb.

Several children played in the fountain that gave birth to the stream. A priest approached Nijon and murmured, "A contribution is expected."

"I am with Princess Nlavi," Nijon responded, and the priest looked down to see the rest of the party struggling upward. Mesech's face was crimson.

"Ah," said the priest. "I shall have a reception prepared."

He disappeared, leaving Nijon to consider the view.

About the pyramid spread the temple complex, of which this was merely the most spectacular structure. Beyond it, the city sprawled, narrow streets and jumbled buildings running to the walls and spilling out beyond. Smoke rose from a thousand places: from bathhouses, bakeries, the workplaces of craftsmen, homes. A permanent haze hung over the town, but the sky above was untrammeled blue.

Almost untrammeled. Nijon saw an object, far in the distance; a bird, perhaps. But something was wrong about it; it seemed distant, yet any bird that distant would need to be enormous.

With a groan, Mesech pulled himself up the final step.

He teetered for a moment, panting and heaving, until two of his soldiers took his arms and steered him toward a couch. Nlavi stepped easily to the platform. "Behold, good Mesech!" she said. "Purasham, at your feet. Lovely, is it not?"

"Ex-exquisite," Mesech gasped, blowing as if life depended on every breath.

From somewhere, a gong sounded, and a line of priests approached. The first bore an amphora, the second bowls; behind, several others carried platters heaped with food.

They spread out as they neared; platters were piled on nearby tables, amber ale was poured from the amphora into bowls. The first priest began to chant to Nlavi in a singsong voice; he spoke in an archaic form of Agondan. Nijon recognized only the occasional word—"gods," "grace," "barley ale." Nlavi responded in the same tongue, and handed the priest a small purse. All at once, the priests fell to their knees, bowed to Nlavi, then turned and bowed seven times to the altar.

Mesech was still panting, but at least partially recovered. He turned to Nlavi, and said, "What means this ritual, O sweeter-than-honey?"

Nlavi began to reply, but at that instant a matron in the line before the altar screamed. She pointed out, into the sky.

She was pointing toward the "bird" that Nijon had spied; it was larger now. At arm's length, Nijon's hand just covered it. It had wings more like a bat's than a bird's, and its sinuous body reminded Nijon of nothing so much as a snake.

"Aiiiiiii!" screamed a priest. "Dragon!"

Suddenly, people were running hither and yon across the pyramid platform. Some made it to the edge and started desperately downward. And some, in their haste, missed a step and cartwheeled down the steep side of the structure, to smash unmoving into the ground below.

For a crown a week, Nijon decided, he would slay no dragons. He sprinted for the fountain. Immersion in water would probably save him from a blast of flames.

There was a gust of wind of nearly gale force; tables and couches went tumbling in its wake. Nijon looked up; the dragon was coming in for a landing.

There were further screams as people scurried out of its way. It landed with its tail draped over the kitchen, and its head facing Mesech. Nijon marveled at its size; it was the length of three elephants, not counting the tail.

"Are you—" said the dragon, in a godlike stentorian voice, but before he could continue, Mesech's soldiers appeared from their hiding places—behind plants, under tables—and charged the monster that menaced their lord.

Axes bounced futilely off scales.

"Oh, bother," said the dragon, inhaled, opened his mouth—

—and Nijon was treated to a sight he had half-thought was legendary: a dragon's blast of flame. It played out over the pyramid platform, burning a swath through the green and, not incidentally, incinerating Mesech's band.

Mesech looked paralyzed with fear. Nlavi was wide-eyed: half-terrified, half-amazed.

"I say," said the dragon to Mesech, "you wouldn't be a maiden, by any chance, eh?"

In a strangled voice, Mesech said, "Certainly not."

"Ah," said the dragon. "Sorry about that. The old eyes aren't what they used to be, you know. But I can smell one hereabouts. Definitely a maiden here."

Nlavi looked about, as if trying to decide where to run.

The dragon turned his attention to her. "What about you?" he asked. "Are you a maiden?"

Nlavi drew herself up. "The very question is an insult," she said icily. "I am as yet unwed; of course I am a maiden. But do not trifle with me, sir dragon; my father is king of this realm, and should you capture me, half the kingdom shall be the prize of the one who rescues—"

"Excellent!" bellowed the dragon, flames darting from his nostrils in excitement. "Not merely a maiden, but a princess to boot! Why, won't the fellows be jealous."

Without another word, he snatched up Nlavi in one giant claw, hurled himself off the pyramid edge, swooped low over Purasham, then flapped to gain altitude and head for mountains beyond.

17

It was the Feast Day of the Pekhlia. In celebration of fructification and the ripening of the crops, maidens danced before the king, strewing flower petals in his path—in accordance with ancient tradition.

It was no easy task. The king was distraught with grief. Back and forth he paced; each time he turned, the flower maidens were forced to sprint to remain ahead. A finger's width of bruised petals had already built up on the floor beneath his feet, and desperate messages had been sent out calling for more petals to meet the demand, lest the gods grow angry and farm yields suffer.

"The light of my life has been despoiled," Manoos lamented, twisting his hands in his beard.

Nearby knelt the grandees of his realm: the Grand Vizier Vakhan, responsible for taxes and the maintenance of order within the realm; the Chancellor Zhemen, responsible for foreign affairs; Marshall Nyekhon, commander of the armies; and diverse courtiers and ministers of state. All knelt, in due deference to their sovereign; all had pillows, to cushion their knees through these long audiences.

"O Exalted," said the grand vizier, "with all due respect, 'despoiled' is almost certainly the one thing that has *not* happened to Nlavi. No doubt she is safe and hale—"

King Manoos ripped his hands downward, yanking fist-
fuls of hair from his beard. Every male in the room winced
in sympathy.

"Aye, alive she may be," howled Manoos, "but shall I
never see my little Nobby again?"

Manoos fell to his knees—to the relief of the flower
maidens—raised his hands on high, and bellowed, in an-
guish, "My kingdom for my daughter! O Gods, would that
I were a simple man, a worthy tiller of the soil, whose life
were not plagued with such calamity!"

The grand vizier rolled his eyes. "Surely position has its
rewards, my lord," he said.

"I can think of none," said Manoos bitterly. "Woe to
the day I was born!" He rent his tunic, ripping it from
collar to breast.

The grand vizier sighed and addressed the minister of the
household, one of the great lords of the realm with the
awesome responsibility of laying out each day the king's
attire and overseeing the preparation of his food. "What,
my lord, is tonight's repast?"

The minister pursed his ample lips. "To start, eels," he
said, "poached in small beer with limes. A salad, of heart-
of-palm and papaya, with a dressing of olive oil, lemon, and
cumin. Hens, stuffed with raisins and coconut. Roast lamb,
garnished with dates. Assorted pilafs and—"

"So?" interrupted the king.

"A peasant's habitual dinner," said the Vizier Vakhan,
"is millet mush and river water. Once a week, he might
hope to have an egg."

"I take the point," said the king, standing up and retreat-
ing to his throne. Maidens dashed to strew flowers beneath
his feet, then halted as he sat down. "But would not a
peasant regret the loss of his daughter?"

"Certainly," said the vizier. "Even if the two did not
get along, the loss of the bride-price alone would be re-
grettable."

Manoos sighed. "If a peasant may mourn the loss of his daughter, may not a king?"

"Indubitably," said Vakhan. "However, the offer of your kingdom entire does seem rash."

"I suppose," said the king. "The traditional offer is half the kingdom and the hand of one's daughter in marriage, is it not? Very well! Herald! Attend. I, Manoos, King of Purasham, Count of this, Defender of that, and so forth and so on, on this day of whatever it is, do hereby offer the one who frees my daughter from helotry to the vicious wyrm half my kingdom and—"

"Ahem," said the Chancellor Zhemen.

"What is it?" demanded the king irritably.

"Half the kingdom—divided precisely how? A line drawn down the middle of Purasham? The city is by far the most valuable single—"

"Half by population," snapped Manoos.

"Ah!" said the chancellor. "That might be workable. You rule the twenty thousand inhabitants of the city and some hundred thousand peasants outside it. Even if sixty thousand peasants were lost, the exchequer would not be unduly damaged. Still, there is the question of foodstuffs. The realm does not suffice to feed the capital even at the best of times; we must needs import to meet the public demand. And in the current rodent crisis, the loss of half our agricultural capacity . . . Well."

"Quite so," agreed the vizier, to scattered nods and "ayes."

"Oh, very well," said Manoos wearily. "Not half my kingdom. The Domain of Dreyadon, then."

There was a sharp intake of breath from Marshall Nyekhon. "O Lord," he said diffidently, "may one timorously suggest that Dreyadon may not be the best of all possible selections?"

"Why not?" demanded Manoos.

"Controlling the passes through the Metrech Mountains

as it does, it is of vital strategic importance. In any future conflict with Motraia—"

"The Counties of Ik, Ok, and Khaametchonak-hametcho, then," snarled the king.

"But those contain Khaamashan," protested Chancellor Zhemen, "the second city of the realm; in the absence of its tax revenues—"

"Ik and Ok alone," shouted the king, beginning to be red-faced.

"That means ceding the ancestral home of the Clan Oklek; this would not be well received by high-placed members of the clan, who constitute an important part of the royal bureaucracy," said the grand vizier. He did not point out that Marshall Nyekhon—the only man who might have a prayer of overthrowing Manoos—was from Clan Oklek.

"For the sake of Ptemesh, Sak, and Meliantos," shouted Manoos, rising from his throne in fury, "would you have me offer three rice cakes and a sip of ale?"

"I believe the royal fiscus could bear such an expense," said Grand Vizier Vakhan, nodding.

"That would smooth the problem vis-à-vis Motraia," said Chancellor Zhemen, "since Nlavi could still be offered to the Satrap Mesech."

"That would not militarily weaken the realm," said Marshall Nyekhon approvingly.

Manoos slumped back in his throne, moaning in unbelief.

Detros and Nijon, enjoying their day off, were in the Demite marketplace. Nijon stood by, a little bored, while Detros haggled with a stallkeeper over a pomegranate.

"Two sequins," the woman insisted.

"Ah," said Detros, "two sequins is a good price, for pomegranates worth two sequins. But are these? Tell me, are they as sweet as you?"

Startled, Nijon took another look at the fruitmonger; if there was a curve to be seen between shoulder and ankle, he could not detect it. Her lower jaw receded; she looked like nothing so much as a ferret. She giggled, said, "As I see you are an honest man, I shall let you taste of my fruit on account"—and, in handing the pomegranate to Detros, scratched his palm with the nail of her forefinger.

Detros peeled open the fruit, and fished out a seed, his fingers smearing with purple as he did. Holding the vendor's eyes with his own, he set the seed between his teeth, then took it on his tongue, bit it, and slowly licked his lips.

Nijon looked uneasily away, musing on the variability of taste.

"Sir!" came a giggle. "You have yet to buy your fruit!" Detros had the shopkeeper up against a cart piled high with oranges, arms around her, one hand on a buttock, nibbling at her neck.

"I thought I could taste it on account," Detros protested, and nibbled up the line of her jaw to her lips.

"Oyez, oyez," bellowed a bass voice from the direction of the fountain at the marketplace center, "hear the words of Manoos, Exalted of Purasham." The hubbub quieted as the crowd gave the speaker their attention. He was, Nijon saw, a squat man with massive shoulders, flanked by two guardsmen. He read from a clay tablet.

"Attend! I, Manoos, King of Purasham, on this the twelfth day of the Pekhlian moon, do hereby offer the one who frees my daughter from helotry to the vicious wyrm the rule in perpetuity of County Petok, and a substantial cash reward, to wit, ten thousand crowns."

"Piker!" shouted someone in the crowd.

"What about the bread ration?" shouted another—but the herald and his guards were already making for the marketplace edge.

"Cheapskate," Detros said, standing by Nijon. The fruit

seller was in the shadows of her stall, playing with a strand of hair.

Nijon raised an eyebrow.

"Tradition demands half the kingdom and the princess' hand in marriage," explained Detros.

"But ten thousand crowns—" said Nijon.

"Nothing," said Detros. "A reasonable endowment for a nobleman, but far from a princely treasure. And County Petok—it's swamp half the year. Nothing there but rice paddies and peasants."

"Still," considered Nijon, "a way to win your fortune in an instant."

"Or win an early grave," scoffed Detros.

Nijon drew himself up. "Small chance of that," said he, "for I am the son of a god, and am fated for great deeds. Have I told you of the time I slew a lioness, while naked, having run seven—"

"Yes, yes," said Detros hastily. "See here, Nijon; could I ask you to return to the palace alone?"

"Eh?"

"I have—unfinished business," said Detros, looking toward the depths of the stall. The stallkeeper pushed back her hair, and nibbled on a single pomegranate seed.

"I see," said Nijon.

"I'd like to see the prince," said Nijon.

"Ah!" said the majordomo. "A worthy desire."

"It is a matter of some personal urgency," said Nijon.

The majordomo wandered over to a slate-clad wall, which was marked up with chalk in Agondan characters. "I think we can fit you in next month," he said.

"Next month!" protested Nijon.

"Yes," said the official, making another mark on the slate, "six days after the new moon, in the morning. You must be here before dawn, and be prepared to wait all day if necessary."

"But—"

"Of course, I cannot guarantee he will see you then. The prince's time is highly prized, you understand; it must be rationed."

"Rationed?" said Nijon.

"Ah!" said the majordomo, studying the slate. "Wait. If I move the Morchite delegation here, and shave Magister Nokhen's time a bit, perhaps I can squeeze you in tomorrow. . . . No, no, it is too risky. To run the risk of offending highly placed folk, a man should be—*compensated*, think you not?"

"Yes, of course," said Nijon, annoyed. "Compensated. How much?"

The door swung open. Poran appeared there, clad in the cloak and hose of a hunter. "Ah, Nijon," he said. "There you are. I've been meaning to speak to you. Come."

With a rude gesture in the majordomo's direction, Nijon followed the prince.

Poran strode briskly down the corridor. Servants and visitors scurried out of his path, dropping to one knee as he passed.

"Exalted," said Nijon, "I wish to request—"

"I am dispatching an expedition to the Vagon plain," said Poran. "This way." They turned a corner. "To capture some weasels like your pet. If we can do something about the rat problem—I want you to go along. You know that land, of course, and must know something of the habits of these creatures."

"Ah, I was considering addressing not the rat problem, but the dragon one," said Nijon.

Poran looked sidewise at him. "What?"

"The reward the king has offered—"

"Bosh!" said Poran. "You don't want to go near that. Every year, the detestable dragons forage from the hills and kidnap a dozen maidens or two. Every year, a dozen starry-eyed idiots venture forth, to slay themselves a dragon. Every year, a dozen fools are flambéed. This year there will be many more, no doubt, drawn by my father's reward to the dragon's fire like the moth to the candle."

"But—"

"Consider the scale," said Poran. They trotted through an opening into a courtyard. A saddled horse was waiting, along with a party of mounted men and ladies. In one corner of the courtyard, a small baggage train awaited; ox-drawn wagons, laden with food and ewers of ale. "A few dozen maidens— the kingdom can spare that. But the rats? Famine threatens. Moreover, we may hope to conquer creatures smaller than ourselves, but dragons? That's a quest for the witless."

"What about Princess Nlavi?" inquired Nijon, a little scandalized at this familial callousness.

Poran mounted up. "Poor Nobby," he said kindly. "The dragons treat their captives well, you know; she'll not suffer deprivation. And at least it gets her out of marriage to that monstrous Motraian."

"Still," said Nijon determinedly, "I beg your leave to depart Purasham for the mountains, in search of the dragon."

Poran scowled. "No, certainly not," he said. "You're going to the Vagon lands, and I'll have no back talk about it. I positively forbid you to leave the palace grounds before I return."

Poran turned to the mounted party, and shouted, "Hola, my companions! Shall we make merry on the banks of the sacred Uk?"

They gave glad assent, and made for the courtyard gate, the ox train laboring behind.

At least a dozen men were in the armory. One kicked a wheel, spinning a whetstone against which he held the blade of an axe. Others wrapped handles in hide, wetting the leather so it would shrink and make a tight grip. Several sat on benches by the windows, to get better light, cutting delicate strips of feather, setting them in arrows, and gluing them into place. No fire burned in the fireplace; it was summer, and metal was cast elsewhere. The armorer scurried about, scolding and offering encouragement to his subordinates.

"Good morrow," said Nijon. "Would there be a bow of the Vagons in your store, master craftsman?"

"No," said the armorer, studying a fletcher's work, without looking up. "You couldn't draw it, anyway."

"Of course I could," said Nijon, offended. "All of my tribe are trained from infancy in the use of—"

The armorer looked up and scowled. "A barbarian," he said.

"A noble warrior," countered Nijon.

"A savage who butchers women and children and burns border towns," said the armorer. "Yes, I have such a bow. And no, you may not—"

"I had understood that members of the guard might requisition items for weapons practice."

"True," said the armorer.

"I would like to requisition such a bow."

The armorer spat into the straw on the floor. He stood for a long moment, reddening. "Ptemesh," he swore at last. "That I should see the day that the king's stores arm blood-thirsty savages."

He went to fetch the bow; it was bundled in leathers, against the wet. Nijon unwrapped it.

Unstrung, the weapon would not be recognizable to one unfamiliar with it. It was shaped like one end of a narrow oval, with little space between the ends of the bow. At the center, the oval's point, was the handle, reinforced with bone. Nijon ran his hand along the smooth shaft, which thickened toward the grip, then narrowed toward the tips. It was made of wood, horn, and sinew, laminated together in a fashion known only to the Vai.

The string, plaited from the manes of Vai horses, was

half the thickness of Nijon's little finger. He looped one end of the string around a bow tip. "I will need your help, good sir," he told the armorer. Scowling, the man came near. Nijon knelt, set the grip on one knee, and grasped each bow tip in one hand, holding the bowstring against one tip with his fingers. He ran the bowstring under his leg, then pulled down simultaneously on both tips, bending the tips down. That narrow half-oval began to form a wider oval, then a semicircle. Then it curved into a stranger shape: the area around the grip remained concave upward, while the tips actually curved to point outward, forming a convex curve at the limbs. Nijon was turning red-faced with the strain, but the bow was still not curved quite enough. With all his might, he pulled downward, his knee feeling as if it were about to collapse under the pressure. At last, the armorer knelt, took the unstrung end of the bowstring, and slipped it about the second bow tip.

Gingerly, Nijon released the tension; the bow remained taut, held by its string. He stood up, raised his leg, and pulled the bow off over his foot.

"It is a fine bow," Nijon said.

"Here is a case of arrows," said the armorer. "Have them all back, and the bow, in perfect condition, by nightfall, or I shall have your skin tanned and used to haft weapons. And try not to murder anyone, if you please."

Insincerely, Nijon assented.

By nightfall, he, his horse, and Brother were well away from the city walls.

His purse was empty again; he'd spent his last sequins on supplies, and a meager lot they were. But had he not survived on the plain with nary so much as a stone knife? If worse came to worst, he could overcome a peasant and steal his food.

Ahead lay the Metrech Mountains; a hawk stooped in the crimson sky.

A hawk? Perhaps not.

18

The Metrech Mountains lift high to catch the clouds, squeezing water to support a forest. Cedar and fir arch upward, blocking light from the forest floor, where little but needled carpet lies. Nijon's road led down a slope through dimness.

The road was little more than a track; patches of bare rock and tree roots ran across the way. Still, the road was rutted, showing that it bore wheeled traffic. A cow pat indicated oxen were not far ahead.

Nijon kept out a wary eye. He had passed a half-dozen adventurers so far—all, like him, off to slay themselves a dragon. None had impressed him unduly, yet Nijon feared one might decide to waylay him, to reduce the competition.

The road took a curve, and Nijon saw the wagon ahead, two oxen leading and two tethered behind—relief animals. The wagon was stationary, sitting on a log bridge over a bubbling stream; one wheel was wedged between logs. A man crouched by it, yanking at the wheel and cursing. He wore a Mikhite tunic, but was clean-shaven—unusual, for an Agondan man.

As Nijon neared, Nialo's nostrils flared; she nickered, and looked back at him. Nijon frowned, puzzled by this behavior. They came to the wagon. The man, intent on his task, had not noticed their approach. Nijon's horse nuzzled the nape of the man's neck.

With a yelp, he sprang up, whirled, and stood facing them, one hand to his neck.

This tableau stood for a moment, no one knowing quite what to make of it—except, perhaps, for the horse—until the man yelled, "You thief! That's my mare!"

"Mika Nashram," Nijon said, recognizing him after a pause. He looked different, out of Vai garb, his mustache now gone.

"Where's my money, you scoundrel?" demanded Mika.

Nijon grinned. "*Your* money, Mika? Or Fela's money?"

"Fela's dead," Mika grumbled.

"What would you do if I had the money?" asked Nijon. "Take it away from me?" His sword hung from his belt, his great bow was slung slantwise across his shoulders; Mika stood, apparently unarmed, on the bridge.

Mika scowled. "I suppose you're off to slay dragons," he said.

"Of a certainty," said Nijon.

Mika snorted. "See here, Nijon, help me free my wagon, and we'll call our past differences history."

Nijon considered; he cared not a whit for Mika's good opinion. Still, the wagon blocked the bridge; how was he to get his horse around it without helping Mika?

It was well and truly stuck. The wheel was trapped in a substantial gap between the rough-hewn logs. Nijon squatted and gripped the axle—which protruded a hand or so beyond the wheel—and heaved upward. The tendons of his neck stood out with the strain.

The wheel popped loose. Nijon grunted with satisfaction and began to turn . . .

. . . and caught sight of Mika, standing behind, a boulder raised over his head for a blow.

Nijon raised one arm to shield himself, grabbing for his sword with the other hand.

Mika held the boulder over his head for a long moment—then gave a quarter-turn, and hurled it into the stream. He cleared his throat, and muttered, "Just clearing the path of this, ah, obstruction."

Nijon nodded, apparently accepting this transparent explanation, then said, "So all's forgiven now, eh, Mika?" He grinned and offered an arm for a handclasp.

"Yes, yes," said Mika, obviously relieved. "Thanks for your help." He gripped Nijon's arm.

Nijon grabbed Mika's thumb, bent it painfully back, and pulled Mika close.

"Try that again," he whispered into a shaven but not entirely clean face, "and you will rot unattended beneath these trees."

"Ah—yes," yelped Mika.

Nijon let him go. Averting his eyes, Mika bustled about, packing up some tools he had used in his attempt to free his wagon, then climbed in, tapped behind the ears of his oxen with a switch, and made hurriedly off down the road.

Nijon stood for a long moment on the bridge. Above, a few wisps of yellow daylight made their way through gaps in the forest canopy to the stream. Cedar scented the air delightfully, and the purling of the stream was music; yet Nijon found the scene gloomy. He longed for the brisk breeze and bright sun of the plain.

Brother chittered, as if to ask whether Nijon planned to stay here, so the mongoose might venture into the wood in search of prey; but Nijon sighed and shook his head. There was little forage for a horse, here in the forest; and Nijon had noticed several sacks of grain in Mika's wagon.

He mounted, and rode to catch up.

Nijon rode at a canter. Where was Mika? He should have come into sight by now, Nijon thought; oxen were not fast creatures, especially when pulling heavy wagons. But the man was nowhere to be seen.

Mika passed a cart, a rattletrap affair pulled by two oxen. Its drover was a gray-bearded old man, who snoozed on the cart's bench, hat pulled over his eyes, trusting to his beasts to keep to the path.

Nijon rode onward. Even if Mika had whipped his oxen into their fastest speed, he could not be far ahead. Nijon goaded Nialo into a gallop; she would probably enjoy running for a few minutes, and it couldn't possibly take long to catch up with Nashram.

But Mika was nowhere to be found. Nijon slowed to a walk, and mulled that over. He had not passed Mika Nashram. He could not have failed to catch up with the trader, if the trader were still on the path. But there had been no branch, no turnoff. True, there was little underbrush here, where tall trees blocked light from the forest floor, and the man might have turned off into the woods—but he would not get far, not on leaf mold, with trees strewn randomly in his way, dead branches everywhere. Could Mika be so desperate to lose Nijon that he would risk a cross-country passage?

Ah. The answer came to Nijon suddenly. Nashram was a sorcerer, was he not? Probably not a particularly powerful one, not powerful enough to free his wagon, but . . .

Nijon rode back. After some minutes, the sleeping old man and his broken-down cart came in sight again. Nijon sniffed at the air; as he suspected, there was the faintest tang of magic.

"Ah, there you are, Mika," said Nijon, turning to ride alongside the cart.

Mika Nashram sat up with a scowl, pushing his hat back on his head. The glamour was broken; he sat atop his wagon once more. He muttered insincere greetings.

"So," Nijon said, "can it be that you, too, hunt dragons?"

Mika snorted. "Of course not," he said. "Do you take me for a f . . . ? Ah." He gave a cough.

"Why then do you labor into these mountains with such supplies?" asked Nijon. "I see spears, axes, and other weapons; ropes and food; cooking utensils; and diverse tools. These are not the usual stock of a trader."

"True," said Mika. "But consider. Will not all sorts of fortune seekers be heading into these hills, in search of Princess Nlavi and her captor? Dozens, perhaps hundreds of them, drawn by King Manoos's munificent reward? And will they not need the odd bit of rope, fodder for their mounts, weapons to replace those lost or broken?" He began to warm up, obviously enraptured by his own scheme. "And where shall they find the supplies they need? Shall they travel back, three dozen leagues, to the nearest town?

"No, no, they shall find the wherewithal to pursue their valiant quests here, at the traveling purveyance of honest Mika Nashram, sutler to all and adventurer's friend. At modest prices, modest ones; modest, surely, for those who seek to slay dragons. For the dragonslayer, after all, there are only two fates: death, or riches. If dead, he has no future need for money. If successful, he has a dragon's hoard and a king's ransom, and need not begrudge a coin or two for supplies. So yes, a bag of my millet may cost a full crown—" Nijon choked. "But what of that? What harm in emptying your purse before facing the pyrescent wyrm?"

"I perceive a flaw in your scheme," said Nijon.

Mika raised an eyebrow. "Yes?"

Nijon leaned over and snagged a bag of millet, draping it over his saddle. "Your potential customers are armed and desperate men. What is to prevent them from simply despoiling you of your wares?"

Mika frowned uneasily. "Once in camp," he said, "there will be many folk gathering at my wagon. No doubt each will seek to prevent the others from gaining undue advantage. Together—"

"Ah," said Nijon comfortably. "But we have leagues to

go before we reach the peaks where dragons dwell. Between camp and here, desperadoes might butcher you and take your wagon many times over. No, Mika, my friend, you need a guardian."

"Ah?" said Mika unhappily.

"A valiant warrior," said Nijon, "to defend you from the depredations of the lawless. What luck that we met, good Mika! For I shall be glad to assume the role of your protector."

"Oh happy day," said Mika flatly.

"In return, of course," Nijon said, "I shall require fodder for my horse, and a few trinkets—nothing to unduly deplete your stock, you understand; only such items as I might require in my quest."

"I see," said Mika glumly.

"And after I slay Nlavi's captor," Nijon said, "you may in turn help me."

Mika stared at the young barbarian. "After you . . . ?"

"Yes," said Nijon confidently. "I shall need a wagon to transport the dragon's hoard."

Mika chortled over Nijon's sheer effrontery—and seemed somewhat cheered by the notion that, whatever Nijon's demands at present, he would soon be dead.

"*Aiiiiii!*" screamed Nlavi.

"Please," said the dragon. "That's quite enough of that." His enormous wings labored; the cultivated plain wheeled far below.

"*Aaaiiiiiiii!*" Nlavi screamed.

"I say," said the dragon, "there's really no call for all this fuss." Ahead loomed the Metrech Mountains: long folds in the earth, from this height the size of wagon ruts.

"I'm going to be devoured by a vicious monster, and there's no cause for fuss?" Nlavi said.

"Devour you? Why my dear, ho ho, no, certainly not."

The dragon folded his wings, and they went into a moderately steep dive.

Nlavi's hair whipped in the wind of their descent. "*Aiiiii!*" she screamed.

"Oh, stop it," said the dragon crossly. "I do have some experience with this flying business, you know."

Somewhat chastened, Nlavi simply held her breath as the mountains loomed before them. There was snow still on the highest peaks; the sprinkling of green resolved first into lichen, then weeds, then shrubs, then enormous conifers.

Nlavi felt a scream coming on, but held it in. Once or twice was fine; after all, screaming was expected of a damsel in distress. But to scream now would be otiose—and might startle the dragon at an inopportune moment.

Out came those wings. The dragon guided the dive in a curve, until they were climbing and losing velocity.

The ground rushed up at them as they neared the ridge line; for an instant, Nlavi was sure they would smash themselves on yonder peak—and then they were over the top, the ground falling away again as they headed out over the valley between this ridge and the next.

"I—I had understood that dragons eat people," Nlavi said diffidently.

"Oh, some do, some do," said the dragon. "Myself, I prefer a calf or two, though aurochs is very nice. But eat *you*—that would be silly."

"Why?" demanded Nlavi, a little sharply. "Princess not succulent enough for the sensitive draconian palate?"

"It's just not done," insisted the dragon. He was diving again, more shallowly—toward, Nlavi saw, a great gash in the mountainside.

Clutched in the dragon's talons, she swung forward as he faced his wings into the descent and began to flap, coming in for a landing.

* * *

"Girls! Girls!" bellowed the dragon. "Come meet your new playmate."

Somewhat out of breath, Nlavi picked herself up from the rocky floor, where he had dropped her. Her chiton was smeared with dust, her hair was askew; well, what could one expect?

Several dozen women appeared from within the cavern. They were of all ages, from adolescence to senescence. "My maidens," said the dragon proudly. "A superb collection: blond, brunette, and auburn-tressed; of every land and city."

"Auburn-tressed?" inquired Nlavi, puzzled, for none that she could see was a redhead.

"That's Matli," said the dragon, extending a talon to point at one of the elderly women.

"Aye, 'tis me," she said.

"Quite a beauty," said the dragon with satisfaction. "Rated an eight-point-nine by the board of examiners."

Matli smiled, her wispy gray beard quivering. "That was thirty-three years ago, dearie," she said.

"Have you been here this long?" Nlavi asked, appalled.

"Thirty-eight years, woman and girl," Matli quavered.

"Would you say she is sloe-eyed?" asked the dragon somewhat worriedly.

The other women crowded around Nlavi, and peered inquisitively into her eyes.

"Sloe-eyed is very in just at present," said the dragon.

Matli, who seemed to be something of a matriarch, reported the consensus that Nlavi was, indeed, graced with eyes of sloe.

"Excellent! Stupendous news!" bellowed the dragon, breathing tiny jets of flame in excitement. "A maiden, a princess, and sloe-eyed! Why, her trading value will be enormous. Perhaps now I can induce Khekhamaish to part with his Nardinian wizardress." He launched himself off the cavern lip and dived down over the valley.

Nlavi went to the lip and looked out.

The drop below was sheer; another step and she would dash her young life out on those rocks, so far below. There would be no escape from here.

"A princess," said a voice from behind, rather nastily.

"Hoity-toity bint," said another.

"She'll want us to do her work, I'll wager," said a third.

"Let's push her out," said the first.

Nlavi rapidly backed away from the cavern lip.

"Please, please," quavered Matli. "You remember how it was when you were first captured. We must be kind. Now see here, dearie."

Nlavi looked to the older woman.

"It will be all right," Matli said soothingly, "if you follow but a few simple rules."

"Rules?" said Nlavi. "All right? How will it be all right? To live like this for forty years. . . ." She surveyed the women about her: tangle-haired, grim-faced, infrequently bathed. They were bedecked with jewelry and well fed, but she could not envision a more tedious life than that of a—collectible.

"Would you rather be eaten?" asked Matli sharply. "You must follow the rules. Imprimis, no attempts at escape. Secundus, you must remain a maiden. Tertius, you must sweep up around the hoard and keep it bright and shiny. Quartus, when called, you must be prepared to display yourself for the dragon's visitors, suitably bedecked in jewelry. I see you have brought your own; you may also borrow items from the dragon's hoard, if you wish."

"And if I disobey?" asked Nlavi.

Matli shrugged. "You'll make some dragon a nice breakfast."

There was a buffet of wind from the cavern opening; women shrieked and ran for the walls. Great gusts blew inward as the dragon landed once again. Each foot gripped a dead cow; he dropped them on the floor, bellowed a cheery "Bon appetit," and launched himself into the sky again.

"What's that?" Nlavi asked, rather shakily.

"Dinner," said one of the younger women shortly. "Come on." She gave Nlavi a knife, and went to work with another knife to butcher the cow.

Nlavi went wan as blood pooled on the floor. She held out her own knife awkwardly. "You can't expect me to . . . to. . . ."

The woman, already bloodied to her elbows, cocked a head indifferently. "Cut your own meat," she said, "or starve. Makes no difference to me."

"Ick," said Nlavi.

19

The oxen labored up a long set of switchbacks, straining to keep going up the mountain. At one point, the road became so steep that the animals were unable to haul Mika's heavy wagon. Mika descended and heaved from behind, bawling curses at his oxen; the wagon inched slowly forward. After watching magisterially for some minutes, Nijon condescended to dismount and lend a shoulder. Thereafter, they made faster progress.

The trees became shorter, then scantier and twisted, as they rose higher. Blueberry bushes abounded, and men and animals alike paused to eat their fill—save for Brother, who rejected a proffered purple berry, then scampered among the bushes in search of mice or lizards.

After long hours, they reached the peak. One moment, the view to the south was blocked by the mountain slope; the next, a whole new world was revealed. Nijon's breath caught.

He had thought the peak on which they stood a mountain; by comparison to what lay beyond, it was a mere midden heap. Yonder, a great wall rimmed the world. It was no single peak, but an enormous range, extending east and west as far as the eye could see; a solid rampart lofting skyward, breaking into separate peaks only at great height.

Below his feet, the hill he and Mika had climbed curved away into a distant arc of green. A vast valley lay there, filled with pine, firs, and patches of broad-leaf trees. Miles away, the forest began to slope upward. Nijon's eyes followed it up, up; forest shading into shrubs, into bare rock; curve shading into sheer cliff, rock falls, talus; rock shading finally into whitened peak.

"Desolation Ridge," Mika said, then gestured toward the valley. "We'll set up shop down there."

They camped by a convenient stream. The road curved eastward here, paralleling the mountains until, leagues distant, it found a pass through the range. Dragons were known to lair near here, high in the mountains; and those who sought to find Nlavi's captor naturally collected at this spot. Mika quickly attracted a ragtag rabble of customers who fell over themselves to buy his dross at gaudy prices.

One evening, some days later, Nijon left the encampment and climbed upward. The dragons were said to forage at twilight, and Nijon hoped to catch a glimpse.

The pine-scented air was filled with a mosquito drone. Nijon had rubbed himself with a salve that Mika claimed repelled the insects, but the substance's efficacy was not apparent. He slapped at a bite, his own blood spattering as he hit an insect.

Wind soughed in the pines above; distantly, there came the *chok-chok-chok* of men felling trees. No doubt, they cut wood for fire, and to build crude shelters.

There was a break in the forest cover, and Nijon saw what he had come for: a glimpse of Desolation Ridge. Down here, it was already twilight: The valley lay in the shadow of the hills to the north. Above, the ridge was sunlit, the snow of those noble peaks dyed orange in the dying light. Nijon scanned the skies, searching for a scallop-winged form. . . .

"Prithee, master," said a voice. "Are you—are you a *hero?*"

"Beg pardon?" said Nijon, turning slightly. A young man had accosted him, perhaps fourteen. The boy had a terrible, scraggly beard, matted hair, feet both filthy and heavily callused with long maltreatment; a coarse-woven cloth was draped about his midriff. He was a peasant, clearly.

"Zounds, is that a real Vagon bow?" asked the lad with awe in his voice. "Is it? I pray you, sir, may I hold it?"

"Ah, yes," said Nijon embarrassedly. "That is, no. I mean to say. . . ."

"Will you slay the dragon?" asked the boy worshipfully. "And rescue Princess Nlavi? Will you do it with your bow?"

"Ah . . . Go away," said Nijon.

"When you kill the dragon, may I watch? Please, sir?"

"No," said Nijon.

The boy pouted at that, shifting from foot to foot while Nijon returned his gaze to the sky above. Divining his purpose, the boy said, "This is a good place to watch the dragons from. See! There is one now."

Nijon looked, and cursed. A sinuous form was arrowing through the air; he had hoped to spot its lair but, distracted by the boy, had not seen it launch into flight. It swooped down over the valley, batlike wings laboring, then began to climb.

Fascinated, Nijon watched the dragon rise. "Is he not large?" asked the boy. "How long would you say he is from tip to tail? A hundred cubits, sir? A thousand?"

The dragon flew in the shadow of the valley, but climbing now, pulled upward—and in a dazzling instant, passed into the sunlit air above, scales suddenly glistening red and gold.

"He breathed fire! He breathed fire!" shouted the boy excitedly.

"No, no, don't be foolish," said Nijon. "He merely—"

"I saw it!" said the boy dreamily. "He breathed fire. A huge jet of flame! He must have roasted an eagle!"

"Why would a dragon want to—"

"How will you defeat his flame? Will you carry a bucket of water?"

"See here," said Nijon. "You're not wanted."

"I know!" said the boy, gesticulating wildly. "You can build a shield of cloth, and soak it in water!"

"Go away," said Nijon with more force.

"Then when the dragon breathes fire," said the boy excitedly, "the water will keep your shield from burning, and—"

"This is very annoying," said Nijon. "I don't want your—"

"And then, you can bellow your war cry," shouted the boy, dancing and waving an imaginary sword over his head, "and slinging your mighty blade, rush forth to valiant battle with the fell enemy of all humanity—"

"*Shut up! Go away!*" Nijon bellowed.

The boy was crestfallen. He backed away, then turned and sidled into the woods, glancing accusingly over his shoulder, his face a study in betrayal.

Nijon sighed and shook his head. The sky was empty now, no serpentine form flitting through dimming light. Shadows crept up the mountains as the sun sank lower; Nijon waited long moments, hoping for the dragon's return, but his hopes were not rewarded.

He stared out there, where he had seen the dragon, seeing it still in his mind's eye. What was it his father had said?

"You need never fear a serpent, for it is in your nature to slay all of that kind."

Yes, that was it. Alas, he had not thought to ask Mongoose: Are dragons serpents?

Mika was in the middle of a spiel when Nijon arrived. His audience was rapt. "Dragonsbane!" Mika shouted, waving a handful of stems that glowed with internal light. "Rarest of magical herbs, culled from the growth at the mystic springs of Micaea, where resides the spirit of Meliantos, goddess of fools and heroes. Powdered and sprinkled on the wind, so 'tis said, it wards off even the most ferocious dragon. When infused in hot water and hurled into the monster's mouth, it instantly quenches the flame within." There was an excited murmur from the crowd.

Nijon went up to examine the bundle of herbs, which Mika had laid on the bed of his wagon. The glow was magical, no question of that. He sniffed at the herbs; yes, they were what they appeared to be: sun-dried mint.

"I have but a smidgen of this fabled substance," shouted Mika. "What hero will buy it from me? For there is sufficiency for only one."

"A crown!" shouted a grizzled veteran who was missing an arm.

"Two!" shouted a pudgy craftsman, who looked as if he had never seen a weapon, let alone borne one, until yesterday.

"Please," said Mika in an injured tone. "The very offer is an insult. I could not possibly accept less than ten."

"Ten!" said a black man in quilted armor instantly.

"Twelve!"

"Fifteen!"

It went for twenty crowns six sequins. Nijon shook his head in disdain for such gullibility, and wandered off.

The camp was bedlam. There were at least a hundred folk, drawn here either by the hope of slaying a dragon or by the prospect of making money off would-be heroes. Stumps showed where trees had been cut; the earth between them had been churned to mud by boots and horses. The main odor was of campfires, but mixed with it were the smells of dung and cooking.

There were rabbits roasting on spits, clothes drying on rocks by the stream, people tottering through the mud with skins and pots of water. Some sharpened blades, or spread out wares for sale; others drank ale, or ate, or begged. Fistfights did not seem uncommon.

Nijon approached a fire, tended by a middle-aged woman. She had a copper pot in the flames. She ladled out dollops of stew onto bread trenchers, offering the result to waiting men. Coins were exchanged. "How much?" Nijon asked resignedly.

The woman eyed him before answering, perhaps judging how much money he might have. "Two crowns," she said.

Nijon grimaced and turned away. He had a few coins now, extorted from Mika, but the price was absurd; he'd sup on his own jerky and a bowl of boiled millet, if need be. On the morrow, he could always hunt game.

"One crown six," she called after him, but Nijon did not turn back. Mud sucked at his sandals as he made for his gear.

Halfway there, the wind gusted unexpectedly. Nijon looked up—

This was no natural breeze. Wind gusted again as the dragon's wings beat down. With leviathan slowness, it drifted across the sky. Screams and shouts rang out across the camp.

Almost lazily, the dragon sailed onward, its talons reaching down toward—

Mika shouted something and crouched in his wagon. Talons crunched amidships. The wooden cart was lifted upward. Two oxen had been tethered to it—not in the traces but roped, to stop them from wandering. One was dragged along for several paces before the rope parted, while the other actually hung in the air for several moments, before falling and lying bleating on the earth.

Mika was shouting something incomprehensible. The dragon's wings were beating faster now, violent downdrafts buffeting the camp; the creature drifted toward the fringe of trees around the clearing, laboring, laboring upward. It was not clear whether the wagon would clear the treetops.

It did, just barely. And then the dragon was gone, out there, somewhere in the night—with the wagon, the supplies it contained, and Mika Nashram, still fearfully crouched within.

With terrified faces, adventurers came forth from their hiding places.

"It—it's so *big*," said one would-be dragonslayer.

"Did you see the size of those teeth?" quavered another valiant hero.

"I wonder if I can get my apprenticeship back," whined a third great warrior.

None had raised so much as a boot knife against the monster. Nijon blinked, and realized: neither had he. His bow was over his shoulder still. He scowled, though truth to tell, he doubted a shaft would even have pierced the dragon's belly scales.

The ox that had fallen continued to bleat in pain. He heard a *chok*—someone had taken an axe to it. "Beefsteak tonight," came the call.

When Nijon rolled out of his cloak the following morning, the boy was crouched by his fire, feeding it sticks and warming himself by its blaze.

Nijon grimaced, then went to fill a pot with water at the stream. The boy trailed afterward.

"Sir," said the lad seriously, "I am accustomed to hard labor, and indifferent to inclement weather. I can carry supplies, make a camp, and start a blaze. It has been my dream since infancy to witness deeds of derring-do—"

Nijon stirred a handful of the millet he'd taken from Mika into the water, and set his pot, somewhat precariously, amid the burning logs of his fire. "I am a man of the Vai," he said. "I am accustomed to caring for myself, and have no need of a valet."

"Surely you would travel more quickly," said the boy humbly, shifting from one foot to another, "with one to take the burden of such necessary and time-consuming chores. I—"

While waiting for the water to boil, Nijon fed millet to his mare.

"Surely I would travel more slowly," said Nijon, "with the need to coddle a peasant child with no experience of the wilderness."

"That's not fair!" protested the boy. "I'm not a child! I wouldn't be a burden." He looked about, seized a stick from the ground, and prodded at Nijon's pot. "I'll prove it. See, I can cook—" He nearly upset the pot. Nijon growled and the lad jumped back, tripping over Nijon's bedroll and nearly breaking his neck.

Nijon picked up a stick himself, and stirred the millet mush. "I have no need of a cook," Nijon said irritably, "I who have dined on raw antelope liver, the unskinned flesh of prairie dogs, snakes eaten whole."

"Yuck," said the boy. "Did you really?"

"Of a certainty," said Nijon, stirring the contents of the pot. As he continued, he snatched the pot and set it down outside the fire's perimeter, quickly enough to avoid a burn. "For am I not Nijon Oonitsaupivia, whose birth was attended by portents, half-divine, the slayer of lionesses, mastodons, and aurochs, warrior and—"

The boy was listening slack-jawed, shining-eyed. Nijon broke off. "Enough of that," he said, a little embarrassed at having been carried away with his own oratory. He began to scoop up driblets of gruel with a leaf.

The boy stared beseechingly, still standing awkwardly nearby, licking his lips.

"All right, all right, all right," said Nijon wearily, and shoved the pot toward the boy, who thrust his hand within and smeared greedy handfuls over his face and scraggly beard.

Shaking his head, Nijon packed up his gear. He was surprised at the quantity; he had extracted more from Mika than he had realized.

Nijon bent down and extended a hand; Brother ran up his arm and leapt to the saddle. The boy watched this feat wide-eyed. Then Nijon saddled up and clucked his horse into motion.

The boy trotted alongside. "Are we going to kill the dragon now, good sir?" he asked. "Do you know where its lair lies? What of Mika Nashram—do you think—"

"Good-bye," said Nijon.

"But I thought—"

"Absolutely not."

"You'll need someone to help, climbing those cliffs. They say you shouldn't scale such drops without a part-ner—"

"*No! Go away! I shan't tell you again!*" Nijon roared, half-standing in his saddle.

Blushing in shame, the boy watched Nijon go.

No path led toward Desolation Ridge. Nijon was forced to make his way through the wildwood. Few folk lived here-abouts, so no one had cleared the trees of their dead lower branches, which were forever swatting Nijon in the face. He was soon compelled to dismount and lead his horse.

Off in the woods there was a crack: the sound of some-one stepping on and breaking a stick. Nijon whispered to his horse, drew his sword, and moved silently into the woods. He had quite a quantity of supplies; other adventur-ers might well want to ambush him for them. Nijon had no intention of walking into a trap.

Nijon ghosted through the woods, looking for his am-bushers. Again, he heard a noise; a sort of thump. He circled round, downwind, and sprang round a tree, sword raised, the battle-light in his eyes—

The boy shrieked and cowered. One foot was caught in a rotten log.

Nijon lowered his sword, glowering. "Please, sir," the boy said, arms raised to ward off a blow, "do not slay me! I mean no harm." He tugged at his limb.

Nijon snarled wordlessly and stamped back toward his horse. "Sir!" came a voice from behind. "Sir! I can help you! I know how to start a blaze, and—" With a crash, the boy finally yanked his leg free and fell over into the underbrush.

By all the gods, Nijon thought, if I cannot lose this cretin, I do not deserve the name of a man of the Vai.

By evening, Nijon had begun to climb the flank of Desolation Ridge. For several hours, he had neither heard the boy nor seen any sign of his presence. Satisfied to have lost his follower, Nijon made camp by a tiny flume, its water clear and cold, borne from the snows of the Desolation Range. Trees parted about the flume, offering a view of the mountains. While ox meat cooked—it had been cut from Mika's fallen ox, and would require long boiling to be edible—he climbed a tree, to better his vista.

Those damnable mosquitoes were out in force. Nijon scanned the mountainside, dark green firs growing orange in the setting sun. There was a flip of motion—and Nijon saw it, the dragon launching out.

A cavern was visible high up the mountain flank: an opening, oblong, gashlike. The dragon hurled itself out and down, away from the cliff, gliding—

It dives to pick up speed, Nijon observed with interest; it cannot fly from a standing start. Now, how might he turn that to advantage?

There was a distant shout. "Halloo! Nijon! Sir!"

Nijon's eyes widened. Was that fool still with him? He looked down—to see his cookfire, and a thin tendril of smoke, rising skyward.

He cursed. No doubt the twit had seen the smoke. Foul-tempered, he clambered down the tree.

Within minutes, the boy arrived, looking no cleaner than the day before. "Sir," he diffidently said, "I brought some mushrooms for our repast."

Indeed he had; he clutched a dozen orange-and-red crowns of fungus in his arms.

Nijon blanched. "Set those down," he said carefully, "and wash your hands and arms before you touch your face."

"Sir?"

"Do it now—and perhaps you may avoid poisoning yourself." Why me? he thought. Why couldn't the clod have attached himself to any of the dozens of other would-be heroes at the camp?

"Going to be a little short of provender," Nijon told Brother. "Don't suppose you might catch us a squirrel or so?"

Brother cocked his head, then scampered off into the woods.

20

▶▶▶

One way, terrifying darkness. The other, faint moonlight slanting through the cavern's maw. Rigid with fear, Mika Nashram clutched the bed of his wagon.

At least he was moving no longer—no more hurtling through the sky, moonlit trees below, stars wheeling above, vertigo at every bank and turn.

Two nostrils glowed—absurdly small nostrils, for so huge a creature. The dragon snuffled, its snout lifting over the wagon. A talon reached forth and flipped a barrel of salt fish over the wagon edge. The talon burrowed, probing Mika's goods.

The dragon gave a small grunt of contentment; Mika heard a jingle as his cashbox hit the floor.

Despite the absurdity—his lifespan was likely measured in seconds—he inwardly despaired at the loss of riches. He'd already made a small fortune off those idiot adventurers.

Dragons were drawn to gold, he reflected. To gold, and to maidens.

Nostrils snuffled over the wagon again. They passed over Mika—and paused.

Small flames jetted from those nostrils—not enough to bake him, but enough to provide some illumination. The dragon's head tilted to one side; an eye scanned Mika's form.

Mika felt terror wash over him—this was it. He was a dead—

"You aren't a maiden, are you?" inquired the dragon, a little uncertainly.

—man, a dead . . . A dead woman?

"We dragons, with our keen sense of scent, can tell these things, you know," continued the dragon.

"No, uh, I'm not—" Mika began, then hurriedly adopted a falsetto. "No," he piped, "I'm not a maiden. La, no, a married woman these twenty years."

"Well enough, then," said the dragon. "I'll keep you for later." Those tiny flames played out. There was another jingle—the dragon picking up the cashbox?—and the creature moved away, scuttling deeper into the cave.

Mika began to breathe easier. He managed to sit up and still the trembling of his limbs, then espied torchlight from the cavern depths.

He clambered off the wagon and did his best to hide behind it.

Soon, perhaps a score of women filed near. They were a diverse lot, of all ages from adolescence on, their clothing a mishmash: rich garb that would credit a queen, plain cotton cloth, coarse-woven homespun. They wore no cosmetics, but each was laden with jewelry; Mika's eyes widened as he took in its value.

Their leader was a matriarch, a white-haired woman who bore a cane. "Salt fish," she said with satisfaction, thumping Mika's barrel. "Make a nice change from beef and venison."

"Millet!" crowed another, discovering the bags in Mika's wagon. They fell to, tossing Mika's goods hither and yon, shouting in delight at each discovery. Mika wondered why millet should be an occasion for rejoicing, not

realizing that the dragon, being carnivorous, rarely thought
to provide grains or vegetables to his collection.

Startled, Mika saw that one of the women was the Princess Nlavi; she stood apart, as if disgusted by these antics.
Mika half-rose at the sight of her—and another woman
stumbled into him.

She jumped back and gave a small yip of surprise.

"What is it, Shemli?" called a third woman.

"A—a man," she quavered. In instants, Mika was sur-
rounded.

"Not much of one," said one of the women.

"Man enough," said another in a low contralto, eyeing
Mika in a disturbing way.

"My savior!" said Nlavi, elbowing her way forward. She
hurled herself into Mika's arms.

"Enough of that!" said the matriarch, Matli. With wrin-
kled hands, she clawed at Nlavi, pulling her from Mika's
embrace. Somewhat reluctantly, Mika let Nlavi go, smiling
with lips still tender at the pressure of her own. "Anyone
not a virgin gets eaten," Matli scolded. "Remember the
rules!"

"Fie on your rules!" said Nlavi, heightened color in her
face. "He is here! Soon enough, the dragon's battered
corpse shall lie at his feet, and in triumph we shall return
to Purasham—"

Matli gave a snort. Mika stared at Nlavi with a mixture
of lust and bemusement.

"Slay the dragon?" he said—but Nlavi failed to note the
incredulous tone.

"Long have I awaited this day," she said, half to him and
half to the other women. "From that fearsome moment the
evil serpent snatched me from atop the Hanging Gardens,
I knew the goddess had a hand in things. For if I suffered
the fate that every maiden fears—capture by dragons—still
I had been rescued from an equally vile destiny—marriage
to a dreadful man.

"But I am a princess, of the blood royale; the gods take an interest in the doings of the great. The dragon had stolen away no common lass, but the only daughter of King Manoos; thus do tales of heroism begin. Meliantos, the wise, the tale-spinner, mother of heroes; she would send one to me, I knew in my heart of hearts. A doughty warrior, a noble man, strong-armed; one to rescue me from both dire fates, to slay the monstrous wyrm and carry me to an incensed bower. And here thou art, my savior, my hero, my—"

Mika, hard-pressed to contain laughter through this exhortation, at last lost control. He leaned against his wagon, giggling and wiping at his eyes. "Brava," he said.

Nlavi, offended, stared.

Shemli was puzzled. "Aren't you here to slay the dragon?" she asked. "Why else would you come?"

"I'm not here by choice," said Mika. "The dragon seized my wagon, as you see. I happened to be in it."

Nlavi colored, stunned.

"You're clean-shaven," said Shemli thoughtfully. "He must have taken you for a woman. If he'd known you were male—he'd have gobbled you up on the instant. Having a man around is a terrible danger for a maiden collector, you see; a girl who loses her maidenhead loses her trading value." She smiled at Mika.

"Trading value?" said Mika, wondering at the term. "So matrons have no value?"

"Correct," said Matli.

"What did the dragon mean when it said it would keep me 'for later'?" Mika asked.

The women cackled—except for Nlavi, who still looked stunned, and Shemli, who seemed rather sad. "Until he's hungry," she explained.

Mika gulped.

"You're no hero, no savior!" accused Nlavi.

"I should hope not," said Mika uneasily. "Honest Mika

Nashram, adventurer's friend and sutler to all, at your service." He bowed. "Perhaps *you'd* care to save *me*? Judging by the age of the good mother here"—he gestured toward Matli—"I'm in greater danger than you. You'll be the pride of the dragon's collection, while I shall be a sweetmeat, to whet his palate before he soars off to ravage a village or three."

Nlavi scowled blackly.

"Come," snapped the matriarch, turning to lead the way back into the cavern depths. "You'll want dinner, I expect."

A fire was burning in the chamber and lamps shone here and there, but Mika's eye was caught at once by the great unignorable that lay heaped in the chamber center: the dragon's hoard. Weak-kneed, he stumbled toward it.

It was a jumble, a precious mess. Here were gold ingots, silver plaques, coins of a hundred nations. There were beaten chalices, set with cabochons; intricate toys of wrought gold and silver wire. Mika saw plates, altars, golden idols, great commemorative wheels of precious metal, bearing the profiles and proud boasts of kings, mixed with crude nuggets, plain ingots, struck coins, and the finest exemplars of the jeweler's art.

It was more wealth than Mika had ever seen in one place; more wealth than he could conceive of being in one place; more wealth, he had no doubt, than lay in the coffers of Purasham. But then, he reflected, Purasham had expenses; a long-lived dragon had centuries to accumulate, and little reason to spend.

Dazedly, he thrust his hands into the hoard, and let coins cascade from his fingers—"That will be enough of that!" said Matli sharply.

"Hah?" said Mika.

"The dragon charges us to keep his treasure shining bright; I cannot account the hours we have spent, polishing and cleaning. I won't have it marred by your greasy hands. Come here and eat."

But Mika couldn't help himself; if he could not touch the hoard, he at least could gaze at it. He wandered around it, studying the gems, the gold, the amazing wealth. He understood those would-be dragonslayers a little better, or thought he did; the glory to be won by slaying such a beast meant nothing to Mika, but the more tangible reward of a dragon's treasure meant a great deal. Still, even attempting to fight that monster was sheerest madness.

Although, thought Mika, force had never been his way of gaining wealth.

Hmm. Dragons were thinking creatures, were they not? That meant they could be gulled, as could men. Had he not already gulled the creature into thinking him a woman? Was there some scheme by which he could fleece the monster of at least some small portion of these fantastic riches?

"Come, dear," said a woman, taking his arm and smiling warmly. "The food isn't getting any warmer, and the gold's going nowhere." So he went with her, doubting that he could eat. What purpose was served? To provide a more succulent meal for the dragon? And his stomach churned, with greed and terror.

The chamber was dim now. The lamps were out, and the fire had burned down to glowing coals. Sleeping women sprawled on blankets. Mika prowled.

He doubted he could sleep. He searched the chamber, expecting nothing, but hoping he might find something to give him some slight chance of survival.

The women had quite an array of items, stored here and there. Cooking utensils, pots, a little loom; no doubt the dragon brought them things for their comfort. But the closest he could find to a weapon was a kitchen knife.

Not that any weapon would do him much good, not against such a foe.

Perhaps he should try to climb down that cliff. Could magic help? He had read of a levitation spell once, but had not thought to memorize it; he cudgeled his brains, trying to remember the particulars, but recalled only the first line of the chant. That was less than useless.

Why not essay the climb? The cliff was sheer, but at worst he would lose his grip, fall, and die. Dead one way, or dead another.

Air moved; Mika turned. The dragon strode clumsily into the chamber. He hauled himself onto his hoard, and curled up on the gold.

Mika froze; the dragon seemed not to see him. Then, stealthily, he began to move toward the cavern exit and the cliff beyond.

"Who's that?" rumbled the dragon.

Mika froze again, but knew it was useless. "It's—" he began, then remembered he was a woman. "It is I," he chirped. "The woman from the wagon."

"Oh," said the dragon, lowering his head. "Go to sleep."

Mika sighed; escape was clearly not an option. But a thought had struck him earlier.

Why not ask? What was there to lose? "Sir," he piped. "A question, if I may."

The dragon's head lifted. "Yes?"

"Dragons prize wealth, as they do maidens. Correct?"

"True," said the dragon.

"Would you, perhaps, be willing to *sell* one of your maidens? For a sufficient sum?"

The dragon considered. "I suppose," he said. "Normally, I trade, but occasionally treasure is kicked in to equalize a deal. For a sufficient amount, I might part with one of my collection."

"Excellent!" said Mika. He had not expected a positive answer. How much, he wondered, was Nlavi worth? The king was offering ten thousand crowns, plus—which county was it? Petok, Petok, that was right.

Now, some vainglorious merchant would doubtless pay to receive the title of Count; Mika thought he might get five thousand crowns for that. And the province itself; well, the taxes were small, Petok being such a miserable place, but they could probably be farmed out for, oh, three thousand crowns a year or so. Figuring that was equivalent to the interest on, oh, thirty thousand crowns, Nlavi's market value was at least forty-five thousand.

"As it happens," chirped Mika cautiously, "I am a woman of some means and a patriotic daughter of Purasham. It breaks my heart to see the rose of our realm in a dragon's claws. I would be willing to offer, oh, ten thousand crowns, subsequent to delivery, for our beloved princess."

"Ten thousand?" said the dragon thoughtfully. "No, that's not in the range—"

"Twenty," said Mika quickly.

"Mmm . . . Still—"

"Thirty," Mika said.

The dragon seemed excited; small jets of flame shot from his nostrils. He was silent for a long moment. "I'm sorry," he said at last, "I've already made a deal."

Mika was puzzled. "You've already sold her? But—"

"I traded her for a wizardress I've much admired," said the dragon, "and the sum of five thousand crowns. Your offer is much superior, but—well, I gave my word."

"You sold her," said Mika. "When must you deliver?"

"I have two months."

"In that case, if you could buy another maiden princess, could you substitute her? And sell me Nlavi?"

"Ye-e-es," said the dragon slowly. "That kind of thing has been done. It isn't easy, you understand; with the recent conquests of Motraia, there are far fewer royal houses than there once were. Royal maidens command a scarcity premium. But perhaps it is feasible."

Mika's mind was whirring; another thought had struck—inventiveness spurred by terror, no doubt. "Look here," he said. "Do dragons trade exclusively to improve their collections?"

The dragon's eyes blinked. "What else?" he wondered.

"For profit!" Mika said, almost shrieking. "Look here, suppose Dragon Aleph is desirous of a xanthous beauty, while Dragon Beth has more red-tressed wenches than he cares to possess. Suppose you knew this. You could buy a redhead from Beth, and sell her to Aleph."

"Mmm, yes . . ." said the dragon.

"If each dragon seeks a diverse collection, then each desires different maidens. So one might value, oh, princesses more right now, and another wizardresses—"

"Yes, yes, of course," said the dragon. "That is why we trade."

"But a profit is to be made, by learning the wants of each and matching them! Now, suppose you were to keep an inventory of maidens—not for your own collection, you understand, but as stock-in-trade. Then, others would come to you when they had a maiden to sell, or wanted one to buy. You could become the central clearing house for the maiden market. A maiden exchange, if you will!"

"Why should I want this?" grumbled the dragon. "It's undraconian. Pillage cities, kidnap maidens; that's our way. Good enough for my dam, and good—"

"But you trade," said Mika.

"Indubitably."

"And money can buy you the maidens you wish for your own collection?"

"Yes."

"And a crown is a crown, whether despoiled from some kinglet's treasure house or earned in a clever trade?"

"Correct."

"Then why should you care *how* you earn your crowns? The more you have, the better a collection you may assemble."

The dragon mulled this over for a long moment. "I see," he said at last. "How interesting. Tell me more."

"Here we have an unsophisticated market in maidens," Mika explained, "operating haphazardly, with no public knowledge of prices paid; a market of many competitors, each with enormous cash reserves. The thought is staggering! If we become the central exchange, we will have advance knowledge of the wants and prices all other dragons are willing to pay, and can therefore work and manipulate the maiden market to our own ends—buying up brunettes to ramp the price, selling royalty short when we know new princesses are about to come to market.

"La, sir, the merchants of my realm have all manner of tricks, to smooth the course of commerce—and turn a tidy profit in addition! We have insurance syndication, letters of credit, factors, interest compounding, contracts for forward delivery—why, my dragon friend, the possibilities are infinite! We can sell maidens on credit and collect the interest, offer insurance against loss of maidenhead. . . . By all the gods, we can take your fellow dragons for stupendous sums. And honestly, yet! No need for chicanery here. Good wyrm, good creature, the future is bright for us, bright indeed. With your contacts, and my commercial acumen, there is no end to the money we can make, the maidens we can add to your collection."

Mika and the dragon talked long into the night.

21

▶▶▶

Hard rock, split by stress and long erosion; gray rock, baking in morning sun. Nijon's legs and fingers ached, but he dared not rest them, not here; one misstep and he would roll down the slope, rebounding off jagged outcrops, until he lay still like the shards down below, in the scree that had broken from this rise.

"Come on," sang Dekh, for so Nijon's grimy companion was named. "This way." Dekh climbed limberly up the chute, disappearing above.

"I am not a billy goat," complained Nijon, eyeing the chute unhappily. It ran upward, at a gentle enough slope that, with luck, one might find handholds and pull oneself up. Yet the cleft seemed to narrow farther up; Nijon had no faith it offered safe passage.

He cursed his own curiosity. From the valley floor, Nijon had seen the only way the cavern might be approached was from above; below it, sheer cliff dropped away for at least a hundred cubits, while the slope at its flanks was equally unscalable.

But "might be" was the correct phrase: From the valley, Nijon had not been able to see what was directly above the cave. It had looked as though the slope became less steep there; a few scraggly trees stood above the opening. But the place had been hidden by the contours of the terrain.

Reluctantly, Nijon pulled his way upward. Brother sat, half in Nijon's pack, and eyed the world worriedly. This was neither his nor Nijon's natural terrain.

It was hard going; Nijon sweated in the morning sun. Unlike Dekh, he bore a heavy sword and full kit; the boy was unladen, save for a piece of cloth and a layer of dirt.

The cavern had *better* be approachable from above, he told himself. Otherwise, all this was wasted effort. But if Dekh could climb this face, so could he.

The chute narrowed enough that he had difficulty scraping by, his gear gritting against the rock; but the passage widened beyond, and Nijon came to a place that was actually flat enough to sit down and rest. Dekh was there already, sitting with arms about his knees and humming something.

"Are we high enough yet?" asked Dekh. "What will you do now? Will you stride forth and defy—"

Ignoring the boy, Nijon scanned the slope, peering to the left. Where was the dragon's lair? From this unfamiliar vantage point, Nijon failed to see the opening.

"Where did you get your rat?" asked Dekh. "Is he tame? Can I pet him? Is . . ." Nijon tuned the boy out again.

"There!" shouted Nijon. The dragon tumbled out into space, swooping down along the cliff. The lair was indeed to Nijon's left and a little below their resting place, as he had hoped.

Knowing where to look now, Nijon saw he had been right; the slope did become more gradual. Above the lair was a minor peak, behind it actually a dip, before the ridge began to rise once more. Nijon might well be able to work himself down into the dragon's cave from there.

If, he reflected, he could reach it. Between here and there was hardly easy going. Wearily, he rubbed his back.

"He bit me! He bit me!" shouted Dekh. Brother scurried

away, disappearing in a cleft between two rocks. Dekh brandished his injured hand.

"If you don't try to pull his tail off, perhaps he won't do it again," said Nijon mildly.

Dekh pouted.

It was late afternoon by the time they reached the peak above the dragon's lair.

"At last!" said Dekh, fairly dancing, despite the labors of the day. "The battle of the ages! Nijon, mighty warrior of the barbarous south, against the ferocious, fire-breathing dragon!"

"Be quiet," said Nijon, studying the ground.

There were a few trees here, lichen, and loose talus; rocks falling from greater height tended to collect in this depression. The peak above the entrance to the cave was granite; below it was limestone. Nijon surmised the weaker limestone had eroded away, but the harder granite had resisted, leaving this sharp protrusion.

"HOLA!" shouted Dekh, striking a pose atop the peak.

"Shush," said Nijon.

"VICIOUS WYRM!" bellowed Dekh, cupping his hands and calling into the valley. Was it Nijon's imagination, or did the call echo from the distance? "EVIL DE-VOURER OF THE FAIR!"

"Shut up!" croaked Nijon in terror, sprinting for the boy.

"COME FORTH TO MEET YOUR END!" shouted Dekh, waving a hand in a sweeping gesture. "NIJON, SWORD-BEARER, HAS COME TO SLAY—"

Nijon grabbed Dekh's matted hair and yanked the boy up until his feet were inches from the ground.

"Ow!" said Dekh. "Stop it! That hurts!"

"Do you have wings?" asked Nijon between gritted teeth. The boy tried to pry Nijon's hands out of his hair, but said nothing. Nijon flipped Dekh over and shifted his grip to the ankles. He held Dekh out over space, face down. Nijon avoided looking down, himself; there were a hundred cubits of empty space there, a long drop before one might smash on the rocks below.

"I see you do not," said Nijon. "A shame, for by Ptemesh's six arms and Mongoose's stripe, if you don't *shut up*, you're going to *need* to fly."

"I can't fly," said a tiny voice.

"Then *shut up*," Nijon snarled, shaking Dekh by the ankles.

"All right," said the boy, chastened.

Nijon hauled him in, and dropped him headfirst on the ground. Then Nijon crouched and peered over the peak, down at the cavern opening, half-expecting an angry dragon to shoot forth any instant—but after long moments, concluded that the dragon either wasn't home or by great good luck had somehow failed to hear Dekh.

Nijon turned. Dekh was sitting cross-legged, sullenly rubbing his pate.

Nijon went back to his pack, opened it up, and began to take things out—not looking for anything in particular, but taking inventory in the hope that something would spark an idea.

"A hero would fight the dragon," said a small voice.

Nijon ignored it. There was a pulley among his gear, a bronze wheel he'd taken off Mika with the notion it might prove useful getting up the mountain; it had a metal axle with holes on the ends, so you could tie it to something, and a runnel around the rim, to run a rope through. He also had a substantial length of hempen rope, another gift of the trader. And there was a hatchet, still fairly sharp.

"A hero would bellow his challenge and charge into battle," said Dekh.

Nijon snorted, and considered the few trees nearby and the talus of fallen rock; a thought began to germinate.

"You are no hero," said Dekh accusingly, as if completing a syllogism.

Nijon gritted his teeth. "Bah," he said. "How do you know a hero? I am the son of a god; I ride with my brother, a mongoose; I wield a sword of meteoric iron. By the standards of the legends, if I am not now a hero, I can hardly fail to become one."

"But in the legends," said Dekh, "heroes are bold; you sneak around the dragon's cave. Heroes are honest; you stole your supplies from Mika Nashram. Heroes are kind; you—you're not. . . ." Dekh's lower lip began quivering, and, Nijon saw, it was all the boy could do to hold back tears.

Nijon gave a soundless snarl. "I will be kind to you," he said, "when you stop doing your best to get us both killed. I do not count it theft to steal from a thief. And I shall be bold enough, after I have made careful preparation."

"In the legends—"

"The legends be damned! Do you think heroes of legend failed to lay the groundwork for their deeds? Ballads sing of the glory of battle, not of the untold hours of tedium that lead up to it, but never doubt that tedium existed. Success in every human endeavor requires relentless effort."

"Oh," said Dekh.

Nijon went to work on one of the trees with his hatchet. He feared the noise an axe stroke would make, so he set to shaving the side of the tree. It would take much longer this way, but he would not alert the dragon.

Dekh sat with arms folded over knees, his head between his legs. "But that's why I left the farm," he said miserably.

Nijon looked up. "To avoid relentless effort?"

"Yes."

Nijon snorted. "My friend," he said. "You will likely die tomorrow. I may, too, for I am a hero; but if I do, my death shall be heroic. You, on the other hand, are a peasant. If you die, it will be the brief incineration of a little life. To find your death, you have braved forests, deprivation, and mighty mountains. This strikes you as easier than hoeing dirt?"

"More interesting," said Dekh.

"Ah!" said Nijon, pausing momentarily to consider this. "Perhaps so." He took up scraping the tree again, then said, "But the hours are lousy."

It was dark in the valley down below; up here, the ridge was sunlit yet, though Ptemesh's fiery chariot raced for the horizon and his nighttime rest.

Dekh had made a small bow, and was working with it, a stick, and Nijon's shavings.

"Stop that," said Nijon.

"But it will be cold," protested Dekh. "We'll need a fire."

Nijon grunted. "We'll do without," he said. "It would give us away."

Dekh looked miserable. A dead hare lay alongside him, a gift from Brother. "But we need to cook—"

Nijon gave him a dangerous smile. "No we don't," he said, skinned the hare with a few practiced motions, cut off a leg, and bit into the raw flesh.

Dekh looked green.

"I've eaten worse," said Nijon. "Try it." He cut away a breast and handed it to Dekh. "Have I told you of the time that I ate raw snake, scales and all? I was sorely wounded, feverish with infection, when my father, the god Mongoose, came. . . ."

Ptemesh banked low the fires of the sun, whose embers dyed red the western sky.

"Look!" shouted Dekh, pointing out into the valley.

A scallop-winged shape soared there, glinting in the vestiges of light.

"Down!" ordered Nijon, urgently and low. He scuttled

across the rock, grabbed the branches he had stripped from his fallen tree, and spread them over his gear, to hide it from the sky. Reluctant but obedient, Dekh crouched low.

Nijon pulled Dekh behind a rock, then himself lay just behind the peak.

As the dragon banked, individual scales sparkled with reflected light, winking as the angle between the dragon and the sun changed with the dragon's motion. From the sinuous neck down its flanks, its color ran from dull red to a light cerise, with areas of purple beneath the limbs.

The wings beat slowly; Nijon was close enough now that he could see the backward-bending elbow joint, halfway out the wing, and the five bones that ran from the "arm" across the wing surface, holding it flat against the air. Those wings must be quite thin, he realized, for the bones to be visible so.

He wondered at their strength; birds had hollow, brittle bones. Dragons were thought to be massive, enormously strong; but in order to fly, they must be more birdlike than legend gave credence.

The dragon grew nearer. It must be slowing; those wings were beating now, partly into the dragon's line of flight, but it seemed to be hurtling headlong toward Nijon, perched as he was above the cave. The dragon grew enormously in size; if it was slowing, the change in speed was not apparent, not to Nijon.

For one heart-stopping second, he thought the dragon had seen him and was coming to pluck him from the peak, to dash him onto the rocks below or gobble him whole in midair—but in that instant, the dragon was gone, vanished into the mouth of its lair.

For a long moment, Nijon could not move, partly from that instant of terror, partly for the memory of vanished beauty.

* * *

"You may address me," said Nlavi frostily, "as 'Your Sublime Highness' or, less formally, as 'Exalted.' "

Mika grinned. "You don't like 'sugar'?" he said. "How about 'toots'?"

"Utterly out of the question."

"Stick with me, Your Exaltedness, babe," said Mika cheerily, failing in an attempt to get an arm around Nlavi. "I'm going to get you home. Isn't that what you wanted?"

Nlavi sniffed.

"You sure sang a different tune when I first got here," Mika said ruefully.

"I had assumed," Nlavi said, "that you were a hero of legend, not a . . . a. . . ."

"Canny trader? Man of imagination? Mercantile genius?"

"Mountebank," said Nlavi. "Palter. Confidence trickster."

Mika laughed. "So you still hope some mighty-thewed bonehead will drop from the heavens, dispatch the dragon with a single stroke, and sweep you into his brawny embrace? Come now, am I so unattractive? I would think after a life of courtly tedium, you'd jump at the opportunity to meet a man like me, an honorable rogue, a—"

Nlavi gave a bitter laugh, and stabbed Mika with a fork.

"Ouch!" shouted Mika.

"Keep your hands to yourself," said Nlavi. "And I'll remind you that three short words are all I need to see you dead."

"What?" said Mika.

" 'He's a man,' " said Nlavi. "That should do the trick."

Mika paled. It was true the dragon tolerated him only because it thought he was female. "You wouldn't," he said.

Nlavi smiled.

They heard a stentorian breath; damp exhalation washed over them. The dragon had entered the chamber. He hauled himself over to his customary perch on his hoard, and sat down, nose pointing toward Mika.

"It's set," boomed the dragon. "Khekhamaish and Zdelgemekh have agreed to contribute funds for the venture. I am reluctant to accept, however; this kind of alliance is foreign to our natures. Explain to me again about the joint stock company."

Mika sighed and sat down cross-legged. It would probably be another long night. "Unless you wish to risk your hoard entire," he patiently began, "you need investors to buy a sufficient stock of maidens. . . ."

The pulley creaked. Nijon cursed under his breath.

It was too late to grease the pulley—not that he had anything with which to do so. It was several cubits above him, tied to a frame constructed from a fallen tree. One end of the rope that ran around the pulley was slung about Nijon's waist and shoulders. The other end hung down below; he had tied knots at cubit intervals, to better his grip on the rope.

It was a dark night. The moon was not yet up, and the sky was partially overcast; the few stars shining gave meager illumination. Yet even so, Nijon knew, he was a black shape against the opening of the cave. And, too, darkness did nothing to mask his odor—and dragons were reputed to have an excellent sense of smell.

Nijon prayed, to Dorij and his father. If the dragon were to see him, hear him, smell him; if he were to lose his grip on the rope; if his jury-rigged hoist were to fail. . . .

Hand over hand, he let himself down. At last, he was even with the cavern floor. He secured himself, knotting the loose end of rope to his belt, and peered.

It was dark inside the cave; it took long for Nijon's eyes to resolve anything at all. At last, he realized that the lump on the floor, before him and to his left, was a wagon—Mika's wagon, he surmised.

He caught something out of the corner of his eye—but it disappeared when he looked at it. Nijon knew what the problem was; he had spent enough time watching the stars while guarding the herd at night. It was easier to see truly faint stars when you looked not straight at them, but slightly to the side. Tracking his eyes back and forth, Nijon peered at that place—

He was seeing a dim glow, he realized.

Farther back in the cave, there must be a light; a fire, perhaps, or simply the glowing of the dragon's internal flame. It was reflecting faintly off a wall at the back of this chamber.

Evidently, the dragon slept not here, but farther in. Interesting.

Nijon hauled himself up to the peak, where Dekh and Brother awaited.

22

▶▶▶

Bleary-eyed Ptemesh rode his chariot of fire into be-
clouded dawn. Nijon was tired; he felt that tightness about
the eyes that meant he was in bad need of slumber. The
sun-god, too, looked as if he had spent an uneasy night; he
emitted a wan, gray light through clouded skies. But like
Ptemesh, Nijon was not ready for rest; the god because he
must discharge his duty of bringing the day, Nijon because
he was hopping with energy, unable to refrain from bringing his endeavor to conclusion.

The night had been spent to good effect. To still the
pulley's squeak, Nijon had greased it with fat from the hare
on which he and Dekh had dined the night before. The
design of his contraption had been somewhat refined; unhappy with hauling himself up and down the rope, Nijon
had decided to add a counterweight. He had knotted a net
from some spare rope, and had filled it with rocks and
rubble. Around the pulley now ran a long loop; the net
counterweight was tied to one end of the loop, and the
harness in which Nijon would sit was tied to the other.

"Won't the rocks just put more strain on the hoist?"
Dekh asked.

Nijon sighed. The lad seemed not to understand the
notion of a counterweight. "The rocks and I will be on

opposite sides of the pulley," he tried to explain. "Their weight will balance my weight, so it will be easier to haul myself up and down." Dekh still looked puzzled; Nijon cursed. "Haven't you ever used a shaduf?" he demanded.

"Of course," said Dekh. There were counterweighted irrigation balers all over the valley of the River Uk. The peasant who had never used one was rare.

"Same principle," said Nijon. Dekh began to show a glimmer of understanding.

To the right of the pulley perched a boulder. It was held in place by wooden chocks. The chocks had been notched and rope strung through the notches; a sharp jerk on the rope, a push to the boulder, and it would plummet over the cliff.

"Time to test it," Nijon said.

"Shall we not rest?" complained Dekh, rubbing a grimy eye.

"No," said Nijon. "We must not tarry. Stay here long enough, and the dragon is sure to notice us."

He heaved his counterweight over the edge of the cliff and, hauling on the rope that ran round the pulley, lowered the net of rocks hand over hand down the cliff side. This was a dangerous moment, he knew. The net would descend in front of the cavern entrance. If anyone was there, and alerted the dragon, this venture would come to a rapid and unhappy end. Nijon counted on the dragon to be asleep, and on the fact that he slept not near the cavern lip, but deeper within.

Hearing no bellow of rage, Nijon stepped into his harness, made sure it was snug, and checked the knots that tied it to the loop. Then he sat on the cliff, and gingerly let himself over the edge.

The counterweighting was perfect. He hung in midair, suspended by his harness, the counterweight preventing him from falling. He eyed the wooden frame that held the pulley. It was firmly lashed together, its base buried under rocks; it gave no sign of strain. Still, Nijon was not entirely easy; he was no artisan, and knew he trusted his life to a jury-rigged device.

Grabbing the far rope, he pulled himself downward, pulling the net of rocks upward simultaneously.

The pulley turned smoothly.

Nijon descended until he was just above the cave opening. Now came the most important test. He grabbed the far rope as high above his head as he could reach, then yanked down with all his might.

He shot upward, toward the pulley. Momentum kept him going for several seconds. That should do, he thought with satisfaction as he came smoothly to a halt.

He pulled himself up to talk a final time with Dekh. Brother waited with the boy, bewhiskered face peering down the cliff at Nijon with an expression of concern.

"You know what to do," Nijon said.

"Verily," said Dekh, shifting from foot to foot in excitement.

"Tell me," said Nijon.

"I wait till you shout 'Now.' I yank free the chocks and pummel the boulder. It will fall, and strike athwart the dragon as it darts from the cave, smashing it downward and onto the rocks below. Are you certain this will work?"

"Nothing is certain," said Nijon with annoyance. "But it should. Those wings are thin, the bones must be fragile; surprised by several hundredweight of boulder, a dragon that has problems lifting a wagon should be distressed. With luck, the fall alone will kill it."

"And if all else fails?"

Nijon shrugged. "Hide," he suggested. "Perhaps the monster will content itself with my life."

"We shall triumph," said Dekh firmly, "for did not your father, the god Mongoose, foretell—"

"Yes, yes, yes," said Nijon. "No time for this." He pulled himself down the cliff, toward the cavern, reflecting, not for the first time, that he was entrusting his life to a boy with the attention span and grasp of reality of a demented puppy.

Nijon lowered himself jerkily down into the cavern entrance. A woman of middle age peered up at him, mouth agape; she had been emptying a chamber pot down the cliff. "Good morrow, goodwife," said Nijon courteously. "Has the dragon broken his fast?"

"Another fool," said the woman sadly. "He's just stirring. If you'll pardon me, I'll leave now; I have no desire to be roasted by mischance."

"No offense is taken," said Nijon, making a courteous salute in midair. The woman scurried away. When she had entered a passage at the rear of the cave, Nijon cupped his hands—then paused. What should he say? Almost anything would do, to attract the creature's attention. He smiled to himself, then bellowed: *"Hola! Vicious wyrm! Evil devourer of the fair! Come forth to meet your end! Nijon, Sword-Bearer, has come to slay you!"* He took a firm grip on the loop, as high above him as he could stretch, and waited for the dragon.

A reptilian head poked into the chamber. "Oh, bother," said the dragon. "Before breakfast, too. Have you people no consideration?"

"Free your captives," Nijon shouted, "and I shall spare you, O monstrous toad."

"Toad, is it?" said the dragon, a little offended. The head turned, as if the reptile were looking over his shoulder. "Watch this," he said. Another, smaller, head peeked in: the face of a man, Nijon saw with surprise. He failed to recognize Mika Nashram at this distance.

The dragon took a deep breath. Nijon yanked down with all his might, and sped upward. He cleared the cave mouth, then watched with satisfaction as a torrent of flame raged harmlessly out into the void beneath his feet.

Or—not harmlessly. Flame struck the loop of rope that hung below Nijon. Fibers charred, then began to burn. Nijon's eyes widened; somewhere down there hung his counterweight—

Nijon made a wild grab for the length of rope that hung parallel to him, and only just in time. There was a yank as the counterweight fell away and Nijon's arms suddenly bore the full force of his own weight.

Disaster! Could his plan be salvaged?

A crash rolled out across the valley: his counterweight, smashing into rocks at the foot of the cliff. Dekh must have taken that for a signal. *"Now?"* shouted the boy. *"Now?"*

Nijon looked up in sudden panic. *"No!"* he screamed. *"No! Stop—"* But he could see the chocks falling away, Dekh hurling himself at the boulder, the boulder tipping with deliberate slowness over the peak—

The dragon's head poked out of the cavern opening. It looked around, then tilted to one side; one eye looked up. "Are you still there?" the dragon demanded, somewhat peeved.

The boulder plunged past. The dragon, startled, yanked his nose in. A stupendous *crack* rang out as the boulder hit the cliff base and shattered. Shards tumbled down the mountain.

Moaning in fear and frustration, Nijon scrambled skyward, toward the peak from which an unhappy Dekh peered. Nijon pulled up, hand over hand, arms straining; without the counterweight, it was hard work.

The dragon poked a nose out into space again, tilting his head and blowing a jet of flame. Fire singed Nijon's heels; he yelped, and clambered upward with renewed speed. The dragon breathed again, but could not turn his head sufficiently far to flame Nijon. The monster considered for a moment—then that massive head turned, until the throat was facing the sky. He had rolled onto his back. He took a breath—

With a last desperate heave, Nijon pulled himself over the peak—just as flame raged upward behind him.

"I'm sorry," said Dekh plaintively, half-turned to run. "I'm really, really sorry."

"Shut up," Nijon panted, cutting himself free of the rope and peering out over the cliff with drawn sword. The dragon had disappeared, had withdrawn into the cave mouth. It was over, all over; the dragon would roar out the cavern mouth in a minute, wheel around. . . . Nijon had a flash of what the scene would look like from the monster's vantage, two little mouselike creatures scurrying desperately across the mountain face as he soared above them, sending jet after jet of flame splashing across the mountain's flank, until at last the little creatures squealed in agony and expired—what good was this sword going to do him, this damnable hunk of metal, against a monster that could eat mammoths for breakfast? It had been idiocy even to make the attempt, he saw that clearly now, sheerest arrogant folly.

Dekh was running jerkily to and fro, babbling terrified prayers. Brother had found a crevice and was crouching in it; he, at least, might survive. Nijon returned his gaze to the cavern lip. "What the hell," he muttered. "What the hell." He sheathed his sword and, still panting from his exertions, poised atop the peak, moving his arms a bit to loosen the ache. He tensed. There was a flash of red from the cavern entrance; Nijon flung himself into the air, no rope to break his fall, void beneath his feet. A quick death, a clean death—

The dragon lumbered out into the air, wings unfolding into the dive he needed to gain airspeed—

Something struck his back.

Nijon skittered along scales; a grasping hand latched onto a dorsal fin. The other hand swept around to snatch the fin also.

He choked, unable to draw breath. His wind was gone,

knocked out of him; and he was already winded, from his labor struggling up the cliff. He gasped for air; sight dimmed. . . .

The dragon dived downward, howling in rage.

A circle hung before Nijon's eyes: half fuzzy gray, half fuzzy red. The circle widened, to encompass the world. Nijon panted, sucking great gasps of air as his head cleared. The gray was clouds, that red the dragon's scales.

Nijon's stomach gave a sudden lurch as the dragon tilted into a turn. He wrapped both arms tightly about the monster's dorsal fin—and not a moment too soon. The dragon stooped into a steep dive, pulling in his wings and nosing down toward the valley floor.

Red wings held close in, the wing fringe rippling in the draft, that narrow head held like an arrow, the dragon dived down, down, gathering speed. A gale-force breeze ripped at Nijon until tears ran from his eyes. Ahead, there was the forest green, growing larger, crowding out the sky.

Nijon was almost weightless; his legs rose from the dragon's back, until only his desperate grip on the fin kept him there. At last, the monster broke his dive, wings extending outward. Nijon slammed into his back, sprawling half across another fin. It jagged uncomfortably into his abdomen.

The dragon knew he was there. He was trying to throw him. Nijon realized he needed a better perch; that last maneuver had almost lost him, and his strength was not infinite. The next would get him, or the one after that. . . .

He cast wildly about; if he could make the neck—it was narrower than the body, he could throw his legs about it. And it was closer to the head. . . .

The pressure lessened. They were climbing, now, those wings laboriously beating. For the nonce, Nijon had the freedom to do something other than cling like a leech; but the dragon must be preparing for another maneuver.

A line of fins ran up the dragon's back. Nijon freed a hand and scuttled forward, reaching for the next fin. He made it; thus boldened, he made for the next.

At that instant, the dragon's wings shot out rigid; he broke from a climb into a flat soar. The sudden motion caught Nijon with only one hand on a fin, the other hand reaching out for the next in line; he slid, spinning down the dragon's flank, feet skittering off scales toward certain death—and he managed to grab that second fin. He hauled himself toward it, and wrapped his arms around.

The dragon swept instantly into a turn. The left wing plunged, the right wing rose; Nijon's feet were pulled off toward the right as the dragon curved, but his grip on the fin was sufficient. The horizon plunged wildly down; it swung up again, and the dragon swooped out of his turn.

The right wing plunged, as the dragon curved in the opposite direction. Nijon's stomach lurched, and he found himself forced into the fin as the force of this turn pulled the other way.

The horizon yanked around again. The dragon was turning violently left, then right, then left again, Nijon realized, trying to throw him from his back. For a moment between each turn he felt almost stable.

He took the chance. When that next changeover came, the horizon almost flat, he lunged for the next fin in line. At the next turn, he gained another fin, and another after that—he was a few cubits from the neck when the dragon ended its sequence of turns and began to climb.

Wings pulled high; with each downstroke, Nijon felt a jolt.

They climbed upward; Nijon worked himself forward, until finally he was at the base of the neck. He wrapped arms and legs about it.

They were in the clouds. It was chill here. Nijon could

see no farther than a cubit or two; the wings faded away into the grayness. It was damp; droplets caught in Nijon's hair and beard. The dragon pulled high.

The rope harness was still about Nijon. He drew his boot knife, cut a length of rope, and wrapped it around the dragon's neck.

The dragon plunged into a dive again. The dive was, if anything, steeper than before. The wings were tight against the body; gray air roared past. Nijon was soaked now, shivering in the stiff breeze. The dragon began to spin.

Nijon cast a glance at the wings, and saw they were slightly extended. They were catching the wind, spinning the dragon about its spine.

The world snapped into existence; they had cleared the clouds. In horrid fascination, Nijon stared at the world below—below, and almost directly ahead. Desolation Ridge swung past, around, behind, ahead again—faster and faster and faster, as the dragon rolled. Nijon felt himself pulled away, like a stone in a sling whirled round the head—a stone awaiting its release, to fly through vacant air and splat against the world so far below. Hands clutching the rope he had strung around the dragon's neck, legs wrapped viselike, Nijon tucked in his head and held on, held on, held on for dear life. . . .

23

A sledgehammer smashed Mika into consciousness. He peered groggily into horror: huge teeth, talons, a monster about to devour—

"I have decided," boomed the monster with excitement.

It was only the dragon. Mika sat up and rubbed his ribs; that blow had been the dragon's idea of a gentle nudge.

"Decided what?" muttered Mika, instantly feeling a thrill of terror; he had forgotten to speak in falsetto. But the dragon hadn't noticed.

"I shall invite Khekhamaish and Zdelgemekh over for a—what did you call it?"

"A board meeting," piped Mika. Couldn't this news have waited? He and the dragon had spoken far into the night, and Mika was far from rested. A few hours' sleep more or less might not matter to a reptile that lived for centuries, but for a human, this human, at least. . . .

"A board meeting," said the dragon, savoring the unfamiliar phrase. "Excellent. Shall—"

A bellow came from the cavern mouth; a defiantly masculine bellow. The words were muffled by distance, but Mika caught "vicious wyrm" and something about "evil devourers."

"Drat," said the dragon. "More of this nonsense." It

lumbered down the passage connecting the living chamber to the mouth.

"Oh, bother," said the dragon, to whomever was there. "Before breakfast, too. Have you people no consideration?"

Mika staggered over to see what was going on, and caught the tail of Nijon's diatribe: "—toad."

No, no, no, thought Mika, squinting into the morning light. It's that idiot Vagon. He's sure to muck things up.

"Toad, is it?" said the dragon. Then, to Mika: "Watch this."

The dragon turned, and breathed forth flames; Nijon darted upward on his contraption.

"Stop this," Mika said testily. The dragon moved forward, to peer out the cave entrance, then flamed again. Mika wondered how to stop the fight. The last thing he wanted was the dragon getting distracted at this point. And the gods forbid, Nijon might actually win by some stroke of fortune—or queer the deal, even in losing. There was money enough in the deal; maybe he could pay Nijon off? That would be tricky, actually—the dragon was so fearful of male humans despoiling its maiden collection—but there must be some way. . . .

The women were watching, now, peering out the passageway. The dragon had backed up, into the cave. He began to run forward, as fast as his squat legs would let him—and hurled himself off the cavern lip and into flight. Wings began to unfold—

Nijon fell from above, slamming onto the creature's back. Women gasped at his audacity.

They ran to the cavern lip. The dragon began to climb—then nosed down into a steep dive. Mika rubbed sleep-fogged eyes, and peered until they burned, hoping to see a tiny form hurtling to its death. . . .

"What valor!" said Nlavi admiringly. "To grapple the

dragon in midair, to dive into certain death! He must be a hero indeed."

"Your prince has come, eh, dearie?" said Matli sarcastically.

Nlavi looked the oldster in the eye. "For a certainty," she said proudly. "Why else would he brave these rocky peaks, the dragon's fearsome ire? To rescue the king's daughter, a maiden fair; for her hand, for a kingdom, for glory and renown. He will succeed in splendor, for does not the right always triumph?"

"It is so sad!" wailed Shemli, bursting into sobs.

With horrified fascination, Mika's eyes followed the line of the dragon's flight. It was turning now, violent turns; first left, then right, then left again.

"Sad?" asked Nlavi.

"Oh, the poor brave lad," said Shemli, mopping at her eyes with the hem of her skirt. "He must be resolute, to have come so far. And like all the rest, he will die, young life uselessly extinguished; so it ever is. The best of our city, throwing their lives away on stupid . . . stupid. . . ." She could not continue, but crumpled to the floor, weeping uncontrollably.

"Oh, I hope you're right," said Mika absently, "I do hope so."

Several of the women regarded him with disgust. "You hope he'll die?" demanded one.

Mika hardly glanced at her. "You don't know Nijon like I know Nijon," he said. "No stalwart of unstained honor, he. Besides which, the dragon and I stand to make a fortune—"

"Trading in slaves," spat a woman.

"You have something against slavery?" asked Mika in genuine surprise. "Civilization would be impossible without it."

The women were silent again, as they watched the dragon

pull high, disappearing into the clouds. "Did he throw the boy yet?" asked one.

"I saw nothing fall," said another, shrugging.

They watched for long moments; there was nothing to see but gray clouds above.

"Pah," said Matli at last. "Enough of this nonsense. We have clothes to wash, treasure to polish, meals to prepare. Come!" She turned and hobbled toward the passage—but no one made to follow her. Noting this, she snorted, said, "Watch the boy die, if you like," and continued on her way.

The dragon shot from the clouds with startling suddenness, spinning like a top. Several of the women gave yips of surprise. "How can the boy keep his grip with that?" moaned one.

Over and over and over the dragon spiraled, plunging toward the earth. . . .

Nijon's fingers cramped with strain. His face was jammed tightly against red scales, but to either side of the dragon's neck was chaos: gray of sky, green of tree, ocher rock, flipping over and over and over, the line of the horizon gyrating like nothing Nijon had ever seen. He felt unreal, disoriented by the lack of any stable reference. He could hardly think, too filled with terror and exhilaration; there was nothing but his grasp, the dragon, the anarchic world beyond.

After an eternity, the outward force slackened, that spin slowing, slowing into a lazy roll; then Nijon's stomach slammed into his spine. The dragon was coming out of his dive. Nijon tensed for the next violent maneuver—but the dragon seemed content to soar, for now, flapping occasionally to maintain velocity. He must be tired, Nijon thought.

He inched the loop of rope forward along the dragon's long neck, and pulled himself up behind it. Though he knew he was safer now, he felt more precarious than before, for the ground rushed past on either side, and only the narrow neck and his grip on the rope kept him from falling. He fought down vertigo, and moved doggedly forward.

The neck gave a wriggle.

Nijon tensed. If the dragon were to toss his head, could he keep his grasp? But no toss came; perhaps the dragon must keep his head arrowed forward to maintain stability in flight. "Damnation," spoke the dragon. "This is absurd."

The dragon was in a shallow dive. Nijon saw his destination: a meadow, a patch of grassland in the forest. The dragon was coming in for a landing.

Nijon had made his way far up the neck. The head was close now, almost in reach. Nijon lunged for it—and grabbed the knobby protrusion above an eye. The dragon's wings began to beat, braking speed; his legs were already making the motions of running, pawing at the air. The dragon's talons met wildflowered earth—

Nijon yanked forth a knife—and nearly cut his thigh as the jolt of landing shook his mount.

Trotting through the green, the dragon swung his head far to the left—preparing to snap it right and toss Nijon off. Nijon sank his dagger into the dragon's eye.

The monster screamed with pain. Scalding blood spurted forth, burning Nijon's hand. The head snapped across—and at last Nijon lost his grip, flying violently across the clearing.

A moment of complete panic; and then he crashed to earth, his fall broken by a juniper bush. He felt a sudden agonizing pain in his chest; he was unable to move for a moment, then hesitantly probed his thorax. A broken rib. He would have to fight on despite it.

Nijon sat up. He almost blacked out from the pain.

The dragon screamed and fire roared from his mouth. A tree at the far end of the clearing burst into flames. The monster stumbled forward, thrashing awkwardly through the brush, tossing his head as if to free himself of pain; flame roared forth again, to splash against an anthill.

Nijon saw that that dragon had a long, ragged cut above his eyes; Nijon's knife must have gouged it, when he had been flung from the dragon's neck. The dragon's steaming blood ran into his one good eye; he could not see. For the first time since Dekh had dropped the rock, Nijon felt a surge of hope. He drew his sword, and used it to lever himself to a standing position.

"So humiliating," roared the dragon, almost plaintively. "Blinded by some hairy mammal. Egad, I shall never live this down."

Nijon stumbled toward the monster's right flank. He ran as fast as he felt able—not terribly, in his condition.

"Where are you?" roared the dragon. "By heaven, I shall roast your entrails."

Nijon was close to the wing now. A bird's bones were fragile; were a dragon's? There were so close to the surface, at the wing, uncushioned by flesh. . . . Nijon raised his sword overhead and, with all his might, swung it down, toward the main wing bone. The weapon smashed through the scales—

There was a crack, the bone splintering under impact. Blood spattered onto the meadow, plants blackening and bursting into flame as the scorching liquid hit.

The dragon screamed. His head snaked down, and flame roared forth. Nijon abandoned his sword in the dragon's wound, darted under the monster's belly, and scuttled out the other side.

The monster stood motionless for long moments, perhaps realizing at last that he was in real danger. This suited Nijon; he panted, trying to control his own pain. He had no desire to run again, not for the nonce.

"Calm," said the dragon. "Calm." The words seemed to reassure him. His head moved back and forth, probing the air; he was sniffing. Nijon's eyes widened as he remembered that vaunted sense of smell; the dragon was not vanquished yet.

He had only one remaining weapon. Nijon unshouldered his bow and nocked an arrow. Drawing the string was agony; it took all his strength, he could feel his rib stabbing as he strained. Shoot for the head? There must be vulnerable spots there. He released the arrow—and saw it bounce from the bony plate around the dragon's jaw.

The head jerked around; the dragon had felt the impact, surmised Nijon was off to his left. Those nostrils sniffed—

Nijon was running already, back beneath the monster's belly, nocking an arrow as he ran. He had seen men of his tribe hunt the gharial, a river reptile. Its small brain was behind its forehead bulge; a well-placed spear would kill it quickly. Gharials were not much like dragons; still, a shot from below, into the jaw, might find the brain in the monster's skull.

Nijon knelt between the forelegs, where red scales shaded into violet, and drew his bowstring.

The dragon had heard something. His massive head peered down, under his belly. Nostrils whiffled not a yard from Nijon's face; Nijon could smell the dragon's blood, burning liquid in the monster's eyes. The dragon drew breath, preparing to flame; Nijon felt his heart in his throat, knew this was his final moment of existence. . . .

He released his arrow. It plunged deep into the underside of the dragon's jaw, where the scales were small and light in color.

Nijon raised an arm, futile though he knew the gesture to be. A mere stick of flesh, it would not shelter him from the monster's fire. . . .

Small flames snorted from the dragon's nostrils. At any moment, that fearsome jaw would open, and a final blast would roar forth to incinerate him—but it did not happen. The flames from the nostrils built up, growing hotter and longer. Twin fingers of fire passed to either side of Nijon's kneeling form. He prayed to every god he knew; it was sheer luck that he was centered between the killing jets.

Blisters rose on his arms and face; the air was filled with the stench of scorching hair. Gradually, the jets died down, growing shorter, until nothing remained but flickers of blue fire playing about the dragon's nostrils. His arrow had pinned the dragon's massive jaw closed, Nijon saw with amazement; that was why the dragon had not spat flame from his mouth, why Nijon had survived.

Swiftly, Nijon nocked another arrow, drew and fired again; again; again. . . .

The dragon's head dropped to the dirt.

Nijon looked up; the vast body above him swayed left, then right—

He stumbled to his feet, almost crying out in pain as his broken rib stabbed, and staggered left, away from the body—

The dragon leaned, leaned; it was so large, it took long moments to gather speed and fall. The left legs splayed helplessly in the dirt, and the body crumpled, smashed to the earth with thunderous impact, spade tail whipping long seconds later into scattered flowers. The head remained where it was, tucked awkwardly between the monster's forelegs.

Nijon stood for a moment, tensed, ready for flight, unable to believe the battle was over.

Could his tiny arrows possibly have slain so gargantuan a foe? He had hoped they would find the dragon's brain; perhaps they had, but actually to see the monster fall was . . . unexpected. Nijon waited for the dragon to rise, to carry on the fight; but there was no motion, no breath, no twitch from the reptile's giant form.

As the charge of battle left Nijon, pain and exhaustion crept forth. He knelt, sat down, lay supine in the wildflowers, panting still.

As he regained his breath, the pain within his chest faded—somewhat. Above, the sun broke through the clouds. He lay amid the scent of blossoms and the gentle drone of bees.

The dragon spun, a distant arrow aiming for the valley floor. Mika peered, but it was hopeless; at this distance, he couldn't possibly see Nijon, whether on the dragon's back or falling to his doom.

The dragon broke from his dive, and soared gracefully across green trees. Mika sighed with frustration, aching to know the outcome.

"He must have thrown—Nijon, did you say his name was?" said one of the women. "Why else would he land?"

"Brave, brave—" Shemli wailed, then broke down entirely.

The dragon landed. After a moment, he flamed.

"No!" shouted Nlavi. "My champion lives yet, else why would the dragon fire?"

They all peered, out toward that distant patch of meadow, all knowing they could see nothing, nothing beyond the dragon himself. The dragon moved a bit, then flamed again. Nijon was there, doubtless; doubtless it was a battle royal; but at this distance . . . Long moments passed as Mika and the women stood with bated breath.

The dragon toppled over, onto its side.

There was an instant of stunned silence.

Then there were shrieks and tears of joy; the women clutched each other, babbling thanksgiving, wet faces shining.

"No, no," moaned Mika in dismay. He sank to his knees. From riches to penury, in instants. Gods, he cursed the day he'd seen Nijon, that conniving Vagon jackal, standing by the wagon's path. Why hadn't he had the sense to butcher the swine then and there?

Thrice plundered, thrice; first of Fela's treasure; then of

half his trading profit, when the scoundrel had demanded goods and money for "protection;" and now, of the dragon's hoard.

Or—perhaps not. If Nijon was still alive, he was in that meadow, down there in the valley; a goodly distance off. And here was the dragon's treasure, unprotected, more wealth than a man could carry.

If there was a way to get it down this cliff. . . .

Didn't he have a pulley? Mika wandered over to where his wagon lay, sides splintered from the dragon's talons, goods strewn over the cavern floor. He began to search.

Shock and dismay were etched on Matli's lined face. "No, no, no," the matriarch moaned, golden goblet falling from one hand, polishing cloth from the other. "We are doomed." She plunged her head into her hands.

Nlavi drew herself up in high contempt. "You relished living as a dragon's toy? A hero risks all to save you from slavery, and you bemoan your fate?"

"Keep a civil tongue in your head," snapped Matli. "How much food have we got? How long can we survive, without the dragon to bring us sustenance?"

"Why—"

"There's nothing but cliff, there, dearie, as you may recall. Escape is no likelier now than before."

Nlavi was shaken, but rallied. "He will come," she proclaimed. "He will come and rescue us from this awful place."

Several other women had come with Nlavi. Realization was beginning to dawn on their faces. "And then what?" said one.

"Up at dawn to fetch water, cooking for a dozen men, red knees from scrubbing floors—unceasing labor."

"Penury, abuse, scrabbling for a sequin—"

"The lecherous graybeard my father had planned for me to marry. . . ."

"The fields. Rice planting. Stoop labor from dawn till dusk."

Nlavi sniffed at such ingratitude. She, at least, had no such fears: Her savior drew nigh.

24

▶▶▶

Hyaaaah!" screamed Dekh, plunging past the cavern entrance.

"Yike!" shouted Mika, jumping back as the boy hurtled by.

Dekh yanked to a halt, facedown. *"Aiiii!"* he screamed again, and began to spin gently at the end of his tether.

Mika gaped at the apparition of a boy, none too clean, wearing a backpack and a harness knotted from rope. The face of a terrified mongoose peered from his pack. From his harness, two ropes ran upward, disappearing into the space above the cave. No, not two ropes, Mika saw; rather, a loop. Aha! Nijon had descended on this contraption to taunt the dragon; a pulley must be up there somewhere. Nijon must have nicked the pulley from Mika's wagon; heaven knew, the swine had commandeered enough other merchandise.

Dekh dangled disconsolately at the bottom of the loop, twisting in the air and contemplating his new understanding of the function of a counterweight. "Help," he said gloomily.

One of the women found a broom, and held the shaft out to him. He snatched it, and several women pulled him in. "Thank you," he said as they untangled him.

"It's a boy," said one.

"A filthy one," said another in disgust.

"Are you our rescuer?" asked Shemli.

"I? Not I," said Dekh. "It was Nijon, mighty Nijon, who slew the foul wyrm; he, Vagon warrior—"

"Oh, shut up," said Mika.

"No more from you, my lad," said one of the women, "until you have a bath." They bustled him away.

Mika eyed the loop that dangled, out there, a cubit or two from the cavern lip. He picked up the broom and hauled it in. He gave it a tentative pull; as he had suspected, the loop turned smoothly. It did indeed run through a pulley.

"Excellent," he said. And there were several coils of rope, in the mess that had been his stock of goods. There should be enough to reach the foot of the cliff.

Mika was paying out rope in a loose coil on the floor of the cave. Three lengths of rope were there, tied end-to-end; he intended to add two more lengths. When newly washed Dekh came into the chamber, Mika glanced at the boy, hunched his shoulders a bit, and kept working. Dekh was obviously in league with Nijon; there was no knowing what the boy would do when he realized that Mika was planning on absconding with the dragon's treasure before Nijon's return. Mika wondered whether he would need to kill the boy, and if he could somehow manage it without offending the women.

"What are you doing?" Dekh asked. "Why do you need so much rope? Can I help?" He positively danced with eagerness. Mika studied the boy askance, wondering whether he was disingenuous or truly the dimwit he appeared to be.

Dekh took Mika's silence and uncomfortably piercing gaze for offense. "I'm sorry," he said contritely. "Does what you're doing have religious significance?"

"Religious significance?" repeated Mika incredulously. He looked down at his hands, and realized he had come to the end of one bit of rope. He picked up another length, and tied the two together.

"What kind of a knot is that?" Dekh babbled, moving closer. "Will you teach me how to tie it? What. . . ."

Mika sighed. There was obviously no getting rid of the lad, and perhaps he could be useful. Patiently, he began to explain.

Though Dekh got tangled up in the rope once, they soon were ready. Mika tied the final end of the rope to the axle of his wagon. Then the two of them together pushed and heaved the massive coil over the edge of the cliff.

It plunged, unwinding as it fell—as Mika had planned.

"It's too long," said Dekh, peering downward. The rope ran all the way to the rocks at the base of the cliff, where a length of it snaked back and forth.

"That's all right," said Mika with relief: far better too long than too short. "We can haul some of it back in." And they did, though it was hard work; they were hauling on a hundred cubits of hefty rope, no light load.

They peered down again; only a short length ran across the ground at the cliff's foot.

"Now what?" asked Dekh.

"Untie the rope from the wagon," said Mika. He had only tied it there to secure it temporarily. Dekh skipped over to the axle and began to pick at the knot. Some moments later, Mika sighed with frustration—couldn't the boy undo a simple knot? He headed over to help Dekh but, with a little crow of victory, Dekh turned around with the free rope-end in his hand—and, in proffering it to Mika, managed to drop it onto the floor.

The weight of a hundred cubits of rope hung down the cliff. This end was secured by—nothing. In a long moment of frozen terror, Mika gazed as the rope end moved, scrabbling over the cavern floor, pulled toward the edge of the cliff. His body seemed stolid, immovable, but only because time telescoped in that moment of fear; in truth, Mika was launching himself into instant motion, hurtling toward the rope. If it went over the edge, there went all hope of riches; and possibly, his life with it, for the gods only knew whether they could escape this cave without the rope.

One foot moved in front of the other; the rope gave a little leap into the air as it whipped over the edge of the cave mouth; Mika dived for it.

The rope brushed one hand. His fingers clasped—and missed.

Mika landed, stomach painfully first, on the very cave lip. For a long moment, he balanced insecurely, certain he was about to topple into the void—but at last his weight shifted back toward his knees.

He had lost everything. He—

He noticed that there was still rope running down the side of the cliff. He had landed bodily atop the tag end. With fearful care, he reached down, grabbed the rope, then rolled into the cave, wrapping it around his fist, his entire body shaking in reaction.

"You lackwit!" Mika said with quiet disgust. "You *scatterbrain*! Haven't you the slightest—" By now he was shouting—but a sudden thought made him pause. He peered at Dekh with narrowed eyes. What better way to thwart his plans than by losing the rope? Could the boy actually have *planned* this?

But Dekh was blushing a deep, shameful red, and the expression on his face bespoke a veritable agony of self-contempt.

Mika turned away and gave a shuddering sigh. Oh well, the boy would be hard-pressed to botch the next task. "Take the broom and snag the loop," he said, pointing to the loop on which Dekh had descended, which still hung in the cavern entrance.

Dekh did as told, almost teetering over the edge himself

in eagerness. Mika contemplated the boy, tempted to give him a shove. Dekh was clumsy enough; Mika could pass it off as an accident—but the moment passed. Dekh caught his balance.

"Now, take the loop in both hands, and hold a length between your fists," ordered Mika. When Dekh did so, Mika drew a knife of bronze, and sawed at the rope between Dekh's fists. At last, it parted. Mika took one end, and tied it to the rope that hung down the cliff. He hauled on the free end, drawing it into the cave, and secured it to the axle of his wagon.

"There," said Mika in satisfaction.

Dekh looked down, eyeing the rope that ran down the cliff—then up, at the length that ran to the pulley at the peak above the cavern opening, and the length that ran back down from the pulley and into the cave, where it was fixed to Mika's wagon.

"I see," said Dekh. "Now we can haul Nijon up when he returns."

"Err—yes," said Mika. "Yes. Precisely."

Dekh was happily banging away on the wagon. Mika had explained the need to disassemble it; he doubted the hoist would bear the weight of the whole vehicle.

"But why do you want to get the wagon down the cliff?" Dekh had puzzled.

"So we can take away more of the treasure," Mika had explained.

"After Nijon gets back, you mean."

"Of course, of course, why, certainly. After Nijon gets back."

The cart was held together with wooden pegs. Metal hardware was far too precious to waste on things like wagons; most wood construction used pegs, joints, or glue. Each peg had to be driven out of its hole with blows of a hammer. Unfortunately, Mika had only the vaguest idea what he was doing, and Dekh had none: The boy was wedging his peg farther in.

"No, no, you dullard," Mika shouted over the noise of blows. "The other way." He showed the boy what to do, wondering whether Dekh was help or hindrance. Then he turned to return to his own task.

Shemli was bent over, shouldering a bag of grain. "That's my millet!" Mika protested.

"Matli says—"

"Matli can hang. It's my millet, and you can't have it."

"Do you want dinner tonight?" Shemli demanded.

"I—"

"The firewood is ours. Understand? And the beef. Unless you want to chew raw millet—"

"All right, all right," said Mika, scowling.

"Supplies are limited," said Shemli. "We're likely to run out in a week or so, Matli says, even on restricted rations."

"We should be able to leave before then," said Mika.

The woman stared at him as if he were mad. "How?" she demanded.

Mika motioned her over to the rope, and began to explain his scheme.

Not entirely awake, Mika lay in his bedroll, facing the wall of the cave. From behind him came the noises of morning bustle, but he had no great desire to face the day. He and Dekh had spent the whole previous day taking apart the wagon. Mika wondered when, if ever, he would get enough sleep, and promised himself he'd spend weeks lounging about, drinking ale and eating sumptuous delicacies, once he returned to Purasham a rich man. Sighing, he at last turned over to survey the scene.

Women were loading up bundles of food and treasure. Dekh danced around, offering help and asking pointless questions. The women laughed at him and gave him bits of food, which he greedily consumed.

Mika scowled. The treasure was huge, but between them, the women were loading up a substantial portion. He rose, and went to Matli. "What is this?" he demanded.

"We are leaving," Matli said, rapping him on the leg with her cane. "Out of my way."

"What? But you can't—"

"Certainly we can. That contraption of yours will lower us down."

"Yes, but—"

"No buts about it. Are we to stay here and starve?"

"But if we all work together," said Mika soothingly, "we can transport the entire treasure. Each of you shall have a share—"

Matli barked laughter. "Bah," she said. "Return to Purasham in the company of a man, and a schemer at that? Where women are chattel and men own all? You would plunder us of our portion."

"Do you hope to do better, wandering the wilderness? Defenseless maidens, alone in the wicked world?"

"Defenseless?" snorted Matli. "Try to stop us, and see how defenseless we are."

Pleading, Mika followed them out as they went to his hoist, then worked together to lower themselves down the cliff. None bore more than she could comfortably carry, Mika saw with relief; they were not planning to steal his wagon. Still, he scowled as a good quarter of the dragon's hoard disappeared down the cliff.

At last, only he, Nlavi, the mongoose, and Dekh stood in the cavern. They were in shade still, though the morning sun illuminated the far ridge. "Aren't you going?" he asked Nlavi.

"Not I," said she with a distant smile. "I await my beloved."

"Beg pardon?" said Mika, blinking. Beloved?

"Nijon, hero, dragonslayer, comes to rescue me," said

Nlavi dreamily. She turned to Dekh. "Tell me, is he a prince among his own people?"

"Every Vagon is a prince, or none," said Dekh enthusiastically, "for his folk live together without such distinctions, every man a warrior and every woman a huntress. All are accounted noble, and each accounts himself with nobility, for they are the lords of the plain, the chosen of their own strange gods. In primitive splendor, they remember what we have long forgotten: that virtue goes out upon the generations, that honor is of greater worth than life or limb. Proudly, they roam the wide world—"

Mika made a sound of disgust, and went to look at his disassembled wagon. Those scrofulous, flea-bitten savages—Bah. Mika wished they would be swallowed up by their interminable plain, and Nijon, curse the swine, with them.

Mika stood at the base of the cliff, sweating in the hot noon sun. The net at this end of the rope sprawled on the ground, and a man's weight of treasure with it; nearby stood a pile of the boulders Mika had assembled. Once the net was emptied of treasure, he would have to fill it with rocks, to counterweight the next load of treasure. He had not enough rope to form a complete loop and counterweight things properly; instead, a pile of rocks was growing in the cavern, as the pile of treasure there diminished. Eventually, he'd run out of locally available boulders, and be forced to lower things hand-over-hand—or perhaps not. He'd need to leave soon, with whatever treasure he'd acquired. It had been two days; the dragon had landed a goodly distance down the valley, but Nijon's absence could not be counted on forever.

Mika grunted under the weight of the precious metal, transferring it to his wagon. The cart was far smaller than it had once been. He could not possibly pull a four-wheel cart, not by himself, not down this steep and rocky ridge;

he had hoped to enlist the help of the women, but that was obviously not to be. Instead, he had shortened the wagon, discarding one axle to produce a little rickshaw. It would suffice to transport a good part of the treasure—enough to live in luxury for the rest of his life, at any rate.

"Good day, Nashram," said an unexpected voice.

Mika whirled, eyes wide. There stood Nijon. The Vagon looked terrible: hair half burned away, blisters over face and arms, skin grimy with days of sleeping in the rough. There were deep circles under his eyes; tightly tied cloth bound his ribs.

"I hadn't expected you so soon," Mika said.

"Evidently."

"Well, this *is* good luck," said Mika nervously. "With your help, we can transfer the treasure more quickly; then home, and equal shares all round—say what, old companion?"

Nijon gave a tired grin. "I think not," he said, drawing his sword and taking a step forward.

Mika fled.

"And a good thing, too," said Nijon to himself. Exhausted and wounded as Nijon was, Mika could probably have bested him.

Nijon finished removing the treasure from the net, and seated himself at its center.

"AHOY!" he shouted skyward, and gave the rope a solid yank.

The net tightened about him, and he began to rise.

"Beloved!" cried Nlavi as Dekh helped Nijon step from the net. She flung herself into his weary arms. Brother made meeping noises, and twined through Nijon's legs.

"Beloved?" queried Nijon, pushing Nlavi to arm's length.

"Well—yes," she said, smiling up at him. "You are my

husband, are you not? Or soon will be. May I not call you—"

Nijon's eyes widened. "Husband?"

"That's the way it works," said Nlavi dreamily. "Half the kingdom and my hand in marriage, is that not your reward?"

"Ah!" said Nijon. "I see. Err—unfortunately, King Manoos has not been quite so generous."

"What?" said Nlavi, taken aback. Nijon told her of the reward.

Nlavi's face screwed up in incredulity. "He *what?*" she shouted. *"Ten thousand lousy crowns of gold and County PETOK, by all the gods?"*

"Yes, I—"

"Not half the kingdom," she said with forced calm. "Not a quarter. Not Dreyadon, or Khaamashan. Not even County Uk, gods help us, but the lousiest, malarial, frog-infested scum-sucking *bog* of a wretched excuse for a province! *That's* what I'm worth? And you—you miserable ninny! To risk your life and limb, to face the most fearsome creature in all creation, for what? For a pathetic little patch of swamp? What kind of an idiot are you? And if you think I'm going to spend the rest of my life with you swatting mosquitoes in Petok, you've got another think coming!"

"Thank heaven you're not," said Nijon with feeling. "The reward does not include your hand. You're going home to your father—and to Mesech, your betrothed."

"What?" shrieked Nlavi. *"That obese slug?"* She stamped away.

Nijon sighed, then crouched and patted Brother. "Women," he said. Brother nipped his hand in sympathy.

Dekh peered over the cavern lip. The shadows of clouds crept over the valley floor. "The wagon's gone," he said.

Nijon looked over. "Mika came back for it," he guessed. "And whatever treasure was already down there."

"That's—that's dishonest," said Dekh, shocked to the core.

Nijon snorted. "You will be well off indeed," he said, "if you never again meet a man as crooked as Mika Nashram."

Some days later, Nijon felt well enough to travel. Dekh descended the cliff first, then Nlavi.

Nijon stood in the cavern and watched Dekh, at the base of the cliff, load the net with boulders. When the boy shouted "Away!" Nijon sat in his own net, and gingerly let himself over the edge of the cliff. Dekh held on to the counterweight, and added a few rocks, until it just balanced Nijon.

Letting the others down had been easy enough; Nijon had stood in the cavern, hauling on the rope to lower them away. But there was no one now to lower him. Until he came even with the counterweight, he was fine; he could reach out to the rope that ran parallel to him, and pull upward, raising the counterweight and lowering himself.

Halfway down, the counterweight came even with Nijon. Here Nijon would hang—forever, if he did nothing to unbalance the load. He reached over to the counterweight, cut a hole in its net with his sword, and pulled out several rocks—perhaps ten pounds or so.

Immediately, he began to drop; he was now ten pounds heavier, the counterweight that much lighter.

At first, he felt no fear; a mere ten pounds, how much difference could that make? But then the cliff began to move past at alarming speed, indeed at an ever-quickening pace. Nijon looked down, and wondered how the impact would feel.

He dithered for a moment, then dropped the rocks. Dekh jumped as one landed near him. Nijon continued to plummet—even to gain speed. Cursing, he shrugged out of his pack, and dropped it, too.

The ground continued to approach, but at a slowing rate.

The cliff moved past, slower—slower—crawling now—until, still ten cubits up the cliff, Nijon's net came to a halt.

And then it began to rise. The counterweight must now be heavier than he.

Cursing, Nijon stabbed at the cliff with his sword. It stuck in a crack, and sufficed to hold him steady.

He looked down. Dekh and Nlavi stood there, peering up.

"Throw me a rope," Nijon ordered.

It took Dekh a while to find one—and several throws before Nijon caught the rope, since he dared not let go of his sword; but at last, he grabbed the rope, and tied it to his belt. Dekh and Nlavi hauled Nijon down. They tied the rope to pegs that had been driven in the earth for precisely this purpose.

"But what about the rest of the treasure?" asked Dekh. There was far more left in the cave than they could carry.

"Stand back," said Nijon, stepping from the net. He cut the rope, and sprinted away.

The counterweight fell from the cavern lip, plummeted down the cliff face, and smashed into the rocks at the base of the cliff. The rope fell after, snaking across the ridge.

Nijon stared up, at the now inaccessible cave. "I don't think anyone else will be taking it. Come, we each bear enough to make us rich."

25

Behold Count Nijon, visiting his new domain.

Dust stung the eyes; sweat rolled down backs and faces. In summer, Petok was a desert; worse than a desert, for the sun baked erstwhile swamp to a fine, powdery substance that rose with every vagrant breeze. Count Nijon and his followers wore cloths over mouth and nose, to avoid breathing the stuff. Here and there, desolation was relieved by dead weeds and the skeletons of animals.

Again and again, they passed dried-up streams; down a few, a faint trickle of putrid water ran. Nijon worried about attack; wherever they went, their horses kicked up dust, rendering the party visible for miles around.

Above, the sun baked fiercely down. They had begun the journey with saddlebags filled with water, but now were left with only a bowlful or two.

"They call this a swamp?" grumbled Nijon.

"Aye, aye," said Keeper Meshed, coming up to ride by Nijon. He was a weary-eyed, thin-bearded oldster whose pony looked to be on its last legs. He was, so he claimed, the keeper of Hekhat Castle, Petok's seat of government, and therefore the chief servant of the previous count—and now of Count Nijon.

"It is, it is," Meshed said, "when the winter rains come

and flood the land. Then doth the ptekh-weed flourish and the koaki breed. The people abandon their villages for high ground and make merry sport, netting the eels that run in the thousands and hunting the koaki for their coats."

"Koaki?" questioned Nijon; the word was unfamiliar.

"Huge rodents, not unlike water rats," said Meshed. "They are aquatic in nature, and breed quickly during the rainy season. Their pelts, which colder lands prize for winter garb, are our only export."

"Ah," said Nijon. "A gay and fantastical place, my new realm. Swamp half the year and desert the other half—and its only export is the skins of rats."

Offended at hearing his native land so described, Meshed reined back his horse, to ride with Nijon's followers.

Twenty soldiers rode to Nijon's rear; each cost Nijon a crown a day, and he resented the expense. Meshed had insisted that a count must have a retinue to befit his rank. The oldster had suggested a century of men, but had reluctantly agreed that a score would do. The only positive aspect, from Nijon's point of view, was that he had been able to hire his old friend, Detros.

They rode on in silence, sweltering in the heat, squinting to avoid the dust. Ahead, on the flat and desolate plain, stood a miserable mud-and-wattle village.

"Behold," said Meshed gloomily. "Castle Hekhat."

"That's my castle?" said Nijon incredulously. It was more hovel than palace. There was a moat, of sorts: A sluggish green stream had been diverted to pass to either side of the castle. There was a wall, of sorts: perhaps five cubits high, built of sun-baked mud. And there were buildings, of a sort: half a dozen squat mud-and-wattle structures, all a uniform and ugly brown.

They rode closer, Nijon's heart sinking. "This is it?" he asked unhappily, hoping against hope that Meshed had made some mistake. At close regard it was, if anything, less prepossessing than at a distance. The wooden gate hung off its hinges. The low bridge across the moat had recently been burned; the planking was gone, although a spry man might possibly hop across on the charred timbers.

"Aye," said Meshed, "somewhat the worse for wear. When the old count's retainers did not receive their pay, they looted it, and burned what they could not steal."

Nijon dismounted and gingerly made his way across the bridge. Meshed followed, while Detros and the soldiers set up camp outside.

One of the buildings within the walls was evidently a stable, deserted save for the faint odor of horse dung. Elsewhere were drying racks—"To cure the koaki hides," Meshed said—a kitchen, a tiny windowless structure Meshed called "the bathhouse," a temple to Ptemesh, and "the grand hall"—a claustrophobic structure containing smashed furniture and not much else.

At last, Nijon seated himself wearily on a piece of rubble. He spat into the dust; the liquid almost immediately disappeared, sucked away by the parched earth. "Ah, what luxury attends the nobility of Purasham," Nijon snarled. "Tell me; how by the seven hells did Count Naeren plan to defend this place?"

Meshed shrugged. "Petok has not seen war for generations," he said.

"I'm not surprised," said Nijon. "Who would want to conquer it? What happens when the floodwaters rise? This place is not on high ground."

"The walls suffice to hold back the waters," said Meshed. "Usually."

"Usually," said Nijon. "I see."

"I suppose my lord will want to rebuild," said Meshed.

"Oh no," said Nijon sarcastically. "It's perfect as it is. Of course it will need to be rebuilt, you fool!"

"Just as I thought," said Meshed gloomily. "There are no funds, of course."

Nijon grimaced. "No funds?"

Meshed shrugged. "Would you expect the peasants to pay taxes in the absence of their lord? None have been collected in a year. Then there is the problem of skilled labor."

Nijon raised an eyebrow.

"There are few carpenters, masons, or surveyors here-abouts," Meshed said with lugubrious satisfaction. "They will need to be imported from the city. Accommodations will be required; tents, perhaps. And cooks. Food. The expense—"

Nijon groaned.

The following morning, Nijon grumpily arose, squashing lice between his fingers. He threw on a tunic, then opened the flap of his tent, intending to venture forth and find someplace to make water.

The moment he stepped out, dozens of scrawny, aged men fell to their stomachs, and bellowed, in ragged unison, "Hail Nijon, Count of Petok!"

One crept forward on hands and knees to kiss Nijon's foot. "Stop that," said Nijon in disgust, yanking his foot away.

"My lord," said the old man. "I beg you, grant us relief from our onerous taxes! The drought has impoverished us, hunger is rampant; the children cry out—"

"Do not listen to this wretch!" cried another dotard, pressing his face into the dirt in supplication. "It is well known that the Bekhites enrich themselves off the Khaama-shan trade! They are liars, every man and woman! With-draw from them, I beg, the toll revenues of the northern road. With such wealth, my own village could increase its harvest of koaki skins a dozenfold—"

"He lies!" cried a third. And soon the oldsters were shouting, at each other and Nijon. They alternately threw themselves on their faces before the count, then rose and shook fists at one another.

"Meshed!" bellowed Nijon. "What by all the gods is this?"

The keeper soon appeared, a chicken leg in one hand; Nijon had interrupted his breakfast. "The headmen of your villages, my lord," he said. "They have come to swear allegiance."

"That does not seem their intention," said Nijon.

One codger grabbed Nijon's leg, and stared up at him beseechingly. "My lord, the border between my town and Zako, to our south, was shifted three generations ago in Zako's favor—"

"Naturally," said Meshed, "they take the opportunity to petition their lord for redress of grievances."

Another geezer shoved forward, and shouted, "Planting rights on the left bank of the Dekhan stream—"

"—granaries are empty—" yelled another.

"—that land is Zako Town's by ancient right, thou treacher, thou bastard. Wherefore do you ask the count—"

At least two fistfights had broken out.

"*Silence!*" bellowed Nijon. Gradually, the hubbub died away.

"After I break my fast," Nijon said, "I shall receive each of you, in turn. You will swear allegiance, tell me when you plan to deliver back taxes, and may then present petitions and requests."

The headmen were silent for a moment. Then one asked, "Which of us shall go first?"

Nijon turned to Meshed. "You set the order," he said.

Meshed was clearly surprised. "Delighted," he said, smiling.

Nijon was halfway to the river, where he planned to relieve himself, when he realized *why* Meshed was delighted: He planned to extort bribes from the headmen in exchange for favorable positions in the queue.

Almost, Nijon turned to go back to prevent such exploitation—but then decided that his full bladder and empty stomach were of more immediate concern.

Nijon sat heavily down by the campfire. "Gods," he said. "What I would give for an ale."

"You and me both," said Detros, sniffing curiously at the stew bubbling over the fire.

Nijon was exhausted. He had spent an infuriating day listening to and disposing of the interminable petty disputes of his villagers.

"I had thought the noble's role," he told Detros, "was mercilessly to exploit his subjects, extracting a maximum of revenue, then live a life of indolent ease. I have had enough of this. I am tempted to let them keep their taxes, if only they settle their own disputes."

"Sounds good to me," said Detros. "Shall we head home tomorrow?"

"My lord," said Meshed, shocked, "what of your castle?"

"Let it rot," said Nijon. "What good is it?"

"But my lord," Meshed protested, "when the winter comes, King Manoos will arrive."

Why in heaven's name should the king want to visit this wretched place? "I beg your pardon?" Nijon said.

"During the rainy season, gharials infest Petok—great lizards, not unlike—"

"I know of the gharial," said Nijon.

"King Manoos loves the hunt," said Meshed, "and . . . but come, have you not heard how my master, Count Naeren, lost his estate?"

"No," said Nijon.

"One of the duties of a noble of Purasham," said Meshed, adopting the stance of a lecturer, "is properly to entertain his king when the court doth come to call. There must be feasting, and merriment, and accommodations must be found for all."

"Yes," said Nijon.

"The cost is easily borne by, say, the prince of Dreyadon, with his rich lands and many slaves. Alas, King Manoos enjoys the hunt too well and, two years gone, came forth to Petok during the flood, to spear the gharial, that great reptile that infests our waters. He stayed for nigh on three months."

"I fail to see—"

"Count Naeren, Sak give his soul respite, ran out of funds. By the third month of our sovereign's visit, the castle was down to koaki meat and moldy millet."

"The king took offense?"

"The king was displeased, but took particular offense when Naeren, a hot-tempered man, declared Manoos a parasite and tyrant."

"Oops."

"The king had him thrown to the gharials, and sold his family to Miletian slavers."

"Charming," said Nijon.

"The king will undoubtedly visit us next flood," said Meshed despondently. "He does enjoy the gharial hunt. And he will expect, of course, adequate accommodation in Castle Hekhat. If it remains in ruins—"

"That does it," said Nijon, scowling. "I am getting shot of this pestilential hole."

Late summer in Purasham: slate gray skies, shimmering heat, sweat on every brow. The populace spent midday sitting under awnings and drinking copious small beer; only with the evening did life revive.

King Manoos had ordered that the banquet be held in the gardens, among verdant vines; the palace halls were stifling. Outside it was cooler, but only slightly so; there was no breeze to cut the heat.

Braziers burned around the banquet site, slaves tossing spices onto the coals; supposedly, the smoke warded off insects. If so, the effect was not apparent; all of the guests reached out to slap from time to time.

Nlavi reclined on her couch and toyed morosely with her honeyed yoghurt, scratching idly at a bite.

"So, my poppet," Mesech bellowed, "what do you think of that?"

He had been chattering loudly with a bevy of merchants; she had paid them no attention, preferring the company of her own unhappy thoughts. "Just as my lord wills," she said hopelessly.

Mesech laughed, and returned to his companions.

Idly, Nlavi watched as one of those little weasels Poran had brought back from the southern plains darted beneath the table—after a rat, perhaps, or merely a morsel some diner had tossed to the earth. She sighed.

"Why so downcast, my lady?" asked a voice. Nlavi looked up; standing over her was a man in Motraian military tunic, very tall. He was young and tousle-haired; around green eyes were the lines that come with squinting into the sun, across the plain and battlefield. His shoulders were broad, arms tanned; well-muscled, he moved with unconscious grace. He was, thought Nlavi, extraordinarily handsome.

"I have been to these affairs since before I could speak," said Nlavi, "and it is hard to summon up any emotion, let alone happiness, in this dreadful heat. Come, sit here." She swung up her legs to make room on the couch for the man. He sat down, and gestured toward a servant, summoning bock beer for them both. Nlavi had never been fond of bock's bitter taste, but made no protest. "Are you with the satrap's entourage?" she asked, eyes following the lines of the muscles that corded his neck.

"The commander of his guard," he said, smiling. "My name is Gerekh. I shall be leading the wedding procession."

Nlavi sighed.

"The prospect does not appeal to my lady?"

She looked toward Mesech, who was shoveling chick-pea paste into his ample cheeks with triangles of bread and guffawing at some witticism at the same time. "Is that a man to quicken a maiden's heart?" she said with loathing.

Gerekh looked at her sidelong, with green, green eyes. There was a few days' stubble on his face; Nlavi had pictured "clean-shaven" Motraians as having faces smooth as those of women, but shaving with a bronze edge was no easy thing, and a bit of stubble was usual with them. It made them look not feminine, as she had imagined, but quite strangely virile. "Is it not customary among your people to marry for political advantage?" he asked.

His Agondan was very good, Nlavi thought; he spoke well, but his Motraian heritage left the tiniest accent, enough to sound exotic and alluring. "Yes, of course," Nlavi said.

"Why then does the prospect displease you so?" asked Gerekh, moving a little closer. His eyes were so very green. Blond hair carpeted his sun-dark arms; strong veins ran across them, calling attention to the fine muscles. "We of the satrap's household live well: His kitchen is of the best, he possesses palaces and villas in a dozen lands. Gardeners, slaves, cooks, brewers, and a hundred others toil constantly for the ease and enjoyment of his companions. You will have the choicest delicacies, bards to regale you, instruction in all the world's lore; you may travel anywhere within the Emperor's wide realm, confer with priests of every sect—whatever may please you, for you will be one of the great ladies of the land."

"You make it sound appealing," said Nlavi. That low voice of his was music, his attentiveness charming. Despite the yoghurt, her head felt light, her mouth dry. Was it merely the heat that made her feel this way—or his nearness? "Still, I cannot imagine. . . ." For a moment, she was unable to continue—then finished, in a rush, "I do not look forward to my wedding night." She looked away, blinking to hold back tears.

"I understand," said Gerekh gently, leaning even closer; she could feel his sweet breath on her cheek. "But you have little to fear on such a night."

Nlavi looked at him hopelessly, his face so close to her own. The beads of sweat on his brow, which in another man would have been disgusting, on him looked like the dew on newly opened blossoms.

"You see," Gerekh murmured, his green eyes holding her own, "the satrap is a sensitive man. He would not force himself on the unwilling."

Nlavi could not hide skepticism.

"Yes," Gerekh insisted, giving her hand the briefest touch, "it is so. You do not know him well. Besides—the satrap has little interest in the fairer sex. Quite the, ah, contrary."

A smile quirked forth from Nlavi's lips. The beer appeared, tall beakers of liquid dark as mud, flecked with tawny foam. At the interruption, they broke gazes, moved a little apart. They each sipped, eyes meeting over rims; somehow, Nlavi thought, the bock was delicious, far better than any she had drunk before. "Will you be returning with us to Noshen?" she asked, low.

"I shall," Gerekh said, looking away again to the pipers who played for Manoos.

"And will you guard me on our route?"

He looked at her, and cupped her cheek in his hand. "Your servant," he murmured, "always."

Nlavi smiled happily, and looked out at the diners for a long moment, unable to speak.

Then she said, "Have some of the eel; it is a specialty of our city"—and gestured over a servant. Daintily, she took a morsel and transferred it with her own fingers into Gerekh's mouth, her fingers giving the slightest caress to his smiling lips.

Perhaps, she thought, drowning in green eyes, perhaps I may resign myself to this existence.

26

Nijon sighed with contentment. An awning flapped in the gentle breeze, warding off harsh sun; a fountain tinkled in the courtyard center, its water serving to cool the air. A girl massaged his feet, while another decanted him an ale from an earthen pot. Such pots, kept in shade, cooled liquid below the temperature of the air; Nijon sipped gratefully at coolness.

Shouts of anger drifted lazily from a window at the courtyard's eastern side: Dekh's tutor. It had been a stroke of genius to hire a teacher to field Dekh's infernal stream of questions, Nijon thought. The boy was absurdly grateful. But what was Nijon to do? He could hardly thrust the lad into the street with a hearty farewell. Given Dekh's canny understanding of the wiles of the world, he would be bleeding in the gutter, stripped of his share of the treasure, before the villa's gates were closed.

What should he do this evening? Nijon wondered idly. He had invitations to three parties; the Sharmeshite Players were at the amphitheater; and the temple of Meliantos hosted the Harvest Festival.

Too, he had a standing offer to join Laelai, the count of Ik's daughter, for a lantern-lit dinner on her barge on the River Uk. Yes, that might be pleasant, to take one's ease on cool river waters; and he thought Laelai rather fancied him. There were possibilities. . . .

Something landed on Nijon's stomach; he started, but it was only Brother.

The mongoose looked exceptionally sleek, as well he might; Nijon had set servants to trapping lizards and mice for his relative's sustenance. Brother put his wet nose to Nijon's; whiskers tickled. Then Brother peered over Nijon's side, to the garden floor. Nijon rose to an elbow and looked there. Another mongoose stood, looking up.

It was black from nose to tip, with golden rings about its tail.

"You've found a friend," said Nijon. Brother leaped down and bit the other mongoose gently on the neck, then sniffed at its rump. They twined necks together; and Nijon understood that the other mongoose was female, and the relationship more than friendship.

"I see," said Nijon gravely. "May I be the first to offer congratulations?" He stroked Brother, then hesitantly reached out and touched the other; she warily consented to let him pet her.

That had been a good idea of Poran's, Nijon thought. There were mongooses all over the city now, and the rat population was said to be much diminished. Yet Poran had gotten little recognition for his deed. The imagination of the populace was captivated by the dramatic tale of Nijon's heroism, not by the dull utility of Poran's success against the rats. A popular ballad, "Dragonslayer," was making the rounds; but what bard would choose to immortalize the importation of a weasel? And "Ratslayer" had hardly the same ring. As for Manoos, he lionized Nijon and considered his son a coward for failing to battle dragons.

Nijon's majordomo appeared and bowed low before Nijon's couch. "My lord," he said. "Detros and your guard await without, in the company of a captive."

"Excellent," said Nijon, sitting up. "Admit them, and fetch more ale." The slave scurried off.

They came in, laughing and making rough remarks; Mika Nashram was with them, bound by a length of chain. He carried himself with remarkable dignity, under the circumstances. His eyes scanned everywhere, considering the chances of escape, but he appeared reasonably calm.

"Is this the dog you wanted?" said Detros, hauling on the chain.

Nashram was jerked by the metal collar around his neck; he looked annoyed, and grabbed at the chain with his hands to protect himself from further jerks. He spied Nijon, and instantly his expression changed from annoyance to dismay.

"That's the one," said Nijon.

"My money is well hidden," said Mika defiantly. "I'll not tell you where it is."

"That's not why—"

"Nijon, dragonslayer, mighty warrior," Mika said sarcastically. "Not content with the lion's share of the treasure, you must strip me of mine, as well? Such heroism! Such generosity of spirit! What are you going to do? Kill me?"

"Well—"

"Do your worst, you despicable savage," Mika said, working himself into a lather. "Dance on my butchered body, see if I care. Three times you defrauded me—"

"See here, Mika—"

"If it hadn't been for you, I'd have gotten Nlavi free, and made a bloody fortune, too. Well, you may take your revenge, but you won't see the cash. I'll—"

"*I don't want your money, you idiot!*" Nijon bellowed.

There was a silence, broken only by the fountain's tinkle.

"You don't?" said Mika.

"No."

"What do you want, then?"

"Unchain him," Nijon told Detros. "Have some ale. You, too, Mika." He cuffed one of the servants. "Get some cheese and meat," he ordered.

Detros and the soldiers sucked thirstily at bowls of ale. Mika sat nervously on a stool, and rubbed at the marks his shackles had left.

"It seems that I own a piece of land in the country," Nijon said. "A county south of here. Perhaps you know of it."

"Petok," said Mika. "Miserable place."

"More miserable than you know," said Nijon with feeling. "Far from being a source of tax revenue, it needs thousands of crowns of improvements: dikes, bridges, repairs to the castle. Worse, King Manoos has made it clear he intends to hunt gharials there next spring, meaning I will be expected to house and feed the entire court for weeks at a time."

Mika was grinning. "The bills add up, I take it," he said.

"Precisely," Nijon said. "Now, an uninformed observer might think Petok attractive. A substantial bit of land, good hunting, a castle, the title of count—"

"Yes, yes," said Mika. "Where do I fit in?"

"It occurred to me," said Nijon, "that my problems would be solved if I were to find a buyer for this fine estate. A merchant, perhaps, with a keen desire for lands and a title; or a neighboring lord, desirous of extending his estate. Of course, to close the sale, one would have to present Petok in a speciously attractive light. I doubt my own capacity for dissimulation on such a scale, and therefore wondered: Where might I find a man with the requisite mendacity? And your name came instantly to mind."

Mika grinned. "You want me to unload your white elephant on some poor sap, I take it."

"In a nutshell," Nijon agreed.

"I should be delighted," said Mika, happily. "And my commission?"

Nijon shrugged. "Since I expect you to cheat me regardless," he said, "I see no reason to offer you a commission in addition to the money you will rake off the top."

Mika stopped grinning. "That's absurd."

"Take it or leave it."

"Zero base pay, no commission, no chargeable expenses—what kind of a deal is that?" Mika complained. "Am I to do this for my health?"

"Precisely," said Nijon. "You are to do it if you wish to see another dawn."

"I see," said Mika, after a pause. "I believe I can—ah—live with your terms."

"Well put," said Nijon. "A pleasure doing business."

The shy stars, who daily hid in fright as fierce Ptemesh arced the sky, crept forth to gently shine. The breeze was cool and filled with the green odor of the river; to Nijon's right, across water, loomed Purasham, a thousand dim oil lamps spread over the land.

The sounds of music, laughter, conversation came from aft; Nijon stood at the barge's prow. The bundled reeds of which the craft was made moved slowly through muddy water.

Hearing a squeak and scurry, Nijon looked starboard, and saw a mongoose disappearing around a capstan, a rat in its mouth. Nijon smiled.

He was yet young, Nijon thought, and no doubt tests, triumphs, and disappointments awaited him still; yet for now, he was content. He felt little urge to return to his tribe. He wondered at his contentment, for his father's prophecy had not yet been discharged. "You will lead your people into a glorious future." There seemed small chance of that—he, an outcast from his tribe.

Brother appeared, and nuzzled Nijon's ankle. Absently, Nijon petted the mongoose.

And then, a chill ran down his spine.

What did the words "your people" mean to the god Mongoose? The Va-Naleu, or—the Va-Nipivia, the mongoose tribe?

"Yes," whispered Nijon to his Brother, "your future is glorious." Rat-killers, treasured pets, they would spread all up and down the River Uk. And if, as Mongoose thought, the future lay with city dwellers and not plains nomads, then the future of mongooses was now assured.

Bastard, thought Nijon fondly. His father had played on childish dreams of glory to drive him north, had used his son for his own ends. What else would one expect from a trickster god?

"Why do you brood?" asked a low voice.

Nijon half-turned, and there was Laelai, the daughter of the Count of Ik, her chiton alarmingly tight about her torso. She had a tiny jade inset in one nostril; kohl limned her eyes, and her full lips were tattooed red. Nijon tilted his head and smiled.

She put an arm over his shoulder, took a handful of his hair, and pulled his head down. Lips touched, and tongues played in moistness.

The dragonslayer Nijon, favorite of Manoos, held his first reception. All the best folk of Purasham came, to get a closer look at the hero of the season. Resplendent in a himation bedecked with gold-and-aqua dragons, Nijon met his guests at the door, pressing cool ale and small amulets of good luck into their hands.

"I understand you have sold County Petok," said the merchant Shemsen, combing his gray-speckled beard with the fingers of one hand.

"I have," said Nijon. "Dreadful place."

"Never been there," said Shemsen, shrugging, his golden earrings swaying with the gesture. "I presume you therefore have capital to invest."

Nijon blinked; this was unexpected. Shemsen was

known as one of Purasham's canniest traders; many were those who sought his expertise. "I do," said Nijon.

"As it happens," said Shemsen, "I am outfitting a ship to sail for the Copper Isles, and several shares have not yet been subscribed."

"We must talk later," said Nijon delightedly. Shemsen's previous Copper Isles journey had netted each investor a tenfold return on his money. "Come, partake of my food and ale."

There were six kinds of lager, bock, and ale—and even that rarity, grape wine from Motraia. There was eggplant stuffed with lamb and rosemary; sauces of chick-pea, garlic, and yoghurt; delectable boreks, and cheeses cold. There were puffed breads, stuffed breads, plain breads and sweet; larks' tongues in aspic; whole mice in brine; eels and whitings drowned in garum; seven kinds of fruit; and even, in token of Nijon's origins, a whole aurochs roasted in salt. Later on, as these dishes were removed, there would be more.

The party filled seven rooms and spilled into Nijon's courtyard.

In one room, dancing girls practiced their art to the song of pipes and tambourines; in another, the best musicians in Purasham plied their lutes and drums. Massages were available in Nijon's private baths, and one room was piled high with ice from the Metrech Mountains, imported for the occasion. Servants shaved it, and mixed it with fruit juices, honeyed yoghurt, or ale, as requested. Several rooms were left quiet, where those who preferred the arts of conversation might talk without distraction.

Nijon peeked into the dancers' room. Pipes wailed, and a dancer removed a veil. Nijon grinned; the folk of Purasham considered nudity scandalous, save in the baths, but the head-to-toes clothes of these houris did little to preserve modesty. Dekh lounged there on a cushion, mouth so agape that Nijon wondered if he'd swallowed his tongue. The lad would be occupied for a while, Nijon judged.

As he strolled through the garden, Laelai beckoned him from a couch. It was arranged in the shade of a willow with several other couches, each bearing a youth of the nobility. A constant stream of servants brought food and drink for their enjoyment. "Come, join us, Nijon," she said.

Nijon reclined beside her. She ran a hand down his bicep, saying, "Try a persimmon, my lord." She held the orange fruit to his lips as he nibbled.

There was a sudden, unholy clatter from the entrance foyer: shouts of anger, yells of fear, the clash of weapons. Nijon's majordomo appeared, to knock his head against the slate flags of the courtyard. "My lord," he wailed, "ill-smelling savag—I mean to say, men of your native land demand entrance. They have no invitations, but have already wounded Mishan, and—"

"Show them in," said Nijon, sitting up. His couchmate sat up behind him, and rested her head on his shoulder.

There were three of them.

Conversation died away as they padded into the garden, peering all about in wonder and trepidation. They gawped at the cream of Purasham, merchants and nobles garbed in richest cloth; delicacies piled high on golden platters; lush and exuberant vegetation. In rude-cut buckskins, with naked feet, hair in braids, the dust of the road all about them, they contrasted strangely with their surroundings.

The leader was Jutson, the Va-Naleu chief, looking haggard and unhappy. The others were warriors, ones Nijon had not known well.

Jutson flung himself at Nijon's sandaled feet. "Oonitsaupivia," he said. "We need your aid."

"I see," said Nijon, enjoying the sight of the man who had banished him from the tribe on knees in supplication. Nijon turned to a slave. "Get them a few coins."

"Your mother and foster father are dead," said Jutson,

ignoring the insult. "The tribe is riven. We have been cursed by Dowdin, our herds have been stolen by the damned Va-Tsinva, and we have been placed under the Great Khan's ban. Famine has visited us, and pestilence. Return with us, and help us fight our foes; together we may yet triumph—"

"Do you think I am insane?" Nijon asked.

Jutson's face fell.

"You want me to return?" asked Nijon, unbelieving. "To eating raw antelope liver, instead of the delicacies you see around you? To women who are crones by the time they are thirty, instead of—" He motioned to his couch-mate, who could not conceal a catlike smile. "To living in a skin tent filled with choking smoke?"

"The life of the true people," said Jutson loudly, "in harmony with nature, in the very beat of the earth. To bestride the plain—"

Nijon snorted. "A life of hunger, cold, and fear," he said. "A life of misery and deprivation."

Detros and the other guards had arrived, Nijon saw, no doubt hurriedly summoned by the majordomo.

"We are your kin!" said Jutson, rising angrily. "Have you no—"

"My mother and foster father are dead, you say," said Nijon. "I have no kin, save Mongoose and my half-brother; no tribe, for the Va-Naleu exiled me." He turned to Detros and his men, and said, "Throw these beggars out."

Jutson's face crimsoned. "You fatherless—" he said, and lunged for Nijon, hands outstretched.

Detros tackled Jutson; he hit slate flags at Nijon's feet. Nijon idly sipped ale, one arm around his couchmate's shoulder, toying with her earring, as his guards struggled with the Vagon men. Jutson crashed facedown in a platter of hummos; tan paste spattered several guests. At last, the men were expelled into the street, the villa's door bolted and locked behind them.

Nijon circulated, apologizing for the intrusion and seeing that servants came to clean the clothes of those who had been spattered by Jutson's clumsiness. And then he returned to his couch, where the count's daughter waited, those tattooed lips smiling. A slave appeared, with a cool ewer of chestnut ale; another hovered by, with boreks and vine leaves stuffed with scented meats.

"A tidbit?" murmured the count's daughter, plucking a vine leaf with lacquered nails.

"Please, O moon of delight," said Nijon.

The morsel was followed by her lips; she drew him down, and kissed him as he lay on his back, black hair a tent over his face. Above, a nightingale sang in a gilded cage. Gentle music wafted through blossom-scented air. Nijon felt Laelai's sweet breath on his face.